How Grim Was My Valley

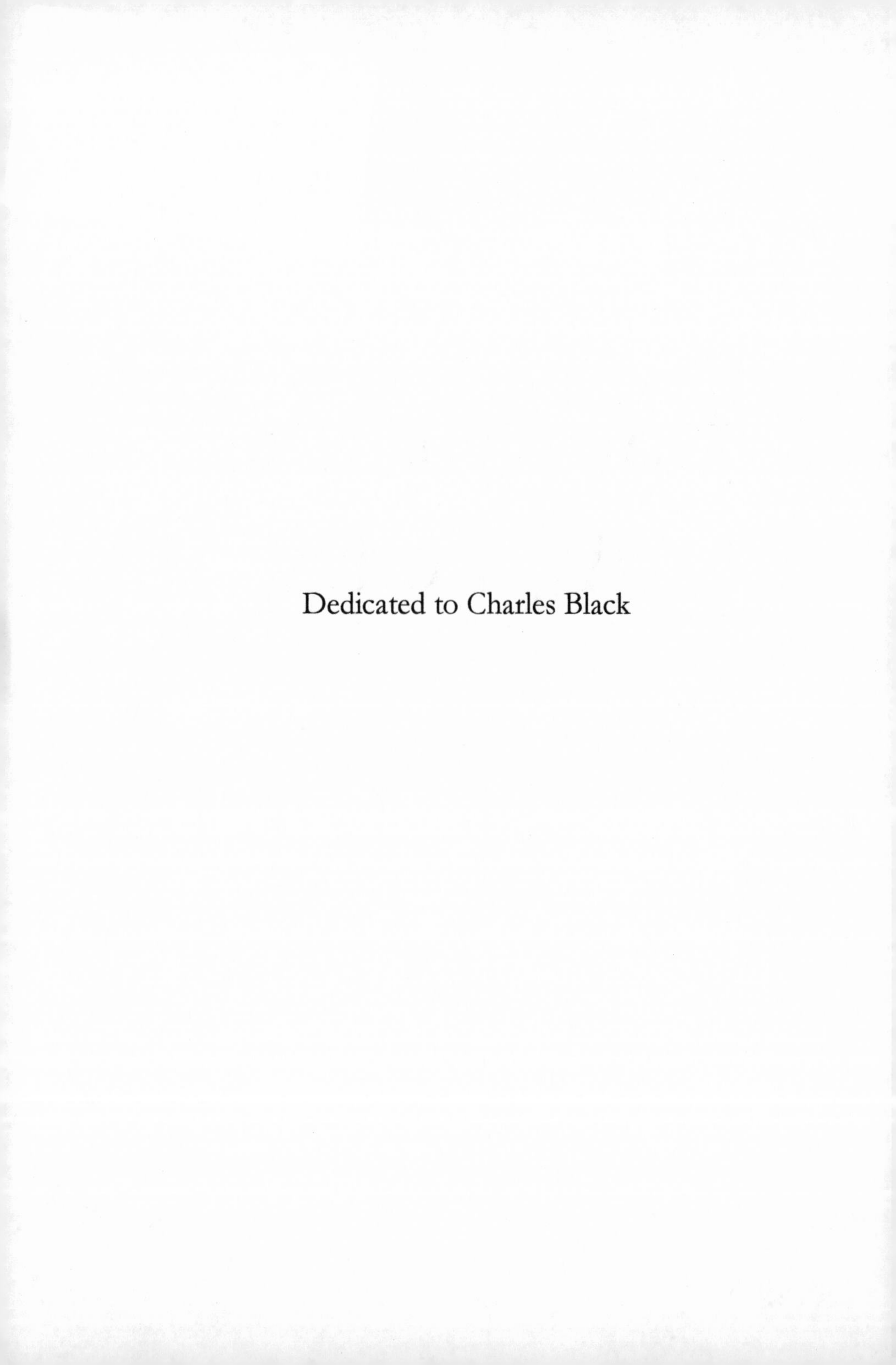

Dedicated to Charles Black

How Grim Was My Valley

John Llewellyn Probert

NewCon Press
England

This edition first published in September 2022 by NewCon Press,
41 Wheatsheaf Road, Alconbury Weston, Cambs, PE28 4LF

NCP283 (limited edition hardback)
NCP284 (softback)

10 9 8 7 6 5 4 3 2 1

The following chapters have been published previously as short stories: "The Men With Paper Faces" originally appeared in *Marked to Die* (Snuggly Books, 2016), "By Any Other Name" originally appeared in *Cthulhu Cymraeg 2* (Fugitive Fiction, 2017), "Learning the Language" originally appeared in *Terror Tales of Wales* (Gray Friar Press, 2014), "The Church With Bleeding Windows" originally appeared in *Great British Horror 2: Dark Satanic Mills* (Black Shuck Books, 2017), "What Others Hear" originally appeared in *Cthulhu Cymraeg* (Screaming Dreams, 2013), "The Devil in the Details" originally appeared in *Demons and Devilry 4* (Hersham Books, 2013), "Forgive Us Not Our Trespasses" originally appeared in The *Eleventh Black Book of Horror* (Mortbury Press, 2015).

All other chapters are original to this book

ISBN:
978-1-914953-28-6 (hardback)
978-1-914953-29-3 (softback)

Cover and internal illustrations by Elena Betty,

Text edited by Ian Whates
Typesetting and layout by Ian Whates

Contents

Author's Note

This is a portmanteau book. It is made up of short stories linked together by a framework that also begins and ends the narrative. Therefore, the reader will gain the most from what follows by reading everything in order.

The geography is accurate as well, by the way, and readers may like to have a map of Wales to hand in order to follow the trail of Robert's increasingly strange adventures as he travels.

Grim With A Capital N

Introduction by Ramsey Campbell

Some creative personalities seem irrepressible. Even in the *Stabat Mater*, Rossini can't wholly contain his ebullience: with a different text, the *Cujus animam* could have found a place in many an opera buffa. Equally, nobody who hears the *Dies irae* from Verdi's Requiem could overlook the composer's roots in opera. By contrast, Michael Haneke's staging of a comic opera (*Così Fan Tutte*) is as austere and disturbing as his films – a chastening experience worth having. In literature, Graham Greene seldom quelled the instinct for dark comedy (the banana skin at the scene of the tragedy, as he put it) that enriched his work. Some artists manage to exclude aspects of themselves: the jokey Lovecraft set loose in his letters is nowhere to be found in his fiction, and for all its merits, Dennis Etchison's prose gives little hint of how much considerable fun he was in person. The last bit is at least as true of John Llewellyn Probert, but I think no reader can fail to appreciate how much he must have enjoyed writing this book.

Its form revives the fix-up, that venerable structure, first named by A. E. van Vogt – a novel constructed from short stories previously published. Some, for instance Aldiss's *Hothouse* or van Vogt's *The Weapon Shops of Isher*, bolt their reprints together without adding extra material. Others – Bradbury's *The Martian Chronicles*, Simak's *City* – cement them with new prose. Among the most imaginative recontextualisations is another Bradbury collection, *The Illustrated Man*, where the surrounding material is as vivid as the tales themselves. It has a powerful although by no means derivative competitor in the shape of the present book.

Its classically noirish opening renders Wales ominously mysterious (which indeed it has been in literary terms since the great days of Arthur Machen) and launches us into "A Cruel Summer". Is that an echo of George Formby we hear at the start? It suggests a voice from yesteryear, more of which we'll encounter later. The story is a flavoursome addition to the sub-genre of the uncanny golfing tale exemplified by H. Russell Wakefield's "The Seventeenth Hole at Duncaster", but gains extra strength from the fraught relationship that invades its antihero's stag weekend. One central theme of our field is the past that reaches out to threaten the protagonist, and that's certainly the case here.

Soon we're back on the road, and an art gallery is our next destination. We're offered a modernist observation about narrative before the setting lives up to its adumbrations of dread in "Still Death", a tale whose grimness goes some way towards confounding my initial contention about the author's uncontainable good humour. Of course the act of creation, however dark, can generate energy that is a joy in itself or at any rate a consolation, though not for our painter here. Our author is a different matter, and revels in gathering atmosphere and omens of unease before delivering us into a series of nightmares from which we're finally released by a piece of grisly wit – released, at least, into the ongoing narrative. If its level of gleeful weirdness recalls Amicus film anthologies at their most unbridled, the complex structure takes us back to *Dead of Night*, that Ealing classic.

Will consulting a psychiatrist help our bewildered protagonist? We may suspect we know better than him. His visit leads us into an account of "The Men with Paper Faces" and traps us in the oppressively paranoid mind of its narrator. How real is the world he appears to have been granted the ability to see? It's imbued with the daunting vividness of an inescapable hallucination. A crowded street brings no relief, nor does a homecoming – either the narrator or the world has grown deranged, unless both have. Disconcertingly, the end of this story doesn't return us to the psychiatrist's office. Instead we're pounced on by another tale, "By Any Other Name". We might read this as a thematic reversal of its predecessor, replacing the papery horrors with a watery variety and locating the monstrous in an everyday element. While it recalls the notion of a djinn, I for one have never previously encountered what's released from the bottle. It and the author distil the occult essence of a teenage tale of mine, and I'm flattered and touched that so much could be found in my youthful fiction or, more accurately, improved upon.

Writing the account brings its narrator no relief, and its secrets threaten to invade the surrounding picaresque. Inklings of them send its errant hero on his way, but his stops en route vibrate with hints of unadmitted terror, and when has it ever been advisable to room at an inn overnight in our kind of tale? We might refrain from playing a mysterious cassette in a lonely room, but then we wouldn't experience the next tale, "Learning the Language".

It epitomises the author's sense of Wales as a numinous landscape, very much in the grand Machen tradition. Also Machenesque is the sense of religion gone wrong or reflected in a distorting mirror, one of that Anglican author's concepts of evil, and the notion of a version of Welsh older and more occult than contemporary usage would surely have appealed to him. Monuments, apparently innocent, prove to conceal a secret significance – street signs too. Horror fiction can convey a sense of revelation, and this instance delivers a series of them, not least the reason Welsh folk may view the English as they do. Watch out who takes you for a Welsh walk if you're English.

An increasingly ominous encounter with the local drinkers helps prepare us for "Somewhere, Beneath a Maze of Sky" (an enviably splendid title). A ghastly evocation of a hangover – Lucky Jim Dixon suffered no worse – precedes a terrible trek even sobriety wouldn't improve. Losing our way is a terror most of us may well have undergone, in which case we'll recognise how ill-disposed even the open countryside can turn. Far worse lies in wait for our ill-fated wanderers – a doom all the more fearful for its lack of explanation. Often sheer unfairness is the heart of horror.

Disorientation invades the surrounding narrative too, betraying retrospective uncanniness in a classical reversal of perception. Our wayfarer continues his journey, gathering untold tales in the process before homing in on one, "The Church With Bleeding Windows" (a title that could well have graced a giallo). The story takes no time to clutch the reader in its claws, and its monster doesn't hang around for long before renewing its attacks in as breathlessly relentless a tale as these pages contain. The first explanatory flashback hardly slows things down, especially not the thing that's on the rampage, but soon we're regaled with some exceptionally grisly humour – our author has never been more himself. Will comedy or horror, assuming they're separable, win the day? I leave that judgement to the reader.

By now our roving protagonist has become a reader too – the psychometric kind – at the mercy of the occult map of Wales, which is poetically evoked by the opening paragraphs of "What Others Hear". The keynote of the tale is claustrophobia, aural as well as environmental (see the cramped accommodation, a synaesthetic metaphor of his condition, that our unlucky organist has to suffer). If only he were just hallucinating his fate might be less hellish. Music is no shield against the demons he has attracted, and the church is no help either. We've come a long way from the religious comforts implicit in the Christian tradition of the genre, represented by the likes of Wheatley (no, not Ben) and his disciple Manchester. While the story starts in Machen's territory, by the end it has entered Lovecraft's. It can be seen as tracing how our field has progressed away from reassurance.

A short drive during which the landscape invades his thoughts if not vice versa brings our wanderer to the account of "The Devil in the Details". In his story notes the author says this wasn't meant to be a comedy. What better evidence of irrepressibility do we need? An atmospheric Gothic opening leads to a decidedly gruesome sacrifice and aftermath, by which point you may be wondering where the comical comes in. Look no further than the doctors' duologues and their grisly bonhomie. Such behaviour should guarantee comeuppance, and in an unexpected way it does, revealing a structural tightness we may have mistaken for enthusiastic looseness. Perhaps the witty title ought to have alerted us.

The tales are coming closer to their reader – the roving protagonist, that is, and perhaps us too. "Forgive Us Not Our Trespasses" is the final tale. I'm surprised if not disconcerted to find that although many fictions (not just Dr Probert's) deal with pregnancy, a recurring theme in horror, very few acknowledge the dogged determination to become a father some men indulge at their partner's expense. The potential monstrousness of maternity is here too, and the spectre of infant mortality, readily roused in any Victorian graveyard. Worse, Victorian surgery returns, coupled with religious fervour, a horrid combination we might like to think we've left behind. Our author often cites Herbert Van Thal's Pan Books of Horror as an influence. Of all his stories, this would surely have taken Bertie's eye (and snacked on it, perhaps).

Before we reach the goal and the reason for the stories, we're led in a metafictional fashion through solutions we may have considered. The purpose of the book-length trek proves to be quintessentially Welsh. Though I once wrote a tale on the theme, it hid from me here until the final revelation. Well done to it and its author! He brings a feast of wonders and horrors, and I'm just the greeter at the door. Welcome and be seated, if you aren't already. Here comes the first course, and before long you'll be replete with imagination.

Ramsey Campbell
Wallasey, Merseyside
4th December 2021

On the Road

Slate sky, steel sea.

Those were the first things he took in when he came round. Those, and the sensation of the gravel digging into his palms and face from where he must have fallen onto the unyielding surface of the roadside. He got to his feet and brushed the dust from his skin. A juggernaut thundered by, far too close for comfort, the vehicle's slipstream threatening to topple him once more or worse, drag him along in its wake, scrape him along the motorway until he was nothing but a smear on the tarmac.

Slate sky, steel sea, grey road.

And blood.

Just a trickle from his nose, splashing onto the back of his hand as he raised it to explore the source, but it was enough to exacerbate the dizziness and threaten another fall.

He closed his eyes, ignored the noise of the traffic, and counted to ten.

The next time he looked the world was drawing into focus. Now he could see the ribbed, roiling cloud cover, the turbulent sea that was actually an estuary with land visible on its far side. He could also see, some distance back, the suspension bridge over which he must have driven.

His car was behind him, too, but much closer. Just a few steps away, in fact. He leaned on the bonnet and peered at his reflection in the windscreen. The car didn't look damaged, and neither did he, just a bit roughed up by the fall.

What had happened?

The driver's side door was unlocked. He got in, and tried to start the engine.

Nothing.

Ah.

That must be it. His car had given up and he had started walking to try and find one of those motorway phone boxes.

Didn't he have a mobile phone?

A quick pat of his pockets confirmed that he didn't.

Best start walking again, then, but be a lot more careful this time.

He got out of the car to discover the air had changed. Mixed in with the petrol fumes was a heavy, damp smell. It was going to rain soon, and rain a lot.

Get moving.

He remembered to lock the car this time before he started walking, away from the bridge.

It still hadn't started to rain when he passed the sign, the great big one with the dragon on it and the bold announcement in two languages:

Welcome to Wales
Croeso Y Gymru

Only now did the irony hit him. Perhaps it was crossing the bridge into foreign territory that had caused his car to pack up. If he had stayed in England it would probably have never happened.

Still no sign of a phone box.

The first few heavy drops of rain were falling when he heard a vehicle close behind draw to a halt. Two sharp blows on the horn made him turn round. The driver of the brown estate car looked to be in his early forties and was beckoning to him.

"Stuck, are you?" The driver had to roll his window down before the words could be understood.

"My car…"

"Yes, I saw it – back there. Need a lift?"

There was a crack of thunder, but still he hesitated.

"Come on – it's going to bloody pour down in a minute. You'll catch your death."

"If it's not too much trouble…"

The passenger door was already open.

"Rhys," the driver said as he climbed in, extending a hand. "Rhys Thomas."

The man's grip was firm and dry. "Pleased to meet you. I'm…" Who was he? He tried to think, scrabbling at the dark out of the way corners of his brain for information that should have been second nature. Was it even there? Hang on… it was coming… "Robert." But that was all. He paled as he realised he had no idea what his surname was.

"Pleased to meet you too, Robert." Rhys didn't look pleased though, he looked worried. "Are you sure you're all right?"

Robert, still unable to remember any more of his name, gave the man an unconvincing nod. "I think so. I must have taken a bit of a tumble. I'm still a bit shaky."

Rhys had one hand on the wheel and was taking a phone from his pocket with the other. "Need me to ring an ambulance? Oh shit, hang on a minute."

The car veered a little as they passed a police car perched at the side of the road and Rhys did his best to conceal the phone. "Bastards," he said once they were past. "Already got six points on my license. Don't want any more, eh?"

"Don't worry about ringing anyone." Robert wondered if he might have been safer taking his chances next to the traffic. "If you could just drop me somewhere there's a phone I can do it myself." He had no idea who he would call. "I'll do better than that. I'll take you where I'm headed. They'll have a phone, somewhere you can sit down, and, most importantly, a bar." That last bit was delivered with a sly wink that suggested Rhys Thomas wasn't averse to a bit of daytime drinking. Hopefully he hadn't already started before he picked Robert up.

"Is it far?"

"Just another mile," came the reply. "Lovely place. Famous, too. Gets used for golf championships, that sort of thing. Do you like golf?" Robert had no idea, but he didn't think so. "Smashing course they've got. You should try a few rounds if you've got the time. I might even join you."

No. "I think I'd better get my car sorted out." Robert rubbed at his nose. The bleeding had stopped, but if he was having memory problems he probably needed checking out. "Do you know if they have a doctor at the hotel?"

"No idea, but Newport's not far. They've got the Royal Gwent there. Fabulous hospital. When my mate Mark got into a bar fight back in Ponty they fixed up his face good and proper. You can hardly see the scars if it's dark enough"

Robert couldn't tell if that was supposed to be a joke. "What's the hotel called?"

"Celtic Manor." Rhys pointed ahead of him. "We're nearly there – look."

Off to their right, Robert got his first look at their destination. The building was impressive, built into the side of a cliff and surveying the roads that ran beside and around it from its myriad windows. Were there faces staring out from some of them? And even if there were, why should it bother him? Was it because he couldn't tell if it was the glass that was the same pallid grey as the sky and the sea, or the faces themselves?

Stop it. People can look out of their bedroom windows if they want to. Even if their faces seem too small to be pressed up against the glass like that.

"We're here." Rhys was waving a hand in front of Robert's face. "You sure you're okay? You were staring off into nothing there for a moment, Mr Spaceman."

"I'll be fine. Thank you for the lift." Robert began to pat his pockets for his wallet.

"Hey now, don't you think you owe me anything." Rhys was already getting out. "Least I can do for someone who's overdone it." Again that wink, that implied double meaning that didn't apply to Robert. At least he didn't think so. "Come on, I'll make sure you get as far as the main desk. Then I've got work to do."

The receptionist was called Anna. She had her blonde hair in a pigtail and regarded him with sympathetic eyes as she reached for a telephone to ring for a breakdown truck.

"Are you sure this isn't too much trouble?"

"Not at all, sir. Give me your details and they'll bring the car here."

Details.

Like his name.

His full name.

He patted his pockets once more, certain he had felt something when he had been about to give Rhys some money for his trouble.

And there it was, in his inside jacket pocket. A wallet.

With nothing inside it but some cash, a driving license, and a small piece of crumpled paper.

"This should give you everything you need." He handed the license over, eager for its return so he could be reminded of his surname.

Anna smiled at him as she talked to whoever was on the other end of the line. "Yes, and his name is Robert –"

"Excuse me!"

A broad man carrying an even broader display board squeezed past, giving Robert a bump as he did so, and headed in the direction of one of the conference rooms. By the time Robert had turned back Anna was putting down the receiver.

"They're not sure how soon they can get to your car, sir, but they hope it should be in the next couple of hours."

"Hours?" Was that good or bad?

"There's a bar through there." Anna was pointing to her left. "You're welcome to have a drink while you wait."

Robert took back his driving licence. "I don't seem to have any money."

"Well, there's some sort of book convention on today." She was already looking behind him at the next person in the queue. "I'm sure they won't mind you wandering around."

Perhaps he could. But first he needed to find out who he was.

It was too dark in the hotel foyer to read the tiny type (although Anna had somehow managed it). Robert retreated to a window near the entrance and held the card up to the feeble sunlight. There was his picture, there was his date of birth, there was his name.

His blurred name.

Was it his eyesight or the card? He could just make out 'Robert'. The surname seemed to start with the letter 'P', but then the print degenerated into a faded remnant that was all but illegible.

What had Anna said to the breakdown man?

He looked over at reception. She was busy with another client, and the crushing embarrassment of walking over and asking her what she thought his name was, in front of other people as well, was just too much to contemplate.

When the breakdown truck got here, with his car, they'd call it out, wouldn't they? Over the public address system the hotel no doubt had. He just had to calm down and have a drink.

No money.

They'd have water, wouldn't they? At last he had a plan. Calm down, have a glass of water, and wait for his memory, his identity, and his car to return. Which they all would.

The bar's main drinking area was relatively deserted, with just a few desultory drinkers on stools whiling away the tepid afternoon. To the left, an old man in a rumpled grey suit sat staring at a half empty glass of something that was fizzing its last gasp. To the far right, and occupying the majority of the space that had obviously been cleared for it, was the book convention Anna had mentioned.

It was a hive of activity. Men in frayed jackets and women wearing enough cheap jewellery to add several pounds to their already considerable weight were eyeing battered hardbacks with lusty expressions while gently turning pages with podgy fingers that seemed too large for such dainty movements. Two of them appeared to be arguing with one of the booksellers, currently safe behind his table of rarities.

The bar, then.

The man serving nodded as Robert approached.

"What'll it be, sir?"

"Uh…" It was so difficult. He had never been in this situation before. Or at least not one he could remember. "Your receptionist, Anna," (that's good – blame her), "said I could wait in here. My car's broken down and it's being towed."

"And you've got no cash, is that it?"

Robert nodded.

"No cards either?"

Yes to that too.

"Then I'm afraid I can't serve you anything, sir."

"Not even a glass of water?

The barman pointed to a sign that read 'Water For Residents Only'. "Are you a resident, sir?"

"No."

"In that case…"

"I'll buy the young man a drink!"

The old man in the grey suit had shuffled out from his seat and was now at Robert's left shoulder. "What'll it be?"

Robert shook his head. "I couldn't possibly presume to…"

"Not at all! Not at all!"

"I've nothing to pay you back with."

The old man raised an eyebrow, causing the skin of the entire right side of his forehead to concertina. "Not even your company for a short time? For a little chat with an old man who has been sitting here since eleven this morning slowly being driven mad by that lot over there and just wants someone to chat to who isn't drunk or obsessed with first editions? I assure you, that's all I want. I also assure you that I am not selling anything, I have no contagious diseases, and I am not trying to engage in a relationship where we end up going on a camping holiday together."

That last bit caused Robert to laugh. It was the first time he had even managed a smile since coming to.

Oh, why not.

"Gin and tonic," he said. "And thank you."

"Good choice!" the old man was nodding. "Two of those please, barman, and make them doubles if you would. I may as well make the most of having someone to converse with."

As the barman fixed the drinks the old man held out his right hand. "Thomas Jeavons," he said. "Currently on my annual holiday, or rather pilgrimage if you like, to this place. And you are?"

"Robert…" it still wouldn't come. Why wouldn't it come?

"My dear fellow, are you all right?"

"I had a bit of an accident close to the Severn Bridge. I feel fine but I'm just having trouble remembering a few things,"

"Like your surname?"

"Yes." *And lots of other things, too, such as where I live, what I do for a job, and why I was coming over to Wales, but I'm hoping they'll all come back very soon in one of those flashes of recovery like you see in films.*

Mr Jeavons took Robert's arm in a surprisingly strong grip and guided him over to where he was sitting. "A G&T and a bit of a sit down will work wonders, my boy. You just let an old man ramble on and I'm sure at some point everything will come back to you."

Robert sipped his drink. "I'm afraid I'm not much of a conversationalist. At least, I don't feel like one at the moment."

It didn't seem to bother Mr Jeavons at all. "That's fine! As I said, what I really want is someone to talk to, by which I mean you do the listening. Is that all right?"

Robert shrugged his shoulders and nodded. "I don't have much else to do at the moment."

"Excellent!" Mr Jeavons gave him a broad smile. It quickly turned cold as his attention moved to the book sale. "It's them, you see. They've got me thinking."

Robert glanced over his shoulder. "Do you know them? Old enemies or something?"

"Oh nothing like that, and I can categorically say I have never seen any of them before in my life. It's the books, rather than the people."

Robert squinted, but he couldn't make any titles out. "Are they rare?"

"Some are, some aren't. It's not so much the prices, as what the books are about." Mr Jeavons paused and sipped his gin. Then he stared at the glass, his mind obviously elsewhere.

"Which is?" Robert prompted gently.

The words were so quiet as to be little more than a hiss of the old man's breath, and Robert would have missed it if the activity in the bar hadn't ceased for that precise moment.

"The macabre."

The general hubbub started up again, and Robert tried hard not to think the room had been silenced just so he could hear that word.

"You want to talk about the macabre?"

This time, when Mr Jeavons looked at him, the old man's eyes held a glint of tears. "In a way, by which I mean I want to talk about what happened to me. Many years ago." He looked around him. "In this place."

"This hotel, you mean?" Presumably he didn't mean the bar.

"Oh this bar was here back then as well, and it only looked marginally less cosy than it does now. But yes, I do mean this hotel. Tell me, Robert," and now he was leaning forward conspiratorially. "Do you believe it's possible for a man to be cursed?"

He seemed to be waiting for an answer and Robert didn't know what to say. "I suppose so. It depends. Do you mean like a magic spell or something?"

No he didn't. "I mean performing an action that, as a result, can damn you for the rest of your life, fill you with guilt, condemn you to returning to the scene of your crime."

"You mean you cursed yourself?"

A wry smile at that. "I suppose you could say that."

"By doing something bad?"

The smile became a cynical laugh. "Oh I did something bad, all right. Something very bad indeed. Would you mind terribly if I told you about it?"

Robert had nowhere else to go, nothing else to do, and right now he owed this man something for the drink he had in his hand. As he nodded the room seemed to darken. No doubt it was the result of a cloud passing in front of the sun. It was probably Robert's imagination that the background noise was receding to the point of near silence, and that the old man's voice had suddenly taken on a new, clearer timbre. Suddenly it felt as if there was nothing in this room but Robert and Mr Jeavons.

And, of course, the story.

A Cruel Summer

It was hot.

Tom Jeavons mopped his brow and tried to ignore the sensation of his shirt sticking to his back. The handle of the beige suitcase at his feet had darkened from the sweat of his grip in just the short journey to the hotel foyer.

"Turned out nice again!"

That was Bob, at the front, signing the four of them in. Always the organiser was Bob, which was one of the reasons Tom had picked him as Best Man. Always the joker, too. In between looking through the paperwork, the pretty girl behind the desk flashed Bob a smile. Tom grinned. There'd be no stopping the banter now.

"Of course, it said on the news that it would be." Bob assumed a mock-serious expression and imitated the words of the radio announcer. 'It is the thirteenth of July nineteen seventy six and there seems to be no let up in the heatwave that is currently leading to water shortages in parts of the country."

"There's none of that here, is there?" Adrian was short, plump, and a bit of a moaner, truth be told. "Water shortage, I mean."

"Don't you worry, Ades." Matt clapped a meaty hand on the little man's shoulder. "You'll soon be able to have a lovely wash after that bus ride, get all the sweat out of those nooks and crannies." The numerous prods and pokes that followed just left Adrian looking all the more upset.

Tom remembered he was the man of the moment, that next weekend he was getting hitched to Katy, and that he was here celebrating his last weekend of bachelorhood with his three best friends. He raised his hands and called for calm, as much to save the receptionist from Bob's terrible chat up lines as Adrian from the bruises he was probably incurring from Matt's over-zealous attack of tickling. "It's not as if we're going to be drinking much water this weekend anyway, are we lads?"

The four of them bellowed a 'No!' that echoed around the foyer and made the receptionist wince.

"Sorry, love," said Bob. "It's just that Tom there," he pointed to the back of their little queue, "it's Tom's stag weekend, so we're expecting to stagger out of here on Monday morning feeling as if we've been visited by the wrath of God."

"That's okay, sir," she gave him a sweet smile as she flipped through a sheaf of yellow forms. "When are you planning to do the golf tuition? This afternoon, or when you're feeling a bit the worse for wear tomorrow?"

"Golf?" Matt's face had lit up.

"Golf?" Adrian looked miserable. "I've no idea how to play golf."

"That's why I booked the training session," said Bob. "As a surprise." He gave the receptionist a pointed glance before swinging his smile around to Tom. "Happy Stag Weekend, mate!"

Tom beamed. He had guessed that was why Bob had suggested they come here. After all, the place had one of the most famous golf courses in Wales. He didn't have a clue how to play and wasn't that interested, either, but it was the thought that counted, and there was always the chance he might actually turn out to have hidden world-class golfing talents.

"Fantastic, mate!" He raised an imaginary glass. "I haven't a clue if I'll be any good at it, but fantastic!"

"I'll stay in the bar, thank you," said Adrian.

"Oh no you won't, my chubby friend." Matt's target leapt out of the way surprisingly swiftly before Matt could grab him once more. "You're coming with us and liking it, especially if Bob has gone to the trouble of paying for us."

"You've all paid for it," Bob said. "That was what the collection at work was for six months ago, remember?" Matt and Adrian finally did, but it took some prompting.

"Bollocks," said Adrian.

"That's the spirit," Matt slapped him across the buttocks. "Are we checked in yet?"

The response was a volley of room keys. Tom and Adrian caught theirs, Matt dropped his and was rewarded for his early insult by a swift kick up the behind from Adrian as he bent to retrieve them. He gave a dramatic pratfall onto the ground to the laughter of all the others.

"Right, no more mucking about." Bob was looking at his watch. "We're on a schedule, here. Get unpacked and let's meet in the bar in half an hour, after which we'll get going with the golf." He swung back to the girl behind the desk. "If that's okay?"

It was.

It didn't surprise Tom at all that he was the first one down. He was too excited to do more than dump his case and head for the bar.

Where his first shock of the weekend was waiting for him.

At first he thought the place was empty. He did a quick scan for his friends and then ordered himself a pint. If they weren't here in time for the first drink of the weekend then it was their loss, wasn't it? The beer tasted all the sweeter for being free (or rather, paid for by the collection back in the office that Bob had organised – another fine reason for picking him as best man) but as Tom glanced around him and saw the figure sitting in a secluded corner the drink turned sour in his mouth.

She was staring at him, the kind of non-committal, blank-faced stare that gave nothing away. All manner of things could be going on behind those eyes – joy or hate or nothing at all.

He guessed it was probably hate, though.

"Hi, Molly." He could hardly ignore her, could he? Especially now they had made eye contact. "What are you doing here?"

"I would have thought that was obvious," came the reply, as well as the obvious fact that she had no intention of getting up, that any ensuing bitterness would be projected across the room, catching anyone in the crossfire who happened to be in the way, including his friends.

His friends.

A wave of horror plunged through him as he slid off the bar stool. He couldn't risk his friends knowing she was here, couldn't risk them finding out what had been going on between them, couldn't risk it getting back to Katy.

"Not really," he hissed, once he was beside her. "You know this is my stag weekend."

"Of course I do." Molly sipped her white wine. The fingers that gripped the glass were tipped with long magenta-painted fingernails that had left marks on Tom before now, which had taken some explaining. "It's all they've been talking about in the office for the past couple of weeks, after all."

"Then why?"

"Because you're getting married next weekend, that's why!" Her face no longer held its blank impassivity. Now those eyes were imploring, the lips quivering. Lips that, although Tom had sworn he would never kiss them again, even now seemed unbearably tempting. "Which means this might be my last chance to persuade you not to."

"And do what? Come back to you? To all the arguments and the shouting? All those nights of saying you were busy when I knew full well you were off with other blokes? Do you think I'm stupid or something?"

Tom shook his head as the full memory of what life with Molly had really been like – the life outside the bedroom, the one that had driven him to drink and a psychiatrist, the one that had made him realise Katy was everything he wanted and needed when she arrived in his life like a gift from some benevolent higher power. Oh no. There could never be any more Molly.

"I'm sorry, Tom." Her voice was icy, now. "But that's simply not good enough." She laid a hand on his and her tone changed again. "Can't we just talk? That's all I want to do, all I need to do."

He pulled his hand away. Same changeable old Molly, changeable to get her own way. "There's nothing more to discuss."

"Well I say there is, and if you don't, I'll tell Matt and Bob and Adrian – especially Adrian, that sad little gossip artist – why I'm here. It won't be long before Katy finds out everything if I do that."

Tom peered round the corner. Still no sign of the others. "They'll be here any minute," he said. "I can't possibly talk to you now."

"Then when?"

"Tonight." It was all he could think of to get rid of her. "I'll pretend I've had enough to drink and leave the bar."

Molly downed her wine and got to her feet. "Room 134. I'll be waiting."

"I don't know what time it will be."

She gave him a wicked smile that both repelled and attracted him. "Like I said, I'll be waiting."

"There he is!"

That was Matt, calling from the entrance to the bar. Tom leapt to his feet and strode to greet his three friends.

"Picked someone up already have you, you dog?"

Tom knew it was useless to fight back the redness he could feel surging into his cheeks, but he tried anyway. "What do you mean, Bob?"

"He means that." Adrian was pointing at the now empty table that had Tom's half-drunk pint on it.

And Molly's empty wine glass. Was it his imagination or was the fire exit door in the corner yet to fully complete its swing shut?

"That was there when I sat down." Tom grabbed his pint and swiftly downed the rest of it. "Come on you lot, you're playing catch up."

"Not just yet, tiger." Bob was pointing to his watch. "Time for our golf lesson."

They would be going away from the bar. Thank God. Tom did his best to feign annoyance. "What, now?"

"Yes now. It was the only time they could fit us in. Besides, I thought we'd get more out of it if we didn't end up clattering round the course half cut. Come on."

Tom deliberately dragged his heels, but it was still Adrian who brought up the rear.

"I don't want to go either," Adrian said. "I bet we'll be terrible."

They were terrible.

So terrible in fact, that by the time they got to the seventh hole Mr Watkins, their instructor, was checking his watch and suggesting they might only have time to complete half the course.

"That's all right," Tom had remained cheery in the face of his and his friends' incompetence. "It's just nice to be out here." More than any of his friends realised.

Watkins nodded. "So whose turn is it to tee off?"

It was Matt's, but as he had already bent one of the club's nine irons out of shape Tom was pushed forward to have another go.

"Now remember what I told you last time," said Watkins as Tom lined up his shot. "Try and ease your body into the swing."

And maybe I'll actually hit it this time. Tom licked his lips. They still tasted of beer, but not of Molly, thank heavens. What was he going to do when they got back?

Almost without thinking, Tom repeated the sequence of movements he'd been shown by their instructor.

He swung at the ball.

To the amazement of everyone, most of all Tom, he hit it.

The ball went sailing through the air and across the course, but in a direction only very tangentially related to where it was supposed to go. It fell to earth in a patch of shrubbery twenty yards away.

"Am I supposed to…?"

"Go and get it?" Watkins nodded a yes to Tom's question. "Otherwise you lose your deposit."

To the jibes and cheers of the other three, Tom trudged across the course, shielding his eyes from the sun as he headed for the rough. He turned just before he entered, intending to wave his club at them in an act of boisterous defiance. For a moment he thought he saw their silhouettes outlined by the nearly blinding sun. Then he blinked and they were gone.

Probably moved onto the next hole. That Watkins bloke looked as if he was getting impatient.

He'd quickly catch them up. All he had to do was find the ball. Tom pushed aside a low-lying branch of a nearby elm, and started to rake his club through the unkempt, thistle-ridden grass.

You would think they'd keep it in better condition than this, even if it is called 'the rough', he thought as he found himself having to move further in. Soon the course had disappeared, the patch in which he had lost his ball proving to be a lot larger than he had imagined. And a lot denser, too. As Tom pushed aside evergreens with his fists, tiny creatures scurried away from the sunlight that exposed the hard-packed earth. There was no ball anywhere to be seen, no promising glint of white revealed by his attempts at searching through the scrub.

Oh never mind. I'll pay the deposit. It'll be worth it to stop poking around in the dust and the heat.

It was only when Tom had made up his mind to go back that he realised he was lost.

This place can't be that big. It's just a clump of rough ground in the middle of the course. Keep going in a straight line and you should come out on the other side.

But rather than finding the tangle of bushes and trees begin to thin out, if anything the rough seemed to be getting thicker. Thorns and branches plucked at Tom's sleeves and trousers, and it was getting increasingly difficult to see where he was going.

Then, suddenly, he found himself in an open space. It was brighter, too, but the sunlight filtering through the oily trees looked wrong, with a sickly violet hue that turned the earth on which he was standing the colour of old blood.

Did the guys put something in my beer?

Tom shook his head. That couldn't be it. He had been alone when he bought the drink. Molly? No, she had been too far away and couldn't have guessed when he'd turn up.

What the hell was going on, then?

At the centre of the clearing was a pit, roughly square and obviously man made. It looked like the kind of tiger trap you might see in a jungle movie.

Tom blinked. Had that just appeared? He was sure it hadn't been there when he entered this place. Beyond it, what now resembled thick rainforest formed an impenetrable wall of wet, black leaves that enclosed the entire clearing.

He kicked at the ground, sending a puff of lilac dust into the air.

"Is someone there?"

The voice came from the pit. Thin and reedy, with an accent that sounded as if it was out of an old movie. Rather than announce his presence, Tom crept to the pit's edge. The violet sunshine was stronger here, and as he peered in he could discern two men standing against opposing walls of earth.

No, not standing.

They were pinned there.

"There is someone. Thank God." It was the one on the left who had spoken, the one who was now staring at Tom with imploring eyes. "Are you from HQ? Have the advance forces landed? Never mind, just get me out of here."

Now Tom could see the insignia on the man's uniform. It helped him place the accent, but it didn't make it any easier to believe. Was he really staring at a British World War II POW?

"Don't listen to him." The other man's accent was American Deep South. His uniform was different, too. Somehow it looked more… modern. "This guy's crazy. Keeps going on about the Luftwaffe and all kinds of shit. Free him if you like, but get me out first, and hurry! The gooks are on a thirty minute patrol and I can't remember when they last passed."

"Where are you from?" It was all Tom could think to ask.

"Alabama, USA. Why?"

"And where do you think you are?"

"What the hell d'ya mean? I'm in this goddamned pit, ain't I? This goddamned pit in this goddamned jungle. I've been here three days, but it feels longer. Should never have come. None of us should."

"He's the one who's mad," said the Brit. "He keeps on about it being over twenty years in the future. He's not even fighting the same war! He thinks he's on the other side of the world!"

Tom looked at the Brit. "Because you think you're in World War Two?"

"See?" That was the American. "He thinks you're as crazy as I do."

Tom turned to the other man. "And you think you're in Vietnam?"

"What d'ye mean 'think', friend? Where the hell else could I be?"

On a golf course in Wales, not that Tom could bring himself to say that. On a golf course in 1976 where he was supposed to be enjoying his stag weekend.

Wait a minute.

Had the guys planned this? Was it some weird kind of practical joke? Tom shook his head. That made no sense. How could they have planned that he would hit his golf ball into this particular part of the rough?

But how else to explain it, then?

He leaned over the pit once more, "I don't know who you are, but I'm guessing you're both friends of Bob's. I don't even know what this is supposed to be, and you've obviously gone to a lot of trouble. It's… er… very good, whatever it is. If I was supposed to get in there with you so you could put the jump on me, tie me up and leave me stuck on this golf course for the night while you lot partied I think I'll say thanks but no thanks. Now if you'll excuse me, I've got my stag weekend to get back to."

The two men in the pit stared at Tom in disbelief throughout his address. When he had finished, the silence lingered. Eventually it was broken by the American, who turned to the Brit and said,

"He's even crazier than you are!"

The World War II prisoner merely took a deep breath and started screaming "Help!" at the top of his voice.

"Goddamn it! You see?" Tom didn't, not at all. "You've started him off again. Quick, get me out of here before the gooks hear him. If they find you here you'll end up in this pit with us!"

That was enough. "Have fun, guys." Tom turned and started walking back the way he had come, through the tropical-looking forest, kicking his way through the dense undergrowth, pushing aside branches wet with rain (a nice touch, Tom thought – he'd have to congratulate the boys on that one). That weird violet light was still disorientating (he'd have to ask them how they did that when he got back) and he realised he had no idea where he was going. Behind him, he could hear the cries of the two 'prisoners' gradually receding into the distance, to be replaced by something else.

Shouts from ahead of him.

Voices calling his name.

With renewed vigour he aimed for the sound. It still felt like ages before he found himself stumbling onto severely trimmed grass, the ground bare here and there from the lack of rain.

He was back, on the nice normal golf course with the nice normal absurdly hot sun beating down on him and his friends beating a path to where he was standing, no doubt looking a bit dishevelled.

"Where the hell have you been?" Bob was the first to get to him, closely followed by Matt, who wanted to know if Tom had found the ball.

"As if you guys didn't know." His words came out more acidic than he had intended and so Tom gave them a broad smile to take the edge off.

"That patch of rough you mean?" Adrian was peering over Tom's shoulder. "But we looked there and couldn't find you. You can't have been in there all the time!"

"Well I was, and I found your little surprise. Sorry, but I'm afraid I'll be joining you for drinks back at the bar rather than spending the night tied up out here like you planned."

Three confused men stared back at him.

"What are you talking about, Tom?"

Tom sighed. "Bob, I saw it all – the pit, those guys. I'm guessing they're friends of yours? Or did you hire actors? I have to say they were bloody good. And how did you get the light to change like that?"

His friends didn't look confused any more. They looked worried.

"Are you feeling all right?"

"I'm fine, Matt. If it's any consolation, the whole thing did really freak me out, so please consider it job done."

"I didn't have anything to do with it," said Adrian. "Whatever you're going on about."

"Listen, mate," and Bob laid a hand on his shoulder. "I swear, hand on heart, that neither I nor any of your good friends here have any idea what you are talking about, but it's obviously bothering you. Why don't you show us?"

Why not? "Follow me."

Tom led them into the rough. He pushed aside the elm branch and made his way through the copse of evergreens like last time, noticing the light beginning to dim like last time.

Then he was out and back in the blazing sunshine on the other side of the golf course.

"But it was there!" Tom was shaking his head. "In there! A pit with two men in it! They talked to me!"

"That's okay, Tom," Bob probably didn't mean to sound patronising. "It's most likely the heat. They said on the news it's been doing all sorts of funny things to people."

"This wasn't a funny thing." Tom pulled his hand away. "This was real. They said they were prisoners. But it made no sense because they were prisoners of different wars, and the light was all weird…"

"Sounds like someone could do with a drink!" said Matt.

"Several rounds of drinks." Bob gave Tom a more manly clap on the shoulder. "Best cure for the pre-wedding jitters."

"Yes." Tom was trying to think. "Yes, I'm sure you're right." He glanced back at the rough. "Just… give me a minute, will you? I still haven't found my ball."

"Oh don't worry about that." Bob was shaking his head. "We can sort it. Adrian can go with one less pint."

Tom ignored Adrian's cry of protest. "No, just let me have one last look. It's important." And it was. "It'll just make me feel less of an idiot. I'll be back in a minute."

Before the others could protest, Tom ducked into the trees. This time it only took him five paces before the vegetation began to change, before the light turned that alien, unnatural violet colour and the trees began to drip. Ahead he could see the broad outline of the pit.

And that was where he stopped, turned, and hurried back to where his friends were waiting.

"Did you find it? asked Bob.

"What?"

"Your golf ball, you nutter." Matt was making a spiral motion with his index finger against his temple.

"Oh. No."

"That's because I had it all along!"

It was rare for Adrian to play a practical joke, or make any kind of joke really, and as he held out the ball he must have somehow slipped into his palm Tom felt he couldn't really slap the smile off the man's face, much as he wanted to. Instead he settled for a "thanks" and pocketed the ball before joining the others as they trudged back to the hotel. It turned out Mr Watkins, the instructor, had long since deserted them as his time of hire had run out.

"But never mind that." Bob was busy explaining what they were going to do next. "A slap up feed in the self-service canteen, plus plenty of water to make sure we're hydrated after being out here all afternoon. Then, my friends, it's onto the most important part of the weekend."

"The drinking!" They all said the words together, even Tom, painfully aware that there was something else important he had to do, or rather someone important he had to meet, and keep it a secret from the others. He had no idea how he was going to do it, and right now all he could think about was what had happened to him in the rough. Of only one thing could he be certain: he had never expected his stag weekend to start off like this

And now he was beginning to dread how it might end.

After they had eaten, Tom suggested they go back to their rooms to get ready for the evening. Hopefully that would give him time to sort out the Molly problem before he had too much to drink.

"All right," said Bob. "I could do with a shower myself to be honest."

"I probably need one too," said Matt.

"I don't." Adrian followed his words with a burp as his steak and kidney pie and chips refused to settle.

Matt wafted a hand in front of his face. "I think you do, mate."

"But no hanging around, right?" Bob was looking at his watch. "Let's all get to the bar by seven at the latest."

That gave Tom an hour. He tried hard not to rush from the canteen as he went back to his own room. He waited five minutes to be on the safe side, then took the lift down to the first floor. His heart hammered against his chest as he made his way down the corridor to room 134, all the while wondering if he was doing the right thing.

If you don't do this, she'll come and find you, remember?

There was no question. He had to sort this out now, even though his mind was still occupied by the prisoners in the pit. Well, the world of the weird was just going to have to be put aside, for the next three quarters of an hour at least.

The first time he saw her door he walked straight past, unable to summon the resolve to knock on it.

Come on, you can't afford to be wasting time like this.

He forced himself to turn around and clenched his fists to stop his hands from shaking.

Back to Room 134.

He knocked.

He waited.

No answer.

He felt a sensation akin to the sudden drop on a roller coaster.

He glanced furtively from side to side, then knocked again.

More waiting.

He was about to leave when the door opened to reveal Molly, clad in a white bath towel and very little else.

"I was in the shower," she said, taking a step back. She frowned when he didn't pursue her. "Well, come in then."

"Wouldn't you prefer to get dressed first?"

"I can do that while we talk. Come on."

Tom couldn't risk staying out in the corridor any longer and so he followed her in. The atmosphere was warm and wet. Steam had escaped through the open bathroom door to fill the rest of the room.

Molly began to remove the towel. "After all it's nothing you haven't already seen, is it?"

Tom responded by turning away to face the closed curtains.

"Goodness me! Getting shy in our old age, are we?"

"At least one of us is." The words came out before he could stop them.

"Oh I'm not so sure about that. I bet with a little bit of persuasion I can get the old Tom to come out and play. But for now, you can relax. I've put something on."

When he turned round Molly was sitting on the bed. Some of her was covered by a white towelling robe.

"I never said I'd put clothes on, did I?" She crossed her legs, right foot tapping away seductively at the air.

"You should, you know. Someone might come in."

She leaned forward. Just a little too far forward. "Like who?"

"For all I know, someone you've arranged to come in so we can be caught together."

"Oh Tom! You really think I'd do something like that? Now that I've finally got you to myself after all this time?"

"It's not 'all this time' Molly, is it? It's only…"

"…two months? Seems longer though, doesn't it?" She regarded the fingernails of her right hand. They were painted the same shade of magenta as her toenails. "What a funny thing time is. I'm sure if Katy was here she would say two months was a very short time ago for you to be screwing somebody else so close to your wedding day."

"Yes, she probably would." Tom took a step to the right, away from the bed and closer to the door. "But she's not going to have the chance. Is she?"

"Well I don't know about that. We're going to need to come to some kind of agreement, aren't we?"

"The only thing I'm going to agree to is that I leave you alone and you leave me alone." Tom took another step towards the door.

Molly stood up. "I don't think either of us really wants that, do we?" Before he knew it she was right in front of him. "Can you honestly say there isn't one tiny part of you that wouldn't like to kiss me now?" Her lips were a fraction of an inch from his own. "And can you honestly say there isn't at least one tiny part of you that you would like me to kiss? Or even one big part of you?" She smiled as her fingertips brushed his groin. "And getting bigger all the time as far as I can tell."

Tom pulled her hand away. "Molly, that's enough! I am not sleeping with you again – not tonight and not ever. There are too many things in this world I don't understand. Hell, there are too many things in this hotel I don't understand, but I know that I love Katy and that I'm going to marry her. So no more of this. Please."

"All right." Molly's shoulders slumped as she backed away, looking dejected. "But you can't blame a girl for trying, can you?"

Tom shook his head and risked giving her the briefest smile. "I'll always think very fondly of you, Molly, you know that."

"Please," she held up a hand. "The one thing I don't want from you is sympathy, all right?"

"You're right," he nodded. "I should be leaving."

"No."

"What, then?"

She held out a hand. "Just stay here with me, a little while longer. For old times' sake?"

"But you said you didn't want to talk about us any longer."

"I don't. Let's talk about something else."

"What?"

Molly shrugged. "I don't know. Anything. What did you mean about there being things in this hotel you don't understand?"

Tom knew he needed to get away, but he also needed desperately to talk to someone about what he had seen. He glanced at his watch. He still had half an hour.

"There's something out on the golf course." He sat on the edge of the bed. "Something only I can see."

"You mean like a ghost?" She seemed to be taking him seriously.

"I don't know what I mean. If it is, then it's a ghost of a place rather than a person. But there are people in it, too. Two of them. Chained up in a sort of pit. They're from different wars, or at least that's what they look like. At first I thought it was a trick the boys were playing, but when I took them to see, it had all gone."

"And this didn't follow some heavy drinking or a fall or… anything else?"

Tom shook his head. "I'd had one pint with you. That's all."

Molly sat beside him and laid a hand on his. Suddenly Tom didn't have the energy to remove it. "It sounds as if the stress of everything is getting to you."

"This isn't stress! It was like there was a gap in the real world, and this… *other* place had slipped through, this piece of somewhere else. But only I could see it. But there must be others who can."

"Why?"

"Because otherwise how did those two men end up in it? It's as if it appeared during those two periods in time and got mistaken for some kind of torture pit. Perhaps it was even created back then."

Molly was shaking her head. "You're not making a lot of sense."

"That's because it doesn't make sense. But I saw it. I know I did."

"Okay. You've said it must have appeared to other people…"

"Yes, but Bob, Matt and Adrian didn't see it when I took them."

"So take me."

"What?"

"Take me. I'm not Bob or Matt or Adrian. Maybe it will appear for me."

Tom shook his head. "I don't think that's a good idea. Besides, someone might see us."

Molly had already shrugged off the robe and was pulling on a pair of faded blue jeans. "There's a fire escape at the end of the corridor. We can use that and bypass the bar, which is the only place your friends will be heading for. You might be a little bit late for your party but I'm sure they'll wait."

Tom tried hard to ignore the waves of lust passing through him as Molly reached for her bra. "Why would you even want to?"

She gave him the smile that had caused him to give into temptation in the first place. "Because it's time spent with you," she said. "Call it our last adventure, one that's outside the bedroom for a change."

Tom was in a quandary. It would be a disaster if his friends saw him with her. On the other hand, he desperately needed someone else to see the pit, if only to prove that he wasn't going insane. He knew what his answer would be. Any time spent debating it would be minutes wasted when they could be on the way there. She had pulled on a thin black polo-neck, her face filled with the anticipation of adventure.

Stop fancying her.

"Okay," he said. "Let's go."

It was just after half past six when they left the hotel. Sunset would not be for another couple of hours, but, as if to aid them, heavy clouds the colour of pewter had gathered to obscure the sun. A grey shadow was cast over the golf course as they made their way to the seventh hole. As they passed the last few straggling golfers on their way back to the hotel after a hard day's play, Tom pulled up his collar and tried to hide his face.

"They're not going to know who you are, silly." Molly was laughing, much more loudly than Tom was comfortable with. "Just relax for heaven's sake. If anyone does accuse you of being with me, I promise I'll deny it."

Was it her words or the way she spoke them that made Tom feel increasingly uneasy? Or was it just because they were approaching the place he now realised he was dreading entering.

"Are we in the right spot?"

"Yes." Despite the heat, Tom was shaking. "Look, I'm not sure this was such a good idea after all."

Molly put her hands on her hips, breathed deeply and looked around. "Well we're here now." She looked around at him as the sun came out and bathed her in its glow. "We are, aren't we?"

It certainly looked right. Tom nodded. "But it only appears if I go in by myself."

"You don't know that." She held out a hand and gave him a trace of a seductive smile. "Come on, let's see what we can find in there together."

Tom took her hand, felt a sensation of lust like warm lightning and knew instantly it was a mistake. Still, he allowed himself to be led into the darkness.

"Was it this overgrown when you were here?"

"Yes. You have to push the branches aside." Grateful for the excuse, he let go of her hand and moved in front of her. "Watch your step, there's a lot of stuff around that could trip you up."

"I'm sure you'll catch me with those big strong hands of yours."

Tom ignored her and pushed ahead. He knew what would happen. He knew that any minute now they'd end up back on the golf course, that Molly would give him an admonishing look, and then they would end up traipsing back to the hotel, where he would absolutely have to say goodbye to her for the last time.

"That's weird."

Tom couldn't believe Molly had spotted it before he did, but she was right. The light was changing, just as it had before. But this time the colour was different. Gone was the gentle violet hue to the shadows, the lilac tinge to what sunlight could force its way through the altered vegetation. Now the light was darker, redder, more like the colour of blood.

"Is this what happened last time?"

"More or less." If the light was different would what they found be different too? "Are you sure you want to carry on?"

"Are you kidding? If I didn't know better I'd think you were taking me to your special little lover's lane for a secret seduction. In fact for all I know that's what you are doing." She accompanied that with a nervous laugh but it was clear she was beginning to feel uneasy, too.

"I don't know what we'll find this time." Tom pushed aside leaves that were much drier, less lush than when he had been here before. Some of them crumbled at his touch while others fell to the ground, taking an unnaturally long time to do so.

The clearing was still there.

And so was the pit.

"Is that it?"

Tom nodded. Was it just his proximity to Molly or was it getting even warmer in here?

She clutched his arm and the temperature rose that little bit more. "I think that's enough. I believe you. Can we go back, now?"

A noise rose from the pit, a hollow croak that sounded like something large and old and birdlike.

"Yes, I think that's best."

They turned, but the forest had closed over where they had entered. Tom clawed at the intertwined twigs, and the leaves that had suddenly become rubbery and unyielding.

Another croak from the pit.

"Tom, get me out of here!"

"I'm trying!"

Tom turned to see Molly take a step towards the black space in the middle of the clearing. "What are you doing?"

"Hey – I think I can see someone down there!"

No! Tom rushed to her, his hands thick with scarlet dust from the leaves. Together they peered into the pit.

The men were there, as before, but they were silent, now. Unconscious, Tom presumed. But that was not what made both him and Molly cry out in horror.

There was something else in the pit, too.

It looked even worse than it sounded. A thing so old and so huge that only its crooked beak and one tapering claw had broken through the pit's base. It was trying to get at one of the prisoners, and the horrid sounds it was making were the result of its abject failure. It snapped at each man once more, and then withdrew to wherever it had come from.

Tom suddenly realised that what was going on in the pit only had half his attention. The other half was on Molly.

Or rather, Molly's back.

She was so close to the pit.

She could so easily be pushed in, this girl who threatened his happiness, his future. She had promised she would leave him alone, but he had heard Molly's promises before. All broken, all either denied or accompanied by the tearful phrase "I didn't mean it."

Was that why the pit had appeared to him? Was that what it was for? A place for the unwanted, the inconvenient?

The hated.

That was all he felt for her now, an all-consuming hate that she should have pursued him here, should have ruined his last weekend as a single man, should have tried to prey on his future like some twentieth century witch.

Tom blinked. In the moment it had taken for those thoughts to pass through his mind, Molly had disappeared.

Into the pit.

Tom had no memory of touching her. One minute she was beside him, the next she was lying on the shining rocky surface through which the creature had thrust its beak. She got to her feet.

"For God's sake, Tom, get me out of here!"

The other prisoners were waking as Tom lay on his side at the edge of the pit and stretched his arm down to her. It wasn't enough.

"It's another one," mumbled the Brit, his words quickly echoed by the American.

"Another one," they said together. "Another one another one another one –"

The ground began to rumble.

"Oh God, Tom it's coming back!" Molly had both arms outstretched as she jumped at the glassy sides of the pit. "Find a rope or something!"

Now the ground was vibrating, being pushed up once more. And something else was happening. Against the wall on the side where Tom was lying another cross had appeared. At the end of each arm of the crosspiece red tendrils writhed.

"Molly!" Her name tumbled from his lips as he regained his senses. He didn't want her to end up trapped down there, to die in the claws of that thing. What the hell had he been thinking? "Stay away from that!"

She couldn't hear him. The noise was too loud. As Tom watched in horror the ground began to rise once more. Molly backed away, straight onto the waiting cross. Something wrapped itself around her neck. In a reflex she raised her arms, only for her wrists to be grabbed by the tendrils and pulled back against the crimson wood.

"Tom?" Her voice was a choked gargle as the beak-thing appeared once more and tried to snap at her. It missed each time, but only by inches. "Tom, help me."

"Yes Tom," said the Brit. "Help us."

"Help us," echoed the American, joining the chorus of three voices, now. Two male and one female, becoming a chant, a mantra, but worst of all a testament to Tom's inability to do what was asked of him. His actions were no longer his own, had not been since he had brought Molly here, a sacrifice for who knew what gods? He could not help them, could not save Molly, could do nothing except what he knew he was fated to do.

He turned his back on them to see the passage had opened up once more.

It only took a few steps this time before he found himself back on the golf course, lit by the sun's dying rays and signifying that more time had passed out here than in there, wherever there was.

And he didn't care.

He didn't care that he would be late for his own stag party. He didn't care that no one would find out about Molly, now. The pit had saved his marriage, it had saved his future. But it had cursed him as well.

Because, as he dragged himself back to the brightly lit building ahead of him, full of laughter and celebration and life, he knew that this was not the last time he would be coming here. He knew the desire to see if Molly was still there, still trapped, and still glaring at him for being unable to help her, would be something he would find himself unable to resist. He thought briefly of going back with a rope, a ladder, anything that might help to get her out, but he knew he could not. There was no way she would keep quiet about such an experience, and even if nobody believed her about that, they'd believe her about her affair with Tom. He shook his head. He couldn't risk threatening the future he had with Katy, the future lives of their as-yet unborn children.

Besides, he doubted whatever had led him there, whatever had shown him that place, would let him.

No, Molly had to stay where she was.

But he would come back to see her, from time to time, because he couldn't help himself.

The pit had saved him, but it had cursed him, too.

And as he made his way back to the future that lay before him, Tom Jeavons wondered how long it would be before the idea of being cursed ceased to be the only thing he could think of.

Valley Interlude No.1

"I've never stopped thinking about it." The old man was regarding his now empty glass with weary eyes. "Every year I come back. Every year I play a round of golf. Every year I check that part of the rough."

"And you've never found anything?" Robert's glass was empty, too.

Mr Jeavons gave him a cold stare. "On the contrary, it's always there. She is always there." He pinched his eyes. "She hasn't aged a day. Except her eyes. I don't believe she even hates me any more. Now, I wonder if she can feel anything."

Robert found it difficult to believe. "You expect me to accept you've been coming back to this place every summer for over forty years, that the girl you trapped in some pit out on the golf course is still there, and that you've never tried to rescue her?"

Mr Jeavons gripped Robert's wrist. "Every year!" he hissed. "I come with the intention of rescuing her every year! But then I get there, and I see her, crammed in there with all the others – because there are more every time – and I find myself unable to do anything. I keep telling myself it's the influence of whatever controls the pit. But I have to face up to the fact that I never really wanted to free her. My world has been a better place with her where she is and, God help me, I cannot help but leave her there."

"But you torture yourself by coming back here?"

A thin smile at that. "A penance, if you like."

Robert picked up his glass and then set it down again. He would have loved another drink but he had no money and wanted to be leaving soon. Besides, drinking on an empty stomach would be a sure way of ending up in an even worse state than he had found himself in to begin with. "You said 'all the others'."

Mr Jeavons nodded. "It's getting very full. There are lots of unwanted people in there now. Even though the pit is bigger, much bigger, there's barely room for them all."

"And what about that creature you described?"

Mr Jeavons looked away for a moment, as if the image the question had conjured up was too much to bear. "It feeds. Every now and then. I've seen it. You don't want to."

The uneasy silence which followed was eventually broken by a sweaty man in stained blue overalls who entered the bar and bellowed in a thick Welsh accent,

"Where's the bloke who ordered the breakdown truck?"

"I'd better go." Robert was already getting to his feet.

"Of course." Mr Jeavons held out his hand to shake. "And thank you. I hope you didn't find my little story too disturbing. If you did, just pretend it's the ramblings of a lonely old man who's had too much to drink and likes to scare the unwary. For all you know, that could be all it is."

Robert shook the man's hand. "Really?"

The old man raised an eyebrow. "Would I lie to you?"

The breakdown truck had brought Robert's car round to the front of the hotel.

"I imagined you'd take it to a garage."

"No need." The mechanic reached in through the open window and turned the key. The engine started first time. "Couldn't find anything wrong with it. Wouldn't have been fair to make you go all the way back to get it, though, would it? So I brought it here." He sniffed. "I'll have to charge you for that, though."

Robert was about to take out his wallet when he remembered his current state of penury. He was about to launch into a lengthy apology when the chunky man who had pushed past him in the foyer earlier suddenly appeared at his side.

"All fixed then?"

Robert nodded towards the mechanic. "Apparently there was never anything wrong with it."

"Excellent! Isn't that sometimes the way? In that case, I wonder if I might ask a favour of you. My name's Stokes, Bernard Stokes, and it's terribly important I get to Newport as soon as possible." He inclined his head toward the hotel. "They've been trying to get a taxi for me for the last half an hour but no luck. It's getting to the point where I'm desperate. I don't suppose you're going that way?"

Robert decided against admitting he had no idea where he was going. "I could be," he said. "But this gentleman needs paying for bringing my car here and I seem to be short of cash."

"Oh goodness me! No problem, no problem at all." Stokes handed the mechanic a sheaf of notes. "Will that suffice?"

The breakdown man glanced at the money in a way that suggested it was much more than enough before tucking the notes away in his overalls. "Fine. Thanks."

"And now, my friend." Stokes was rubbing his hands together. "Unless there's any reason why we should tarry, I'd be grateful if we could get going." He raised a broad portfolio case Robert hadn't noticed before. "Can I put these in the boot?"

"Of course." Robert opened the back of the car. "I remember you now. I saw you carrying a picture into the hotel. Are you an artist?"

"Art dealer." Stokes slid into the passenger seat. He didn't speak again until they were on the motorway. "I don't believe I caught your name?"

"Robert."

"Well, Robert, are you an art fan?"

"There are pictures I like." Robert didn't know what else to say. "But I'm afraid I'm no expert. And when it comes to a lot of modern stuff I'll admit I'm completely lost."

"Oh, but the modern stuff is the easiest to appreciate! Instead of a detailed education in the history of classicism or romanticism, all you have to do is look at the picture and react to it."

Robert gave Stokes a wry smile. "Even if that feeling is that the painting isn't very good?"

"Indeed, yes."

"Or makes no sense?"

"If it makes no sense to you then yes, that too. But I'll bet your tastes are not as prosaic as you make out. Even the fact that we are having this conversation suggests to me that you are a man capable of appreciating the more challenging end of the artistic spectrum."

"Well I would very much hate to disappoint you, Mr Stokes, but I think that's highly unlikely."

"In that case," the little art dealer puffed himself "I shall consider it a challenge!"

The gallery was not at all what Robert was expecting.

Had he ever visited one before? He had no idea. His memory was still hidden behind a thick membrane of jumbled thoughts, blurred visions, and self-doubt. His mind was capable of visualising an art gallery, though. Bright, clean, well lit, modern.

The 'Stokes of Newport' Gallery was nothing like that.

Housed in a hefty old Victorian building on the outskirts of the city, the walls on which the paintings hung were panelled in wood so dark as to be almost black. The oak floor tiles had seen better days, before they had been subjected to the numerous insults which had left scratches and gouges grooved deep within them. While each painting was crowned with a lamp for better illumination, the feeble light did little to stave off the surrounding darkness, and gave each of the images Robert now found himself looking at an eerie presence that was likely unintended by the artist.

"Place needs a bit of a clean." Mr Stokes managed what sounded to Robert like the understatement of the year as he leaned his portfolio case against a wall displaying a worrying crack in the part of it that wasn't in shadow. "All these bloody lights need fixing, too. Bit of polish on the floor, lick of paint on these walls, and it'll all be ready for the grand reopening."

"You've been closed, then?" Robert was staring at a landscape, at that solitary skeletal tree on the horizon. He knew there was something hiding behind it. Something even thinner than the twisted trunk. How could something manage to do that? And why was he so sure it was there?

Despite the chill, Stokes mopped his forehead. "Seven months, now. The pictures are up because I didn't have the heart to take them down. If they're still hanging it means this place is still alive. At least to me."

Was there movement in the painting? A thready, spider-like limb tentatively creeping out from behind the rotted wood? Or perhaps from within the wood itself? A creature that had burrowed up from the depths and was about to take its first few crawling steps in a world that was new to it?

Stop it.

Robert looked away from the painting and at Stokes' shiny face. "Why have you been closed?"

"You mean you don't know?" the art dealer sounded uncomfortable. "I suppose you can't, otherwise you would have said something when you realised where we were going. There was some trouble here a few months back. A couple of girls went missing and it turned out they had been to exhibitions at this gallery shortly beforehand. The police never found anything but you know what something like that can do for the reputation of a place."

"I always thought people flocked to places where that sort of thing had happened."

"Not when they haven't found a body." Stokes sniffed. "Strange, isn't it? If we'd had a couple of good juicy murders here I would have been fighting off the crowds. Have a couple of university students disappear, never to be found, and nobody wants to know."

"It's because people like a story."

Stokes frowned. "That is a story."

"No, I mean, people like a beginning, a middle and an end. No end, no story. That's why. Give it time and the girls never being found will be an ending in itself, but it always takes a while for people to realise that."

Stokes looked impressed. "You know, young man, you may be right."

Robert wasn't sure where such an educated-sounding outburst had come from, and so he just nodded and tried to look wise. "Were you going to show me some pictures?"

"Oh yes indeed!" That seemed to elevate the art dealer's spirits. "Come with me!"

If the main gallery area was dingy and gloomy, it was a haven of well-lit cleanliness compared to the vast storage area at the back. Robert waited at the entrance while Stokes switched on the single bare bulb someone had deemed fit to serve as illumination for the entire room, and brushed the worst of the cobwebs from some nearby stacks of paintings. He crouched to read the labels and finally, after a bit of huffing and puffing, drew one out.

"Now," he said, beckoning Robert over. "How does this make you feel?"

The painting was an abstract. Vertical red streaks on a grey background. It looked as if at some point during its creation a cat had wandered across the canvas and left muddy yellow prints the artist had failed to clean off.

Robert looked apologetic. "I can't say it makes me feel anything, other than wonder why someone would want to paint this."

Stokes nodded. "Well that's something at least." He pulled another one from the pile. There was a clatter as three more canvases fell to the dusty floor.

"Don't worry about those." Stokes was following Robert's gaze. "I'll pick them up in a minute." He held up his next choice. "This should make you feel anger."

It actually made Robert feel slightly sick. Wavy horizontal keys that would never fit any lock hung suspended above a pallid landscape. In the top right hand corner was the suggestion of part of a keyhole.

"The fact you can't see all of the lock should cause you to feel immense frustration."

Robert shrugged. "I'm sorry. I guess I'm just not cut out to enjoy modern art." He bent down to help Stokes replace the paintings that had fallen. As he did so, he happened to glance at what one of the pictures portrayed.

And felt something akin to an electric shock.

"My dear fellow, are you all right?" Stokes took the painting from Robert's trembling hands. "Would you like to sit down?"

"No." There weren't any chairs nearby anyway, and the filthy floor wasn't an option. "I'll be fine."

Stokes glanced at the picture Robert had picked up. Then he stopped. "I'm not surprised this one gave you a fright. It is a bit extreme." He laid it to one side. "And do you know, if I'm not mistaken it was one of the pictures we had hanging in the gallery back then when there was all that trouble. I thought the police had taken them all away as evidence. They must have missed this. I'll put it away."

"No." For some inexplicable reason Robert needed to look at the painting again. "Let me see."

Stokes handed the painting over.

It was horrible. But at the same time it was sad, and moving and… beautiful? Robert could understand why the police would have wanted to confiscate it in the light of a missing persons case. It was just too disturbing, too weird. So weird he could imagine it turning the mind of someone susceptible, to send them running from the building never wanting to look at another painting again.

And it wasn't just because of what was depicted by the oils, it was because the picture told a story.

Robert wished there was a chair nearby now, as images flooded his mind.

He knew what that story was.

The story, and so much more.

Still Death

In the drawing room of a lavishly appointed country house somewhere in the depths of rural Wales, a beautiful woman was waiting for the telephone to ring.

The house was old, and a closer look at the room in which the woman was sitting would reveal that its upkeep was not, perhaps, quite as meticulous as initial impressions might suggest. The dark maroon wallpaper with gold trim that cloaked the walls was the 1890s original. The passing of over a hundred summers had caused it to crack a little, and there was the occasional hole here and there where mice had bitten into it. The furniture, while undoubtedly of good quality, had seen better days, before bumps and scratches incurred during several house moves had rendered it more worn than was strictly presentable. The rugs that mantled the oak parquet floor (itself scraped and stained here and there) were slightly frayed at the edges, and just a little too threadbare to escape notice.

The woman, too, on closer inspection, was perhaps not quite as beautiful, nor quite as elegant, as one might have assumed from a single glance. A little older, a little less glamorous, but nevertheless still possessed of a tremendous resolve and determination, and of a wish to present to the world (what little of it she encountered these days) an image that suggested fashionable society would once have been most desirous of her company.

Her eyes, hazel flecked with gold, glanced nervously between the antique telephone on the occasional table beside her and the large and draughty bay windows revealing grey, rain-lashed gardens beyond. From time to time her gaze came to rest on the object that stood between her and the door, and once again she had to resist the urge to chew on one of her elegantly manicured fingernails.

The storm worsened.

The windows rattled.

Still the telephone refused to ring.

Marion Morgan got to her feet and rested her fingertips on the lip of the open coffin.

"She's very late," she said to the silent occupant recumbent within its rosewood casing. "Perhaps the weather's too bad. Perhaps the girl isn't coming at all."

But 'the girl' was indeed on her way. She had just managed to get herself a bit lost.

Once Gemma Parkyn realised she could no longer see the road, even with the windscreen wipers going full pelt, she looked for somewhere to pull in. Which was how her green Fiat Panda ended up off the road and nearly in a field.

She should be okay here for a minute, she thought. Beyond the rusted iron gate she could see damp sheep huddled together. She couldn't imagine a farmer wanting to get into this field in this weather, but you never knew with these country types. It was probably best to be quick.

She opened her road atlas. The signal for the SatNav had died half an hour ago. What had that last sign said? A470? Gemma resisted the urge to light a cigarette. She had given up two days ago and had been feeling terribly proud of herself until she got past Talgarth. Then the craving had set in with a vengeance. Her eyes strayed to the glove compartment where she had secreted her 'emergency pack' but she was determined to hold out at least a little bit longer.

With a shaking fingertip she traced her route up from Exeter, along all those nice big motorways and the okay A40 and then onto the most winding, nausea-inducing route she had ever had the displeasure to drive. It looked as if she was on the right road, but it was difficult to tell.

She looked up from the map. On the opposite side of the road an abandoned petrol station filled her with thoughts of cannibals and pillagers, living off city folk like her who had got lost and stopped on the side of the road.

Who on Earth lived in this part of the world?

Marion Morgan did. Why had Gemma agreed to visit her? Was it out of some misplaced guilt over Maddy's death? Or what had happened after? Or was there, perhaps another reason?

The downpour worsened, accompanied by a crack of thunder so loud it made Gemma jump. The map suggested she was nearly there, but it was probably best to sit tight for a moment until the weather improved.

Sit tight and remember how it had all started.

The paintings were horrible.

That was the best word to describe them. It was especially the best word to describe the one Gemma had been standing in front of when she had been approached by the woman she was now intending to visit. The picture showed a beautiful girl viewed side on, seated in a cane garden chair and surrounded by the vivid green of exotic plants. The glass wall of the conservatory beyond betrayed that the subject was indoors. A summer's day, light filtering through the subject's shoulder-length blonde curls. The trace of a smile on her lips, her expression pensive. The delicate porcelain fingers of her right hand stroking her chin in thought.

The girl had no legs.

They were not hidden. Not tucked up beneath her or obscured by foliage. Her lower limbs ended high above the knee, the stumps encased in black hosiery, a stark contrast against her short white dress. From the girl's position and expression one would assume the insult to her anatomy was something that must have happened long ago, some event many years past which she had so come to terms with that it now felt as if she had never been able to walk.

Except Gemma knew that wasn't true.

Because the girl in the painting was her sister.

There were other pictures of Maddy at the exhibition. None showed her before the illness had taken hold, before the treatments that had rendered her progressively less of a human being and more an atlas of tissue in differing stages of disease, all to be increasingly trimmed back as her condition worsened.

The artist was Maddy's husband.

Maddy had married Tobias Morgan before her condition presented itself. A whirlwind romance while Maddy was at university (studying early English literature) and Tobias was at art college. It was only months after they tied the knot that Maddy had become ill.

Gemma stepped back and glanced at the paintings she had already seen. They all depicted her sister. There was Maddy standing when she could, and sitting when she eventually couldn't. Maddy holding up a hairbrush when she still had fingers, cradling what remained of her hands in her lap when the fingers had gone. Finally, there was Maddy on her death bed, so little of her left it was amazing she was still alive. Gemma sniffed. All that was missing was a picture of Maddy in an open coffin.

No. That would have been too much.

Tobias had insisted on using his skills to document the ravages of each stage of his wife's disease. Maddy had assented, explaining to Gemma during one of their rare telephone chats that it was helping Tobias cope, that it was helping both of them by doing something that felt constructive. Surely that was worth something. Better than just spending each day taking pain killers and enduring visits from the cancer nurse between visits to hospital and getting over each operation. Only to be told she would soon be needing another, counting down the hours until there would be nothing of her to cut away. At least now there would be something left behind when she went, something she could bequeath to the world as a sign of her passing, to say that she was here once, that she had lived in this world, and that she hadn't gone without a fight.

"Do you like the pictures?"

Gemma always felt uneasy in Marion Morgan's presence. In late middle age, knowingly attractive, and dangerously predatory where any man was concerned, Gemma and Maddy had taken to calling her the Black Widow behind her back. As well as the figure, Marion had the voice to go with it – confident, persuasive, and ripe with the threat of double meaning.

"I can't say I like them." It was best to be honest. "But they are very good."

"They are, aren't they?" Was Marion's smile one of mock sympathy or sincere disdain? "You know, I like to think that this exhibition is as much a tribute to your sister's life as it is to the genius of my son."

No she didn't. This whole thing was all about Tobias. If his paintings of anyone or anything other than Maddy had not already been disposed of Marion would be exhibiting those, too. Tobias had always insisted his portraits of his wife weren't for sale. But he had never said anything about them not being shown to the public. They were all that was left. Everything else had gone. Even Tobias. Marion's son had killed himself two weeks ago, grief-stricken over his wife's death. Hence this exhibition in his memory.

Not Maddy's.

"I'm so glad you could come, Gemma. I know Tobias would have appreciated it."

"I haven't seen most of these paintings, so how could I say no?" It was true. As Maddy's illness had worsened, so the couple had become more reclusive. Gemma sipped her drink as an uneasy silence descended. Shouldn't Marion be chatting to some of the other people here? There were plenty of them. "I didn't even know Newport had an art gallery."

"Anywhere can be an art gallery if there is work worthy of display. Tobias said that. He always found our house sufficient, which was why he refused to allow these paintings to leave it."

So Tobias and Maddy had lived with Marion, then. To the end?

"Do you think he would be happy with you bringing them here?"

Should Gemma have said that? It didn't look as if Marion minded.

"I wanted the world to appreciate his genius," she said, "and I wanted Maddy's family and friends to be able to see these beautiful paintings as well."

They could be considered beautiful in a way, but not by anyone who had known Maddy when she was whole and well and… alive. Certainly not their parents.

"Mum and Dad couldn't come," Gemma said. That bit was true. "They had a holiday booked and couldn't cancel." That bit wasn't, but they had asked her to make up some excuse so Marion didn't feel snubbed.

"I understand." What did she mean by that? "It's a shame none of Maddy's friends could make it, though."

Gemma shrugged, "She never had that many friends to begin with, and they kind of drifted away after…" She gestured to the people around them. "Are these all Tobias' friends?"

"These? Oh no. These are just people who love great art. I'm hoping for some write-ups. The man from *The Observer* said he was coming –" Marion performed a theatrical look around the room for him "– but it doesn't seem as if he's turned up."

"Perhaps he got lost?"

Gemma had only meant it as a polite response, but Marion didn't take it that way.

"I should hardly think so. It's straight down the M4 from London. We may be in Wales but it's hardly the back of beyond. Not like where I live." Marion seemed almost embarrassed to admit it. "It's a little out of the way, but Tobias and I liked living there, and so did Maddy when she moved in. We were all happy, even if it was for so short a time. So short…"

More silence. Despite the background chatter Gemma could hear the fizz of the bubbles in her prosecco glass. "Is that where you had the funeral?"

It seemed Gemma had touched another nerve. "It hasn't happened yet."

"Oh?" Should she be prying? "Why not?"

"The post mortem." Marion's eyes glittered. "It's taken that bloody hospital until now to release the body. Some fuss about having to be thorough with suicide cases, eliminate the possibility of suspicious circumstances, I don't know what." A tear threatened to escape down her cheek. Marion dabbed it away. "They say we should be able to have the funeral next week."

"Would you like me to come?" The words were out before Gemma had given them proper consideration. A phrase uttered out of politeness that she almost instantly regretted.

Marion's change of expression was like the sun coming out from behind an especially grey cloud. "Oh Gemma, that would be awfully kind of you."

The storm was getting worse. Now the rain sounded capable of punching holes in the roof of Gemma's car, and the wind was blowing so hard it felt as if her little vehicle might get overturned.

If she drove away now it probably would.

Best to keep her engine off and her fingers crossed for the moment.

Marion had drifted away after that final remark, almost as if securing Gemma's attendance at Tobias' funeral was all she been waiting for, and now she was free to charm the men and deliver veiled aphorisms of the greatest bitchiness to the other women. Gemma was relieved to be finally rid of Marion. She no longer felt like talking, and the paintings were starting to make her feel dizzy. What did they call it when art overcame you? Stendhal Syndrome? It wasn't so much the exquisiteness of Tobias Morgan's technique, though, more the crowd and Marion and Maddy and everything being just too much. So Gemma had left. She could think up some excuse as to why she couldn't attend the funeral later.

The invitation arrived the next day.

The card was edged in crimped gold and had the arrangements described in a florid font. On the back, written in lilac ink, were the words 'So glad you said you'd come. It will be a very small affair and your presence will be so valued – M'.

None of this explained how the card had arrived so quickly. Gemma frowned as she read it. Marion must have posted the thing as soon as they had finished talking yesterday. Perhaps that was where she had vanished to.

Or perhaps she had sent it before she asked.

The idea sent a wave of fury through Gemma. How dare Marion assume Gemma would say yes.

Don't you want to go and finally see where Maddy and Tobias lived together?

Yes.

Don't you want to see where your sister spent her last days?

Yes.

Don't you want to support Marion in her hour of need?

No, not really, but Gemma was aware she still hadn't bid a proper farewell to her sister. The funeral in Aberystwyth had been a rushed affair, with Gemma having to drive her parents back to Devon that night. There had been little time to reflect, let alone say goodbyes. She needed to sit by Maddy's grave and have a good, long, final chat with her.

Well, now you have a good reason to go.

She did. Never mind Marion. She would do it for Maddy, and for Tobias, of course. Gemma had only met him twice and he had seemed a bit odd, but totally devoted to her sister, which was all Gemma had cared about.

Time to say those goodbyes.

Gemma started to compose her RSVP message. Wales in November, she thought. Hopefully the weather wouldn't be that bad.

It was starting to get dark. The leaden sky that had glowered over the gloomy landscape all day now began to turn charcoal. Was the rain letting up a bit or was she just being optimistic? Either way, Gemma needed to get to Marion's before nightfall or she'd never find the place. Time to get going.

Gemma switched on her headlights and manoeuvred the car out of the gateway.

A figure was standing in the road.

Gemma hit the brakes. It was difficult to see in the gloom, even with the lights and the windscreen wipers set to maximum, but she felt sure she could see someone just up ahead, dressed in what had to be black oilskins that gleamed in the glare from the headlamps. The head was cowled and the body cloaked, the shining black reaching to the ground. Dragging along it, in fact. That was what it had to be, surely. The train of a long, wet, shining cloak being pulled along behind it as the figure came nearer?

Gemma blew the horn.

The figure raised a twisted arm beneath the shining black. Did it need help? Was it waving?

No.

The concealed limb seemed to be describing a pattern in the air, heavy rain dripping from the flaccid blackened sleeve that concealed its hand. A circle? A circle with… some sort of symbol inside it?

Maybe there were road works and they didn't have a sign. Or perhaps there was a diversion. Whatever lay ahead, the man wasn't making it very clear. Gemma got into first gear and edged the car forward. As her headlights illuminated the figure more strongly, so it seemed to become less substantial.

Weird. A trick of the light?

And now something else strange was happening. As Gemma crawled forward, the figure looked somehow further away. By the time she reached the point in the road where she was convinced it had been standing, she realised the figure was even further distant. It had stopped making shapes and now just stood there, its left arm held out at right angles beneath the leather cloak.

Was it pointing?

Relief swept over Gemma as she realised what was going on. Probably some bloke who worked for Marion, sent out here onto the road to make sure Gemma didn't miss the turning.

Sure enough there it was – a narrow gateway off to the right that Gemma would most likely have missed without help. She wound down the window to ask if the man wanted a lift up to the house.

The figure had gone.

Probably making his own way back, or perhaps his cottage was down here. Either way, Gemma felt grateful to him as she negotiated the stone-pillared entryway. The weather was too bad to see what creatures were perched atop the limestone, but in the near-darkness it looked as if they had far too many legs. Whatever sculptures were capable of producing such weird outlines, she didn't fancy seeing them by daylight.

The single track driveway made a sharp bend to the left once Gemma was a hundred yards in. The overarching trees blotted out what feeble daylight remained, and she had to rely on her headlights to guide her.

After ten minutes she wondered if she was in the right place.

After twenty minutes she concluded she wasn't.

The track was too narrow to turn round, and now it was so dark either side of her that for all she knew there could be a steep precipice, or running water, or nothing at all.

That final thought chilled her as she realised she had no option but to keep going. Besides, the road had to go somewhere.

Didn't it?

Up ahead the road bent to the left. Gemma kept going, trying not to think about how the darkness felt like a palpable thing, pressing in on either side of her car, trying to break the windows so blackness could come dribbling in through the cracks and ooze towards her, rendering everything it touched the same shade of absence as itself. What would happen when it touched her?

There were lights.

And a lawn.

And a big house beyond it.

Gemma almost wept. Stupid girl! What the hell had she been thinking? It wasn't as if she was usually the over-imaginative sort but things had really started to get to her back there. As if by way of reward, the rain stopped as Gemma pulled up in front of the house and got out of the car.

A figure stood waiting for her in the open doorway.

"It was very good of you to come, Gemma."

"Not at all. I'm just sorry I'm so late." Gemma put her bag down and looked around the poorly lit hallway. The well-worn grandfather clock sitting in shadow by the staircase had seen better days, with the hands having stopped at some long-forgotten ten o'clock. "I'm glad that's not the time." She forced a smile.

"But it is." Marion looked confused. "That clock keeps perfect time. Always has, although I'll admit I've only just started using it again. Tobias couldn't stand the sound it made. He felt every swing of its pendulum was taking away another tiny sliver of Maddy's life. It's working now, though. Can't you hear?"

Yes, she could, now. The dull repetitive clunking was unmistakable. How had she not heard it before? More importantly, and far more worryingly, how had it taken her six hours to get from the A470 to Marion's house?

"Are you all right, Gemma?"

"Yes… no… I think I must be tired."

"Those roads are enough to exhaust anyone. You've come a long way through some dreadful weather." Marion picked up Gemma's case and headed for the broad staircase. "They say it should stop by tomorrow."

But it had already stopped, hadn't it?

Now, behind the measured beats of the grandfather clock, Gemma could hear the downpour. Maybe the rain had paused for just a minute, enough to allow her to get inside. That had to be it.

"Are you coming?" Marion was already halfway up. "Watch out for the sixth step, the rod's come loose and I haven't had time to get it fixed yet."

Gemma took care as she followed. Which one had Marion said? Never mind, the carpet was threadbare to the point of coming apart, so it was probably best to be careful all the way up, especially as she could hardly see where she was going.

The light on the landing wasn't much better, with the corridor disappearing into blackened gloom in both directions.

"Your room is down here."

"It's not…" It was difficult to put it delicately. "It's not…"

"It's not Tobias and Maddy's room if that's what you're worried about." Marion came to a halt. "This is a grand old house with plenty of grand old rooms."

Gemma's eyes widened as Marion took out a key. "You're not going to lock me in are you?" The words came out before she could stop them. She topped off the sentence with a nervous giggle.

"Warped." Marion tapped the doorframe. "They all are. It's the damp, you see. The hinges are tilted so the doors won't close properly. Unless you lock it you'll find it swings open in the middle of the night." She reached in and flipped a switch.

The room looked surprisingly comfortable. There was a four poster bed, and a rug that covered enough of the otherwise bare boards that Gemma shouldn't get splinters in her feet.

"The bathroom's just down there." Marion nodded towards impenetrable darkness. "Light switch here." Gemma missed exactly where. "I'll leave you to get settled in. It's a bit late to eat but I suppose I could find something if you're desperate."

She was but she had no intention of being a bother if it really was so late. "No that's fine."

"Anything else you need?"

It could be a bit brighter for her to see. "Are the lights on dimmer switches, or is the power out here a bit weak?"

"No dimmer switches and the power supply is just fine." Marion turned on her heel to leave. "It's the house." She was halfway down the corridor but Gemma was sure she heard Marion's parting words correctly, even if they were patently ridiculous.

"The house doesn't like light."

There was something at the window.

Gemma turned over in bed and tried to ignore the scratching sound. Probably a tree branch or a loose bit of guttering. Very persistent guttering. Whatever it might be, it was interfering with the sleep that she wasn't managing to get any of.

The heavy bedclothes protested as she pushed them away, trying to fall back into place to trap her, but she was too quick. The rug felt rough beneath her feet as she padded over to the window, where she expected to see the jagged outline of whatever was making that tapping noise.

Nothing.

At least the rain had finally stopped. The moon glared at her as it lit up the landscape, the tousled silver hair of the unkempt grassland, the charcoal outlines of the two apple trees close to the house.

And the figure standing between them.

It resembled the one she had seen standing in the road, although this one seemed to hold even less shape beneath its black waterproofs.

Waterproofs it still wore even though it was no longer raining.

Gemma scarcely had time to wonder what it might be doing there when it raised a limb and pointed at her.

A hand emerged from beneath the coverings. Blackened and charcoal-thin and with too many fingers.

That was what made Gemma bite back a scream. Spider-thin and multi-jointed, it was difficult to tell how many digits the thing actually possessed, partly because it was moving them quickly, and partly because, as it did so, they seemed to blur, joining and then separating, fusing and then splitting into even further, thinner, appendages.

She had to be dreaming.

She had to be, because now the apple trees were moving as well. Because they weren't trees at all, and never had been. Stick-thin creatures with too many limbs and emaciated streaks of bodies, they began to crawl towards her while the thing in the middle looked on, if it could see through that black cowl-thing covering its head.

Unless, of course, that actually was its head.

As the cowled thing's servants wormed their way closer, Gemma saw that they did indeed have faces, tiny ones balanced atop scorched-looking necks surely too thin to support them. But that was not the worst.

The terrible thing was that Gemma recognised them.

Now she screamed – a long drawn out howl that she hoped would wake her.

It didn't work.

The 'cloaked' thing on the lawn was describing that pattern again, the one she had seen on the road. A circle with some kind of symbol inscribed within it. Over and over. Meanwhile the spider-thing on the left had wrapped probing limbs around a nearby drainpipe and was pulling itself upward towards her. It tilted its head back – too far – looked down its rotted beak of a nose at her with eyes that were nothing but void, and pulled its face into a hideous semblance of a grin.

Gemma backed away towards the door. She flicked the light switch. Nothing. She pulled on the door handle. It wouldn't budge.

The scraping, tickling sounds of spider limb against brick were coming closer.

You locked the door.

Of course she did, just like Marion had told her. Gemma twisted the key and pulled. The door opened and she was out on the landing. The pitch black landing. Where there might be other things.

Never mind, she thought. One at a time. There were definitely creatures coming up the wall and they would be in her room in an instant. She closed the bedroom door and locked it just as she heard something bulky and dry land on the rug. Why had she not heard the window break?

There was tapping, and scuttling, and then an awful, awful scraping noise on the other side of the door.

Gemma felt around for a light switch but found none.

Just run, then.

So she did, arms flung out in front of her, bare feet treading as lightly as possible, Gemma made her way down the corridor, feeling along the wall to where Marion had said her room was.

From behind her came a horrible creaking sound. Gemma gulped back a sob. If they could do that to a door what might they do to her?

She found a handle. Could it be Marion's room?

It'll be locked anyway, idiot.

Never mind that. Gemma pounded on it.

"Marion! Marion! Let me in!"

The door should have been locked but it swung open. Gemma dashed inside and closed it behind her. The light switch worked, the glow as dim as the rest of the house, the house that didn't like the light. Gemma grabbed a stool and wedged it under the handle, then turned to apologise to her host.

"Marion I'm sorry but I… there's…"

It wasn't Marion in the bed.

Tobias stretched out withered arms hung with rotten flesh to bring her closer. Maddy couldn't do the same because she no longer had any limbs, but she welcomed Gemma with a smile redolent of rot and decay. Both had the same faces as the things that, even now, were scratching at the door.

"You're not real." Gemma didn't know what else to do, what else to say. "You're not real. None of this is real."

The rotting corpse of the Maddy thing shook its head. Words came from a throat partially eaten by disease.

"No, Gemma. You are the one who isn't real."

"Did you sleep well?"

No, not at all, not with her nightmares of things climbing up the wall, and Maddy, and…

Best not to think about it.

Gemma nodded and managed to force out an affirmative as she slowly buttered a piece of toast.

"I'm so glad." Marion seemed a different person this morning. Affable, enthusiastic, and more light-hearted than Gemma had ever known her. If nothing else it helped to make up for the weather.

The rain still hadn't let up. Heavy drops wept from clouds so black and thick that had it not been for the kitchen clock telling her it was nearly nine it could almost be the middle of the night. Perhaps it was. Gemma checked her watch, just to be sure.

"Not thinking of leaving, are you?" Gemma shook her head as she reached for a murky-looking jar of gooseberry jam. "Good."

"I'm sorry." Why was it such an effort to speak?

Marion raised her eyebrows. "What on Earth are you apologising for?"

"For being late yesterday. I wanted to be here in time for the funeral. I'm sorry I missed it."

"Oh my poor sweet thing, you haven't missed anything. I wouldn't dream of having my son's funeral without you."

That made no sense. "But what about the vicar… the church… the mourners?"

"Gemma." Now the old patronising Marion was back. "There is no vicar. There is no church. Or any other mourners. We're having the funeral here."

It was a bizarre thing to hear. It also was the eye-opener Gemma needed. Suddenly she felt alert.

"Here?"

Marion nodded, her eyes unnatural in their brightness. "It was what Tobias would have wanted." Really? "To be buried in the grounds." Oh yes? "In the absence of any silly religious rites." Right. "His body is currently in repose in the drawing room." *Shit.*

"I beg your pardon?"

"Oh don't worry." Marion poured some more coffee. "You can finish your breakfast before you get to see him. It's important that you eat. You must keep your strength up, after all."

Yes, thought Gemma, yes she certainly did need to. Just in case Marion had something a little too weird planned in this house that didn't like light where time didn't work properly and the dreams she had were just a bit too vivid to be dreams. She'd need all her strength just in case she needed to run away from all of it. Now that her thoughts were turning to escape, it was probably worth checking her car as well. And perhaps, when she checked it, she might just ease herself behind the wheel, try the engine and…

"I just need to pop out for a second." Gemma got to her feet and patted her trouser pocket. The car keys were still in there.

Marion looked startled. "Pop out? Where? What for? For heaven's sake it's pouring down out there."

"I left something in the car." Gemma gave a nonchalant shrug while she tried to think what the hell it could be.

Which, of course, was Marion's next question.

"The card I brought." Well done. "The sympathy card. I don't want to wait until it's time for me to leave to give it to you. That would be really rude."

Was Marion buying it?

"Oh Gemma that's so kind of you, but I couldn't possibly ask you to go and get it with the weather the way it is."

"Really, it's no bother."

"Oh it is." Marion sounded more severe as she pointed towards the entry hall. "That front door is locked and is staying locked until the weather cheers up. There is no way I am going to have your suffering from pneumonia on my conscience."

Locked. Damn. Was it just slightly dotty kindliness that stopped her from opening the door? Or was there something else going on?

This is Marion Morgan we're talking about here.

Be on your guard, Gemma.

"All right," she replied. "As long as you promise that the minute the rain lets up I can go and get it." And get away from here. Far, far away.

"Of course." Marion was smiling again, quite unnervingly so. "Now, not another word until you've finished your toast. Then I can take you to meet Tobias."

Gemma almost choked as her mind flashed back to last night and the image of Marion's son with his half-decayed face and flesh-ripped arms reaching out to grip her tightly.

She took as long as she could finishing her breakfast. By the time she was emptying the dregs of her fourth cup of coffee she could see Marion was starting to become impatient.

"I think that'll do." Gemma got to her feet once more. She gave Marion the broadest, most sincere smile she could muster under the circumstances. "I'm in your hands."

That seemed to please Marion immensely.

"He's been waiting to meet you," she said as Gemma followed her from the kitchen. "Not actually Tobias himself, of course, that wouldn't make sense, would it? What I mean is I've had him ready to meet you, all prepared and laid out, for the last week or so."

In the art gallery hadn't Marion said the hospital had only released him just the other day?

"We've both been so excited about you coming. And by both I mean, well, if you'll excuse a mother her indulgences but it's been so lonely here since he passed on and I can't help it if I've been talking to him a little bit, can I?" Marion had been happy rambling on her own but she seemed to be seeking justification for that last part. Gemma gave her a kindly nod. "Of course I can't, and even though he's no longer resident within his body I do very much feel that he hasn't left this house, and that he hasn't left me. Because he wouldn't. He couldn't. I could never imagine him doing that."

Gemma felt a pang of sympathy as she followed Marion across the hallway. It didn't stop her casting a glance at the locked and bolted front door, but it did make her feel sorry for the woman, stuck here in this isolated dreary corner of the country with only her dead son for company. The place was already having an effect on Gemma and she hadn't even known there was a dead body in the house. So, as Marion Morgan paused at the entrance to the drawing room, she was granted a brief moment of sympathy from the girl who was effectively her prisoner.

A very brief moment.

Until Marion opened the door.

Gemma peered into the room. It was difficult to see because the heavy curtains were closed. Cracks in the material allowed threads of feeble light to pierce the room here and there, creating streaks of pale grey amongst the dark and giving the coffin that stood dead centre an eerie, blurred outline.

The open coffin, the bier of which stood on bare floorboards.

On which a shape had been drawn.

It was familiar to Gemma now, even if only from what she still believed to be her own fevered imagination. The chalk circle enclosed the bier and the four heavy black candles that had been placed at the head and the foot of the coffin containing Tobias' motionless form. The circle had been divided into quarters. In each was inscribed one of the sigils Gemma had seen the formless figure making on the road, and outside her room last night.

"What is this?"

Marion was already lighting the candles. "Close the door, Gemma, or the draught might blow them out."

Gemma was doing nothing of the sort. Marion pushed past her, looking unhappy, and did it herself before returning to Tobias' coffin. Now the flickering flames lent an orange tint to the gloom, and there was a smell of incense as well. Gemma took a step back.

"For heavens' sake girl, you're not going to be of any use to me over there. Come here. Or am I going to have to bring you?"

The idea of Marion touching her sent a chill through Gemma sufficient to make her force one foot in front of the other until she found herself standing at Tobias' feet.

"That's better." Marion was at the head end of the coffin, close to the drawn curtains. "Now stay there until I need you."

Marion picked up something torn and crumbling. It took Gemma a while to realise it had to be a very old book. With infinite care, Marion opened the cover and took her time lifting tissue-thin pages until she came to the part she wanted.

Meanwhile Gemma was looking at Marion's son.

If anything, his embalmed corpse looked even worse than the version of him she had seen in her nightmare. At least, she hoped he had been embalmed. The waxy yellow of his skin had to be the product of chemical treatment, didn't it? The hands clasped over his chest had fingernails that were not just ragged, but crumbling. His face was so mask-like that it seemed more an approximation of human features than something that had once been alive. Slack and pliable, it presumably had not received the mortician's attention. The eyes were closed, and Gemma was very glad of that.

She was also glad he was dressed in traditional funeral black that covered the rest of his body. She had no wish to know if his arms were the flapping flesh-torn things of her dream, nor if his chest was as open and gouged as when he had risen from his bed to clutch at her.

Marion was reading something. Aloud.

"Is this the funeral service?" If so, Gemma couldn't understand the words. "Shouldn't we be waiting for a priest or something?"

"We have no need of a priest because this is not a funeral service." Marion sounded annoyed at the interruption. "These words have another purpose."

"What?"

"I am calling Them." She was still scowling. "They who said I could keep my son. If I gave you to Them."

Gemma edged back to the door. "Gave me to who?"

"I've locked the door, Gemma." Marion sighed. "You can't escape."

Gemma tried the door handle anyway. "What are you talking about?"

Marion lowered the tattered volume. "The world is thinner in some places, and there are parts of Wales where the barriers are nothing more than tissue paper. This house sits on the borderland between one reality and another. They can come here, and we can go there, if we choose to."

Marion was mad, that much was certain. Best for Gemma to keep her talking while she considered what to do. "Who would want to go there?"

"There are many of us, those who feel this planet of ours is doomed, that its deterioration into chaos is merely part of an overall divine plan. Their plan. Salvation through entropy."

"Entropy?"

"Randomness. Death. Disease. Chaos. That is how they live. It is what they thrive on. It's what they did to your sister."

What was Marion raving about? "How could they have done anything to Maddy? She got cancer." It still shook Gemma to say that word. "An aggressive form of cancer that spread quickly."

Marion shook her head. "She was especially receptive to the entropy of the other plane, and when she came to this place They claimed her. The doctors couldn't explain it. They put it down to a rare kind of tumour that ate into her tissues. But it wasn't cancer that killed your sister…" Marion looked around her "…it was this house, and the closeness it bears to a dimension other than ours."

That was enough. If Gemma couldn't get out through the door there might be another way. She ran up to Marion and shoved her as hard as she could. Marion Morgan fell backwards, as much from shock as from the force of the blow. Gemma stepped over her and pulled the curtains back.

The French windows were locked, the rain still hammering defiantly against the glass.

The glass…

Gemma grabbed a chair and flung it at the windows with all her strength. There was a crash as it sent a scatter of shards out into the garden. Gemma kicked away the remaining splinters and stepped through.

"It's no good!" Marion shouted from behind her. "They won't let you leave now! They know you're here! They've already tasted too much of you!"

Marion's voice faded as Gemma ran. She was close to the end of the garden, a high hedge ahead of her, before she realised something strange.

It wasn't raining.

The grass beneath her feet was dry.

And the sky was an angry shade of pink.

Gemma turned back to look at the house. There was Marion, screaming at her from the hole in the windows, rain still streaming down the outside of them.

The outside of them.

But not here.

Gemma felt dizzy. She turned to face the hedge again.

The hedge had come closer.

It was starting to change as well. Breaking up into pieces, each one moulding itself into a shape, each shape becoming horribly familiar. The cowl-things.

Six of them.

Gemma was close enough that she could see, by the light of that unnatural sky, that their appearance was not due to garments at all, that in fact their shape was formed from a skin of dark leather that glistened in the gloom, that the trailing matter about their base was a mixture of frond-like tentacles curled around blackened twigs that probed their surroundings. None of them had what could be called a face.

As one, six of the things moved toward her.

Gemma stumbled backwards, looking to the walls that bordered the garden on either side.

But they had changed, too, red brick and crumbling mortar blurring together to form something fluid. The thick, red-brown substance was starting to leak across the lawn in spurts that made Gemma think of a haemorrhaging wound.

Was that what was happening? Was that other universe Marion had been telling her about leaking into this one? Or was it the other way around?

Gemma gasped and turned away from the creeping beings. The only place still recognisable as part of the normal world was the house. Marion still peered through the glass. She wasn't screaming now, though. She was smiling in triumph. Because Gemma had nowhere else to go.

Herded by the creatures, careful not to let them touch her, Gemma made her way back. She didn't need the encouragement, but that didn't stop Marion.

"That's right, Gemma. Now you know there's no other option I hope you're going to be a good girl and do what you're told." She kept talking as Gemma climbed through the broken glass and back into the drawing room.

The cowl-things remained outside.

"Don't they want to join the party?" Gemma spat.

"Even if they did they cannot. As well as existing close to the borders of the other dimension, this house affords us protection from it as well. Except in dreams, of course."

At least that explained the previous night. "But you said you were calling them to get me."

"No, I was calling them so they could exert further influence over you. Which they have. You have spent long enough now in their company that their effect on your tissues should soon begin to exert itself. Do you feel it?" Marion's eyes glittered with lunatic zeal. "The entropy flooding through you? Does your skin feel dry? Your throat like paper? Can you still see with perfect vision? Soon it will go, just like your hearing. That was why your sister didn't want to see you close to the end, because she knew if you came here the same thing would happen to you. And that I wanted it to happen."

Gemma rubbed her fingertips against her thumbs. Was it her imagination or did they feel drier than before? Ready to flake? To crumble? Was she already dying? Would she soon need the ministrations of the knife and the bone saw to cut the dead tissue away? To keep her alive for a short a time, like Maddy?

"Why?" Gemma asked. Marion seemed confused by the question. "I mean, I can understand you wanting your son back. Any mother would. But was this the only way?" In some weird parallel universe dedicated to randomness, Gemma reasoned, surely all logical bets would be off?

"It was not just to bring him back that I invited you here." Marion gave her an evil grin. "But to give Tobias a reason to go on living. You see, Maddy's gradual deterioration sickened my son, but it inspired him, too. In your case I intend it to merely inspire him. I would hardly be a good mother if I brought him back without something to occupy him." She pointed to the things outside the window. "I hope They will be pleased. His paintings of you and your gradual submission to the entropic universe will be our offering to Them."

Gemma was beside the bier, now. She could feel its wooden border digging into her back. She didn't want to see those limp, jaundiced features again but she couldn't help herself. She had to know that Marion's son was still in there, that he was still lying motionless, that he was still dead. She turned and looked into the coffin, and that was when she finally screamed.

Because the coffin was empty.

Marion covered the gap from the broken window to the bier in a single stride. She looked in, and a broad grin split her manic features.

"He lives! My son lives!"

Perhaps, but where was he?

From the darkened corner to the left of the door came a sound, the scraping of shoes not long worn, accompanied by croaking from a dry throat too long unused. Gemma was about to make for the door but Marion had her arm in a vice like grip as something unsteady on its feet and unsure of its surroundings shuffled into the lilac light flooding the room from the garden.

"Oh, Tobias..." Overcome by what was happening, Marion released her hold on Gemma and ran to her son. The thing in the black suit responded by raising its arms. Mumbled sounds escaped from its slack lips. Its sunken eyes were yet to open.

Gemma glanced round the room. The cowl-things were still at the window, observing the proceedings within. Beside the coffin sat the book.

Don't even think about it. You'll only end up saying the wrong thing and causing the real world to crack in half. If there's any of it left.

If only there was something Gemma could use to get the door open, though.

And then she realised.

The bier was on wheels.

Marion was still fully occupied with her recently reanimated son, trying to get him to walk a few more steps with her aid. He wasn't doing terribly well. Good. That should occupy Marion's attention for a bit.

Gemma moved to the head end of the coffin and with trembling fingers grasped the wooden lip. She checked she had a clear path to the door, then she checked Marion, then she checked the door again.

Go. Now.

Gemma pushed the coffin on its bier as hard as she could. There was a sharp squeal of protest as castors desperately in need of oil began to move, then the whole thing shot forward.

Straight into the drawing room door.

The wood panel cracked but didn't give way completely.

One more go.

"What do you think you're doing?"

Tobias was still leaning heavily on Marion, so all she could do was watch as Gemma rolled the coffin back to its starting position and then rammed the door once more.

"Stop that!"

This time it worked. The crack Gemma had opened up on her first run split apart and the coffin went crashing through, with Gemma following.

She stood in the entrance hall, the grandfather clock ticking her life away just as it had Maddy's. From the drawing room came shuffling sounds as Marion whispered words of encouragement.

"That's better. Good. Now you're opening your eyes! Oh you are a good boy. Now let's go and see where that wretched girl has got to."

'That wretched girl' had decided it would be a bad idea to get trapped upstairs and had instead made for the back of the house. Maybe there would be another way out, one that hadn't yet been swallowed up by those things and their world. Gemma pushed at a door and found herself in what she initially thought was an enormous conservatory.

It was two storeys high and easily the size of the rest of the house put together. Three of the walls were composed entirely of glass, tiny hexagons bound by wire that admitted so much of the purple daylight that it was almost as if Gemma was standing outside. There was very little furniture in the room. Just a chair, and a small table beside it with a white cloth draped over it.

But there were lots of paintings.

Gemma remembered how overwhelmed she had felt in the art gallery. This was ten times worse. Back there, it had been a combination of the art and the memory of her sister. Here it was just the art, the paintings of all these different girls.

And their mutilations.

Gemma held a hand to her mouth in horror as she walked a maze of easels, each one proudly displaying a life study. Sometimes it was of the same girl, but there were so many paintings, and so many subjects, it was often difficult to tell.

All of the subjects had endured amputations.

Just like Maddy.

Gemma had noticed there weren't any pictures of her sister here. Was that because Marion had thought they were the only ones good enough to sell?

Or the only ones that could be used to trap another victim.

The door to Tobias' studio opened and Marion entered, her son shuffling behind.

Gemma, far back in the labyrinth of macabre artwork, crouched and prayed. Perhaps she could make her way round to the exit as they looked for her.

"You've found my son's playroom, then?" Marion had the clear and confident voice of a predator convinced their victim has no chance of escape. "He was always a sickly child. He died for the first time many years ago. You understand now that They have given him back to me many times?" Did Gemma detect a trace of sadness now? "Each time a little more of him is lost. Not from his body – that will be revitalised once he has started working again – but from his mind. Tobias was always prone to depression. Artistic types so often are, don't you find? But each time he has come back to me the episodes have been worse. And then he gets so attached to his models. He has even married some of them. Well, one of them." Gemma kept her eye on Marion and what was left of her son as they began to search the workroom. "What am I saying? Of course you know that. Just as you know there will be no escape. You may as well give yourself up. Hiding like this is just being selfish. My son needs you, needs the inspiration that will bring light back to his eyes, love to his heart, and fervour to his entire being."

As her son continued his mumbling, staggering search of the room, Marion retreated to the table. "I even have everything ready so we can get started right now."

With that she whipped away the cloth. Gemma was now against the wall near the door and she crept closer to get a better look.

One half of the table held paintbrushes and rags for cleaning them, tubes of oil paints in a rainbow of colours, a mixing palate.

The other half was filled with surgical instruments.

"Tobias is really bad this time, Gemma. There's no time to wait for your rot to become serious enough that it needs to be cut away. No time to wait for us to take you to the hospital, for the doctors to treat you, for you to be brought back here to recuperate. Besides, you know too much. You've seen all this. You're the only human being to witness this room in its true state other than my son and me. It proves you're special, if nothing else."

"Or that those things in the garden are on the verge of breaking through, of turning this part of the world into part of theirs!" Gemma couldn't stand it any longer. She emerged from behind the paintings and began to walk towards the door.

"Tobias! Get her!"

Gemma was no longer afraid. That part of her emotions had been burned out of her by everything she had seen. Not even the stumbling, flopping caricature of a man she had once known making its hesitant way towards her could scare her anymore.

"I'm leaving." Gemma said. "I don't care where I end up, as long as it's not here." She opened the conservatory door and stepped through.

To find herself back in the conservatory.

Tobias was closer.

Marion was grinning.

Panic gripped her. Gemma turned and went through the door again.

Tobias, arms outstretched, guttural moan of desire issuing from his throat.

Marion, still with that awful grin on her face, shaking her head from side to side.

Gemma turned.

And turned.

And turned.

And turned.

She was still trying to escape when the purple light faded to nothing but darkness.

"I didn't know they had an art gallery in Aberystwyth!"

The girl was young and pretty. Her name was Annabelle. She had declined the prosecco and opted for the orange juice.

"It's an Arts Centre," Marion smiled as she topped up Annabelle's glass, "they don't just have plays and films here, you know. Do you like my son's paintings?"

Annabelle wrinkled her nose. "They're very… evocative."

"Of what?"

"Well, for want of a better word, hopelessness. You get the impression that the subject feels she has no way out, that the end has come for her. It's such a shame, isn't it? When people get such horrible diseases so young?"

Marion nodded. "Tobias is affected by them too. I think that's how he's able to express the emotion so well on canvas."

Annabelle's eyes brightened. "You know the artist? Is he here?"

"He's my son, and no, he isn't here. He's a very private person. He doesn't like to leave the house. But we don't live far from here. If you'd like to meet him I might be able to arrange it."

The girl beamed. "Oh that would be marvellous! I need a subject for my end of first year dissertation. You don't suppose he'd mind, do you?"

Marion remained non-committal. "I'm not sure about that, but what I do think is that he might be willing to let you pose for him."

"Really!" The girl suddenly turned shy. "But I'm not a very interesting study. I've been told that."

"I'm sure Tobias will be able to find some aspect of you interesting." Marion was scribbling down her address and phone number. "Just let me know a few dates and we can fix something up."

"Wonderful!" Annabelle was beaming. "I don't know how to thank you. And now I have to ask a very embarrassing question indeed. I hope you won't think I'm too stupid."

Marion shook her head. "Not at all, dear. What is it?"

Annabelle gazed again at the picture they had come to a halt in front of, the one where the subject was propped before a window, her tear-stained eyes staring from what remained of her face into the most beautiful lilac-lit garden.

"It's just that I've forgotten," Annabelle said. "What do you call this kind of art. Is it Still Life?"

"No, dear." Marion gave her a sympathetic smile. "But you almost got it right. Almost."

Valley Interlude No.2

"They're in Aberystwyth."

"I'm sorry?" Stokes frowned.

"Those girls." Robert shook his head and put his fingers to his temples. "They're in Aberystwyth. Except they're not, not really. They're somewhere… else. But the only way to get to that somewhere is in a house that's close to Aberystwyth."

"You're not making any sense, you know." Stokes waved a hand in front of Robert's face. "Are you sure you're all right? You were staring off into space there for a moment."

"A moment?" It had seemed like hours, days even. "I'm sorry." What else could Robert say? "I think I just found myself daydreaming for a bit." But it hadn't been a dream of any kind. If so the images should have been fading rapidly from his mind now he was awake again, but if anything his visions of those horrible things, and of what had happened in that windswept country house, was just as strong, perhaps even stronger.

"I can't say I've ever seen anyone affected in quite that way by one of my works of art before." Stokes was trying to make light of the matter despite his obvious concern.

"Perhaps you haven't been paying close enough attention."

"I beg your pardon?"

"No," Robert shook his head and laid a hand on the other man's shoulder. "I should be begging yours. You were kind enough to pay for my car and here I am snapping at you because I'm probably tired and have had a bit of a weird time today. Would you accept my apologies?"

"Of course, my dear fellow! Can I get you anything? I have half a bottle of reasonable whiskey in the office?"

No. No more drinking. Not with those things still in his head. "A cup of tea would be marvellous."

Mr Stokes beamed. "Then a cup of tea you shall have!"

Mr Stokes' office was no better lit or any less cluttered than the storage room, but it boasted a kettle that actually worked and a couple of rickety chairs. Robert was grateful to be able to take the weight off his feet. He leaned on a desk covered with papers and sipped the hot bitter liquid.

"Feeling better?"

Not really, but he didn't want to inconvenience Mr Stokes any more than he already had done. "A bit. I'll just finish this and then I'll get going."

Stokes pulled up a chair. "And where is it you're planning on going?"

It was almost as if the man already knew.

"Aberystwyth." The word came out as a croak.

"Because that's where you were going in the first place, or because of what you think you've just seen?" Robert knew Stokes had the answer to that one as well. "You told me on the way here your memory has been shaky since you woke up by the bridge. Don't you think your next port of call should be a hospital?"

No. No hospitals. Robert couldn't say why but the mere thought sent a chill down his spine. "I'll be fine."

"I don't think you will, my friend. Memory loss? Strange visions? Staring off into space? Someone needs to take a look at you." The man's hand was straying to a grubby white telephone receiver half buried beneath a stack of final demand notices.

"No hospitals!" Robert had grabbed Stokes' hand. He released it immediately and apologised. "I'll be fine, really."

"I'm still not convinced." Stokes took out a pen and began scribbling on the back of one of the unpaid bills. "Look, if you're determined to venture out there, could I ask you to do one thing for me?"

Robert wasn't sure. "That depends."

Stokes passed over the paper, which now boasted, in scrawling blue ink, an address and a phone number. And a name."

"Dr Rebecca Harrison," Robert read aloud, "who presumably practices at this Cardiff address?"

Stokes nodded. "She's very good. Helped me out once. And if you're still insistent on going out to the hinterlands of Wales it would be on your way."

"I don't need a psychiatrist."

"Don't you?"

Was Robert imagining it, or had something about Stokes changed? Suddenly the man seemed more intense, as if there was a far older, wiser individual lurking just beneath this chubby man's jolly exterior.

"All right. I'll go and see her."

"Promise?"

"Yes!" Why was the man suddenly being so insistent?

Probably because he's worried about you. Calm down.

"I'm sorry." Robert slumped in his chair and the wood gave a worrying creak. "I must be tired."

Stokes looked at his watch. "It's only mid-afternoon. If you set off now you could see Dr Harrison and then stay overnight somewhere in Cardiff."

Robert gave him a weary smile. "You're determined for me to go, aren't you?"

"Because I'm worried about you my dear fellow!" Cheery jolly Stokes was back but it was too late. Robert had seen something else in the man, just like he had seen something else in the painting, and something else in Mr Jeavons who had told him that golf course story.

Robert drained his mug and got to his feet. "All right," he said. "You've convinced me."

"I am not in the habit of seeing patients after hours, Mr…"

"I'm afraid I'm not really sure of my surname. That's one of the reasons I'm here."

"The others being…?"

"To be honest I'm not too sure about those, either."

It wasn't a very good start, but then Robert's journey from Newport had been fraught with difficulties as well. There had been a terrible queue of traffic through the Brynglas tunnels and then further roadworks on the slip road into Cardiff had meant he had eventually pulled up in the upmarket side street where Dr Harrison had her practice at close to six o'clock. The young male receptionist had refused point blank to let Robert in at first, telling him the first available private appointment was late next week. Robert had been tempted to forget it and just find a hotel, but what Stokes had said still bothered him, and he had put so much effort into finding the place he was unwilling to be turned away now.

"She was recommended by a friend." He passed the crumpled, biro-scrawled bill over. "He said she would be willing to see me."

The receptionist's grimace at being handed the scrap of paper altered when he looked at the handwriting.

"If you would be kind enough to wait here, sir" he said, his demeanour suddenly much more polite, "I'll see what I can do."

Robert didn't have to wait long before he was shown through into a luxurious consulting room. An oxblood leather couch stood against the wall opposite double windows that looked onto the sunlit street beyond, the view only slightly obscured by a huge antique desk.

And, of course, the woman sitting behind it.

She looked more like a corporate CEO with her sharply cut navy suit, brown hair pulled back tightly from her pinched face, and severe expression. She regarded Robert with glittering blue eyes from behind the small round lenses of her fashionably framed spectacles.

"You aren't making a lot of sense." She held aloft the piece of paper Stokes had given him. "If it wasn't for this I would have allowed my receptionist to send you away with an appointment for a later date, but I know Mr Stokes of old and I owe him a favour, so the least you can do, both for me and for him, is clarify why you should be worth my after-hours time."

That was all the incentive Robert needed to tell her everything, from waking up at the bridge to his bizarre daydream in the art gallery. As he spoke, Dr Harrison's expression softened to the point where she seemed to be relaxing more than he was. That wasn't the way it was supposed to work, was it? By the time he had finished she looked like a different person. Robert felt much the same.

"You have my sympathy, Robert." She removed her glasses. "You've obviously been through a traumatic episode which, for all we know, may not yet have resolved itself."

"You mean it will resolve? I will get my memory back?"

"I would hope so, but it's difficult to tell. Were you ever an especially imaginative individual? As a child, perhaps?"

Robert shook his head. "There's so little I can remember. For all I know I might have been a great artist, or on the other hand I might be someone without a single creative bone in my body."

"Either way, you now seem especially susceptible to suggestion. The story that old man told you in the hotel – was it just words to you?"

No. "It was more like a movie playing out in my mind. I could see every aspect of it, every detail."

"Even details that you weren't being told?"

Robert nodded. "He didn't need to tell me what people looked like – I could see them. And when I looked at the painting, it wasn't like a real dream at all, where everything is jumbled and random and you're left wondering what has just passed through your head when you wake up. This was all as clear as day. I could tell you everything that happened in it right now, if you like."

Dr Harrison got up from behind her desk and opened the top drawer of a heavy oak filing cabinet in the corner.

"Is this a recognised condition, then?" Robert asked as she began flicking through case files.

"Not exactly. But yours is certainly not the first case I have encountered where fantasies have been experienced as a kind of vivid reality." She pulled out a thin manila document wallets. "What we don't want is for you to end up like this man."

That didn't sound encouraging. "I'm guessing he didn't recover?"

Dr Harrison shrugged. "If you want an honest answer, no one knows. All that they found in an abandoned house in Cardiff was this manuscript. There was quite a hunt for the individual at the time but it came to nothing. The document was brought to me by the police for a professional opinion, in case I might be able to help them find him. But they never did. For all we know writing it may have purged him of his delusions and he is now happily married and employed and living in a newly built home somewhere on the nice side of town under another name." She paused.

"But?"

Dr Harrison gave him a steely look. "The chances are, that's not how he ended up. You see, I've encountered this sort of thing before – a situation where a subject's delusions are so overwhelming that they end up losing their grip on reality entirely." She had taken out another folder. "This transcript was brought to me by one of my colleagues for a second opinion. By the time I got back to him he told me that his patient, a woman on this occasion, had vanished. He was convinced that her delusions had most likely led her to…"

Dr Harrison didn't need to say any more.

"And you think I might end up like them?" Robert was finding that difficult to believe. "I mean, I may have lost my memory, but I have a very definite idea of what is real and what is not."

'Do you?" Dr Harrison was tapping her finger against her chin. "I wonder..."

"What?"

"Whether these might help us to reach a diagnosis, whether reading these accounts, written by the patients themselves, might help jog your own psyche – a kind of written Rorschach test, if you like."

"You mean you want me to read those files and tell you what I think?"

She smiled. "Exactly. And in case you're thinking what a terrible psychiatrist I am for breaking patient confidentiality, the names in these documents have already been changed so I can share them more widely with other colleagues should I so wish."

"But you haven't, have you?"

"Not yet. But if I could say I had used them to help you the potential for a new therapeutic technique could be extraordinary."

Robert remained unconvinced. "So you're using me as a guinea pig?"

The smile hardened. "A guinea pig who may well profit from the experience. You do want to recover your memory, don't you?"

He did.

"And you do want to find out who you are?"

He did.

"And why you are in Wales?"

All true.

"All right." Robert held out his hand. "Do I get to take them away with me?"

"Oh no, that would be irresponsible of me." Dr Harrison handed over the folders, switched on the lamp that stood close to the couch, and then retreated behind her desk, where she opened an A4 notebook and unscrewed the cap of an elegant black fountain pen. "I'm going to sit here and observe while you go through the documents."

Robert made himself comfortable, opened the first folder, and began to read.

The Men With Paper Faces

There is another world that exists beneath ours.

Only slightly beneath, mind you. Sometimes only very slightly indeed. The distance from our world to theirs can be a mere hair's breadth. No more than a lick of paint. A film of water. Or a sheet of the thinnest tissue paper.

Paper.

I would never have thought something so innocuous could be capable of shielding something so hideous. But then twenty-four hours ago there were many things of which I was blissfully unaware. The moment must surely soon come when those who have been moving among us all these years will reveal themselves. In that infinitesimal fragment of time between the shock of realisation, and succumbing to the appalling fate which will undoubtedly follow, may merciful insanity descend upon us all.

I was born and raised in Wales. A sickly child, little did I realise at the time that the dampness that settled with such dogged persistence in both the valleys of my homeland and the bronchioles of my lungs might be the very reason they chose this ancient and mysterious land.

The damp helps their faces stay on, you see.

Their paper faces.

Even now I find myself typing those words hesitantly, in between nervous glances from the window to the door and back again. My fingertips hover over the keyboard as if the very spelling of those words will somehow reveal my presence, and my knowledge of their existence, to them.

Let me wait a while, just in case.

There. It is now more than two minutes since the words appeared on my computer screen and there has been no moon face with cutouts for eyes at my window, no scraping of papery, threadbare fingers at my door. Perhaps I will be safe long enough to finish this account. Perhaps then I may also be granted the time to conceal it before they find me.

As I have already said, I was born in Wales, and have remained in my homeland for the entirety of my adult life. The only change in my circumstances is that on attaining adulthood I moved from the isolation of a valley town to the capital city. I will confess that I have spent several reasonably happy years in Cardiff, and it is only very recently that day and night have blurred into one with every hour, both sleeping and waking, filled with visions of people and things and places, and what they really look like underneath.

It all began after the accident.

No, even that isn't right, and if this account is to prove of any use at all to those who find it there must be accuracy, otherwise I may as well spend my final hours making up nonsense about sea beasts and tentacled monstrosities from outer space.

I do not know where they come from.

Only that they are here.

I first became aware of them when I was lying in a hospital bed. True, this was after an accident, but I am unsure if it was the trauma itself that lifted the veil from my eyes, or the surgery that had been necessary to repair the injuries I sustained. Either way, a while after I came to, I caught my first glimpse of a changed world. Even then I imagined it was likely a drug-induced and therefore transient occurrence, a side effect of the general anaesthetic, or of the pain-killing medications (administered to stop me from screaming, I was later told, although I have no memory of this).

I remember waking in darkness, and then realising, as I raised my right hand so that my fingers ought to have been visible before my face, that it was not darkness at all, but utter blackness. The blackness of a coal cellar without light, of a night without stars, of the unending void of nothing that most likely awaits us upon death.

The blackness of the totally blind.

I remember the panic that gripped me as I moved my hand over my face. Then my fingertips came into contact with the bandages that had been taped over my eyes and I heaved a sigh of relief, before fear flooded me once again as I began to wonder why they were there.

I moved my hands lower and felt sheets and blankets. When my fingers explored the edge of my mattress, my skin felt the shock of cold metal. Bars. The kind used to stop hospital patients from rolling onto the floor.

I remember trying to call out, that all I could manage was a dry croak, and that by the time I had swallowed sufficient saliva to make utterance I could hear movement in the room, far away, deeper in the darkness. I could hear the rattling of instruments on a table, a needle piercing rubber, the squirling rush of fluid being drawn into a syringe too quickly. It was only when I asked where I was that the individual performing these actions must have realised I was awake. And in the seconds before a response was given, I heard a strange sound, as of the rustling of coarse newspaper being used to cover something, before a female voice spoke to me.

"You're at St Tristan's," it said. "My name's Sally. I'm one of the nurses here, and you still need plenty of rest."

"What's happened to me?"

There was a pause before the reply.

"You had an accident," Sally said. "You came in a few days ago. You weren't badly injured but, well, you've probably already guessed which bit of you came off worst."

"Am I blind?"

"I can't say." Sally inserted a probe into my left ear. I heard a click and then she withdrew it. Beyond the ringing the action had caused I could hear the scratching of a biro scribbling on a chart. "But Mr Sanderson and his team will be around in a bit. I'm sure he'll explain everything to you."

He did, but not before the dressings were removed and I was able to view my surroundings, as well as those individuals gathered before me to explain my circumstances.

Once my eyes had been given sufficient time to adjust to a glaring white sunlight which held no warmth and flooded the room with the clinical harshness of a light microscope prepared to examine a specimen slide, my first impression was that the hospital must be desperately short of beds. That could be the only reason for the appalling state of the room in which I found myself. It was spacious enough, but the magnolia-coloured paint on the walls was cracked and peeling, and in the worst places, high up and close to the ceiling, it hung in long strips that revealed an underside of glistening dampness, the paint failing in its task of concealing a wall of suppurating red brickwork.

"It is always something of a shock when the bandages are removed."

So spoke the individual who proceeded to identify himself as Mr Sanderson, the surgeon who had operated on me. He was a short, squat man in an immaculate three-piece black suit, the pale roundness of his utterly bald head an anaemic shade of pink. I did my best to concentrate on him, to ignore my dilapidated surroundings, but it was difficult as I could not see his eyes, hidden as they were behind rimless spectacles whose tiny circular lenses were of an opaque whiteness that matched his shirt. I wondered how he could see anything through them, never mind how he might be able to perform delicate surgery.

"Your injuries were fairly minor." His voice was gentle, almost a whisper. But far from finding his tones comforting, I was reminded of serpents from the animated feature films I had enjoyed in my youth. I did not trust him. "Some conjunctival lacerations that in some places extended to the cornea, but nothing that couldn't be fixed with a few micro-sutures. Six of them in fact. Six stitches holding the surface of each eye together."

That caught my attention. Stitches. This man had put stitches in my eyes.

My reaction must have been one of horror as his tones subsequently became even more placatory.

"Nothing to worry about! The stitches will dissolve eventually. Over the next few weeks they will be absorbed by your eyes until nothing of them remains. It will be as if they were never there."

For a moment I wondered if he meant the stitches or my eyes themselves. Then a noise made me aware of the assemblage of nurses and junior medical staff gathered behind him. It was most likely my imagination, but I was almost sure that after this last utterance they all, as one, tittered to themselves, the massed bulk of their bodies heaving with a collective giggle at some joke to which I was not party.

"You still can't remember how you came by them?"

"I beg your pardon?" I had become distracted. By my situation, by the rotting room, and most of all by these almost alien individuals who were at that moment regarding me.

"Your injuries." Mr Sanderson looked concerned, while his accompanying entourage imbibed a moist-lipped, collective intake of breath. "You still have no recollection?"

I had not previously considered it, but now I tried to recall how I had come to be here, in this awful bed in this terrible place, I found I could not summon even the most insignificant fact that might have contributed to an explanation. I tried again.

Nothing.

I shook my head and gave a weak smile.

"Never mind." Mr Sanderson beamed in a way that made me think of a fat white spider who knows its meal is helpless enough for it to enjoy later, when it has had time to develop sufficient appetite. "One more day and we should be able to get you home."

"I could leave today if you like," I blurted, not wishing to remain in this dusty, peeling chamber a moment longer than was necessary. "I mean, I can understand you must be very hard pressed for beds."

Again that horrible, hungry smile. "You worked that out, did you?" The Sanderson entourage mumbled assent as he spoke. "Well, you're right. The hospital is currently so full that we have had to open our new wing a week early. You are the very first patient to occupy a bed here. Well done for spotting how new everything looks. Your eyesight has obviously recovered more quickly than I thought." The smile dropped as he clasped maggot-white fingers across his midriff. "Perhaps you are ready to go home today, after all!"

They all turned to go. I searched for the nurse who had spoken to me earlier, but I could not guess which of the pale, expressionless matrons might be host to the voice I had heard. As the door to my room creaked open, desiccated fragments of rotten, greyish wood fell from where the hinges desperately held it in place. The ward round, with Mr Sanderson now at its head, shuffled out. I pushed the bedclothes aside, intent on leaving immediately.

The nurse bringing up the rear turned and regarded me with tiny eyes set in a pinched face whose skin was the same shade of mottled grey as the doorframe. Just before she stepped outside she breathed something at me.

Even now I do not know exactly what it was she said, but I have narrowed it down to two possibilities. It was either "You may leave" or "You may see". Since departing that horrid place, the implications of either have become increasingly horrific.

But I am getting ahead of myself. I have not even mentioned that when I threw back the bed covers the action raised a powder of particles that were easy to see by the empty sunlight. These particles were not dust, I am convinced of that now. To begin with they were coarser, more substantial than the motes one commonly encounters. These were more like tiny fragments of torn paper, such as might be created if one were to tear a tissue into the smallest possible pieces. As they floated down before me I tried to grab one, but they were too quick.

They landed on the wooden boards of the floor, and I watched in horror as each fragment grew six tiny, gossamer-fine legs, and scuttled beneath the bed.

That was enough. I was leaving. I climbed out of the bed slowly, not wishing to disturb any more of the tiny alien creatures. The scarred boards creaked a warning beneath my naked feet as I made my way to the crudely fashioned wardrobe slumped to the left of the door. It opened with some difficulty, as quite obviously very little care had been taken in its workmanship.

My clothes were gathered in a heap at the bottom.

I picked them up, and shook them out. Sure enough, I found them to be infested with the same 'tissue motes' (I can think of no other name for them), and as I gave each garment a thorough and vigorous shake, the tiny creatures dropped to the ground and scuttled to join their brethren beneath the bed. Once I was happy my clothes were free from infestation, I pulled them on, much happier now that I was dressed in my tattered green corduroy suit, and my feet were safely inside my scuffed brown Oxfords.

My journey through the hospital to the outside world was the stuff of nightmare.

As soon as I stepped out of my room, carefully avoiding the still-splintering doorframe, I realised that Mr Sanderson must have been joking when he had called this place the 'new wing'. Indeed, I had never before found myself in such dilapidated surroundings. The long and empty corridor that stretched ahead of me was high-ceilinged, but many of the insulating tiles had fallen and now lay in fragmented heaps of rotting brown fibres on scabrous floorboards spattered in places with thick black mould. The medical team must have been quick on their feet, for there was neither sight nor sound of them as I made my way along, and there seemed to be no other rooms into which they might have slipped to visit other patients. Instead, on either side of me, I beheld walls adorned with peeling wallpaper of faded pink stripes on a dirty white background. As I progressed, the corridor seemed to become narrower, and I was never able to tell if it was an effect of actual physical dimensions or just an optical illusion created by the nature of the decor. Reaching out to touch the walls did no good, as the damp wallpaper collapsed beneath my probing, suggesting the absence of any kind of solidity beneath it. The moisture that pooled in the thickened folds I created was chill and burned my fingertips such that I did not persist with my explorations.

At the very end of the corridor I expected there to be a turn either to the left or the right. Instead, and quite impossibly, the passageway came to an abrupt halt, and I found myself facing a high window that consisted of nine square panes of glass that were almost opaque with dirt. I was loath to touch the blackened grease that obscured my view of the world outside and yet I felt myself compelled to trace a diagonal line across the centre pane with the outstretched index finger of my right hand. The subsequent grime I acquired would not leave my skin, no matter how hard I rubbed my finger against the fabric of my jacket. Doing my best to ignore the gritty, slimy sensation that seemed to have been exacerbated by my attempts to rid myself of it, I knelt on creaking boards and peered through the glass I had cleared.

I did not recognise the part of Cardiff I could see though the window. I must have been on a high floor of the hospital, as the row upon row of terraced houses I beheld seemed far beneath me. Of course, this could also have been due to the distorting effect the glass had, making the houses seem somehow… wrong. The doors were too narrow, the windows too small, and the buildings themselves were all manner of curious shapes. They were more like a child's crude attempt at models of houses than the buildings themselves, and yet I somehow knew that the structures I could see were real.

But how to get to them? Or rather, how to get out of this awful place? How had Mr Sanderson and his team achieved their egress? Had they found another way out, perhaps behind one of those dripping curtains of pink and white paper? Or had they gone out of the window?

I prodded the glass once more, to be rewarded by a scraping sound as of the blade of a shovel being dragged against concrete. This was accompanied by the glass before me swinging open from hinges along the top of the frame. I poked my head out and coughed as my lungs were assailed with a mixture of petrol fumes and the same dampness I had felt in the corridor, although strangely it seemed to be stronger outside than in, as if a storm had broken but the moisture had been retained by the air molecules rather than falling to be absorbed by the ground.

A rickety metal fire escape led downward. I had little wish to test my weight upon it, and yet it seemed the quickest, and indeed the only, means of escape. The poorly constructed metal wobbled and creaked with every tentative step. The bolts holding it against the filthy, crumbling red brickwork of the building's exterior seemed inexpertly applied, rudely driven in at angles that suggested carelessness. The dust trickling from the attachment points merely served to encourage my haste.

Once I was on the street, the relative solidity of rocking paving stones beneath my feet, I quickly became aware that the members of the general public who buffeted and thronged about me were of two distinct types. The first were as you or I – normal-seeming human beings going about their everyday business. A few were smiling, many had nondescript expressions, a few seemed either angry or depressed, occasionally both. Still, it was more or less a normal mixture of the kinds of individuals one might encounter in any major city.

The other type were not normal at all.

At first glance they seemed so, but one only had to hold one's gaze on them for more than a second to realise there was something entirely alien about them. They were humanoid in appearance, and dressed much the same as those who pushed past and round them. It was their faces that gave them away.

Their crumbling paper faces.

Imagine, if you will, a handful of wadded-up tissue paper that has been dampened and then applied to an inverted white balloon the size of a human head. Poke holes for eyes, nose and a mouth with your fingers, add a smear of wiry grey hair to the scalp and you should have some idea of the creatures I beheld in that dreary Cardiff street. I bit back a scream and felt the pounding in my chest increase as I realised none of the normal human beings had any awareness of the anthropomorphic approximations in their midst. Fortunately, the alien creatures seemed oblivious to my knowledge of their presence and I was able to make my stumbling way along, taking care to avoid the intruders. At a crowded street corner, however, it became impossible and, as I swerved to avoid one, I collided with another. My elbow met with the same sickening, collapsing sensation I had experienced when probing the hospital wallpaper. Unlike the elastic resilience of normal flesh, the intruders' flesh seemed more plastic, more accommodating to changes in shape. I coughed an apology and that with which I had collided grated a polite reply in what would otherwise have passed for a human voice, were I not already privy to the creature's true nature.

I suppressed a shudder and turned to regard the road I intended to cross. It was then I was struck with another realisation.

I had no idea where I was.

I am not familiar with the entirety of Cardiff, of course. I would be surprised if anyone living in a major city is fully conversant with every street. However, I would have hoped that in the event of an emergency any hospital I might have been taken to would be in a part of town I had at least passed through at some point. This place, however, was completely unfamiliar to me.

A nearby newsagent put me straight. I did my best to ignore the appalling state of his shop – the leaking roof, the newspapers, chocolate bars and other snacks teetering in random piles, the dim lighting that meant I could barely find my way to the counter. I also ignored the peeling features of the individual in front of me paying for a chocolate bar and, once they were gone, proceeded to ask the man who owned the shop if they might know the whereabouts of my street of residence. My question was met with a frown, followed by the gentleman responding that his establishment was on that very street, and that my address was but a few houses distant. I knew that this could not possibly be the case, and so strong was my conviction that he deemed it necessary to show me on one of the copies of an amateurishly printed and poorly stapled A-Z street guide that he was telling the truth and that, even more significantly, there was no other street in the city bearing a similar name.

I left the shop in a state of utter confusion, pausing only to note the number before setting off in the direction in which, according to him, my dwelling ought to lie.

Nothing was familiar. I have walked the length of the street on which I live many, many times, and yet now I may as well have been walking the highway of a distant country. To my left the buildings soon gave way to an expanse of recreational parkland. I felt some distant pang of familiarity at the towering oaks, the central lake upon which both dead birds and rudimentary attempts at model boats floated, but I cannot honestly say I recognised any of these things.

When I finally arrived at my address I once again felt no sense of recognition, of homecoming. Instead the Victorian terraced house with my number on it felt as grim and as foreboding as those crumbling buildings I had first viewed on my escape from that terrible hospital. I felt in my pocket for keys, only to discover I had none.

And so I rang the bell.

What else could I do? I had nowhere to go, and it was just possible the house was made up of apartments, and that one of the other residents could let me in. Perhaps even the landlord lived there and might be able to grant me access to my own flat. As I lifted my finger from the buzzer another thought occurred to me. Perhaps my inability to remember my street, the park, my house, could all be attributed to amnesia I had sustained as the result of an accident I still could not remember. If that was the case, then what else might I be unaware of? Was I married? Did I have a wife? Children?

I took a step back as I heard footsteps coming closer on the other side of the door. The sounds were muffled, as if the individual responding to my summons was walking in slippers, or had very soft feet. As fingers fumbled with the latch I poised to make good my escape. The door opened softly, to reveal an empty hallway beyond.

After a moment, I took a step forward and peered inside. Nothing of the house's interior served to jog my memory. Not the brick red squares, bordered in black, that tiled the floor. Not the coat rack to the right of the door that was home to a moth-eaten mustard-coloured duffle coat half-concealing the dusty black cardigan that cowered beneath it.

I called out a greeting, only for the word to be swallowed by the hollow space before me. Despite the absence of a reply, I stepped inside, noting as I did so that the floor tiles were uneven, and actually a little loose. I attempted to kick aside the crumbling cement I had dislodged, only for three of the tiles to come free entirely and skitter away, hitting the scabbed skirting board to my left with a clatter.

I called out again.

Nothing.

Another step inside. This one was even gentler than the last and yet still I felt the crunch of rotten tiling beneath my foot. The door to my left was flaking with inexpertly-applied, magnolia-coloured paint similar in hue to that which had adorned my hospital room. Then I noticed that the wallpaper either side of it, and on the wall opposite and up the stairs to the right, consisted of the same damp-looking pink-striped stuff as in the hospital corridor into which I had made good my escape.

I began to climb the stairs. The threadbare carpet of patterned crimson covering the mildewed wood was preferable to the awful sensation of crumbling glazing beneath my feet. I presumed the condition of the floor was the reason whoever had opened the door had been wearing slippers.

The stairs creaked as I ascended, each step warping at the pressure of my foot and failing to regain its shape once I had moved on. The landing was composed of the same rotten flooring, the same threadbare carpet, and the wallpaper here was more faded than downstairs.

I could hear breathing coming from the bedroom to my left.

By now my throat was so dry I could barely summon a sound. I tried to ignore the deep scratch marks on the door, and pushed it open.

There was something lying on the bed.

Even now I find it difficult to describe. It was human-like, and similar to the alien creatures I had seen on the street. The face of this one was far more rudimentary, though. The nostrils were ill-formed, the mouth little more than a pulsing black dot above a flaking chin, and as for the eyes –

There were none.

As the thing began to rise, as the mouth began to expand and the feathery structures I could see within it began to organise themselves into a rudimentary tongue, I felt a strong impression that this thing, whatever it was, had been caught off guard.

And then it spoke my name.

I am not sure which was more shocking, that the creature knew me or that the voice in which it spoke was female. Either way, as I stepped back I crammed my knuckles into my mouth to keep myself from screaming.

The wasting thing was on its feet now, rubbing at its papier-mâché face with fingers that resembled pale sausages wrapped in wet tissue. When it revealed its features to me once more I could see it had poked holes in the damp paper coverings to allow it to see out.

To see me.

I could taste bile rising in my throat, and over the pounding of blood in my ears I could just make out the thing's gargling, rasping attempts at language.

I dismissed its communications as nonsense. How could this limping, tattered thing that shambled towards me possibly be my wife? I retreated further, realising too late that the door to the bedroom had swung shut behind me. The creature hobbled nearer, squeezing at the sides of its head so that it now possessed rudimentary ears. Then the sausage fingers pulled the mouth into a ghastly parody of a smile.

What else could I do? I reached out to fend off the advances of this horrible thing, and in doing so felt my fingertips dig into the chill moistness of its face.

A face that came away in my hand.

I fought the urge to vomit as the tissue I found myself holding frayed and fragmented into the same kind of tiny tissue motes I had observed in my hospital room. Even as I made the connection, they began to swarm over my fingers, tickling the web spaces with their tiny, multi-jointed, thread-like limbs, imbuing my palm with the sensation that my skin, too, was coming apart.

I brushed the creatures off, slapping at the more persistent of them, and having to physically pick at the ones that were doing their best to bury themselves beneath my nail beds. I would have stamped on them, too, but once they had fallen to the ground, they quickly disappeared between the cracks in the floorboards.

I turned my attention back to what was standing in front of me.

Beneath the creature's torn face lay something quite unexpected. I would not have been surprised to see ripped flesh, bleeding muscle, even exposed bone. Instead, I beheld a pale, waxen rudiment. A bloodless approximation of a face such as a window-shop dummy might have before eyes are painted on and other features added. A template, an approximation, an estimate.

Deprived of its lips, it seemed the thing could no longer speak. Instead it waved its arms at me as if in a desperate attempt to communicate. It was less a conscious decision and more the reflex action of sheer panic that caused me to grab the rusting lamp from the bedside table, raise it high above my head, and bring it down with all the strength I could summon upon the creature's waxen, hairless cranium.

The head did not so much give way as accede to the blow, such that when I raised the instrument again there remained the impression of my weapon as if it had been pressed into modelling clay.

I hit the thing again, and again, but it took many more blows before the creature finally fell to its knees, and thence to the floor. As it did so, an unearthly sound filled the room. As I have already explained, the creature had no mouth, and so I can only guess where the sound came from. It resembled a humming, as of a plethora of tiny insects buzzing too close to one's ears for comfort. It lasted only for a minute, and yet it caused the most blinding headache. Even now, hours later, I am still recovering from it.

I am still in the house.

Because I cannot leave.

In a downstairs room I have found a computer, and that is where I am now writing this account. I can only assume that the sound the creature made in its death throes was a cry for help. When I began writing this I imagined I was alone. Now, however, outside the front and back doors, and at every window, both upstairs and down, I can see them, looking in at me. They have yet to enter, but I know it is only a matter of time.

What are they? If these words are to be of any help to those who find them, to those who must begin to organise the fight against these things, I offer this:

That they are of otherworldly origin I have no doubt. I am also convinced that they are two different species, that there is a symbiotic relationship between the tissue motes and the faceless, wax humanoid creatures they cover, thus creating the semblance of humanity. These symbionts have somehow been able to alter the vision of human beings so that we remain ignorant of the rotten, decaying world these invaders are building for themselves.

They thrive on corruption, of that I am now sure. New buildings are nothing of the kind. What we see as alive is actually dead. What we see as order is actually chaos. Our world is not just falling apart, but is actively being taken to pieces. For what purpose I cannot say, except that it suits their needs.

I just heard a crash upstairs. I should investigate. I would say I will be back in a moment, but I suspect that will not be the case. So instead I'm just going to press the 'Save' button and hope for the best.

There.

All done.

Time to go.

By Any Other Name

It's bad today.

It always is when the rain comes, and today it's pouring down. There's a vicious storm hammering against the windows of my house, every single drop insisting that I pay attention to it.

I can see things moving in the raindrops.

Not nice things or happy things. Perhaps if they were it wouldn't be so awful. I'd still know I was going insane, but it would be better than this terrible, haunting madness, this withering mental horror of hallucination and delusion.

That was what the psychiatrist called it. Not the withering mental bit, but he did say the other words. He said them to me, and after the consultation he said them to my husband, Donald, making sure I was in earshot.

"Mr Bryce," he said in that annoying laid back tone of his that matched his ghastly farmyard-beige clothes, the ones that were presumably intended to project a degree of casualness that would help his patients open up to him. And I suppose they might if they bought their outfits at the same charity shop – if nothing else it would give them something to talk about. "Mr Bryce, your wife is suffering from what we call delusions – beliefs that are entirely false but which are nevertheless fixed in her mind as the truth. There are also some accompanying hallucinations which I find worrying. It's possible this has been brought on at least in part by her stressful position at the university. She is obviously a highly intelligent woman. Unfortunately she also has a vivid imagination that is in danger of becoming uncontrollable."

At least 'vivid' and 'uncontrollable' were correct. I could agree with that. I'd give anything to be able to stop the awful things I see, to stop them squirming, stop them calling, stop them looking at me with those horrible, sightless eyes.

Would you like to know what they look like?

The psychiatrist wanted to, but when I told him I don't think it was what he was expecting. His face just crumpled up, as if I'd told him his child had been run over, or that his wife was leaving him. I was lying on the couch with my back to him but I could see his expression reflected in the tiny mirror on his desk. He tried to keep his voice steady after I told him, but it was obvious he was upset. Good, I thought. That'll teach you. And now you know what I have to deal with all the time.

No, not all the time.

Only when I see water.

I'm not going to tell you what they look like, not just yet. Otherwise your face might crumple up too, and then you'll throw this account away and that wouldn't be a good thing for anyone. Trust me. Just keep reading and I'll tell you my story as gently and as accurately as I can.

I first saw them at the bottom of a drinking glass.

No, that's not the beginning. I'm sorry, I have to go back further. I've given this a lot of thought over the last few weeks and if I'm to write this down – the psychiatrist said it would help – then I must go back to the very start, the thing that I now believe triggered it all off.

It started with the argument.

Couples argue about all sorts of silly things, don't they? Where to go out to eat, what to watch on television, what colour carpet should go in the living room – anything and everything, really. I can't even remember what the argument was about now. I might have thrown something, but probably not. The violence came later, after I started seeing the things. Before that I was the nicest, calmest person you could possibly imagine. Believe me. It's only a matter of a day or so but it feels like such a long time ago now. I didn't used to throw glasses or overturn water coolers, and I didn't mean to break the door on the shower when I kicked it. But I was scared, you see.

Terrified.

The day after we had the argument, Donald gave me a present. He said he'd picked it up on his way home from work, from one of those 'crazy little places' I liked going into so much. I realised he meant an independent shop in one of the arcades. There are quite a few in Cardiff, and I love wandering the covered walkways and imagining I'm back in Victorian times. The shops all look as if they're out of Charles Dickens, and you can find anything from second hand books to designer shoes, sometimes from the same tiny, gloomy little place.

Donald had bought me some perfume.

It didn't say so on the bottle. In fact there wasn't any writing on the glass at all – no label, no raised lettering, nothing. But, he said, the shopkeeper had assured him that was what it was.

I remember holding the palm-sized phial up to the afternoon sunlight. It was a hexagon of the deepest cobalt blue, crowned with a stopper encased in a coating of thick, black wax. The shopkeeper had claimed it was very old and very rare, and that the seal had never been broken. A tiny meniscus close to the top of the bottle's stubby little neck indicated the bottle was full. I had never before been aware that I had a tremor, but as I held the bottle, I realised the liquid inside it was shaking and I had to bring up my other hand to steady my wrist. It was strange, though, because it didn't feel as if I were trembling at all. I should have taken that as my first warning.

"Aren't you going to try it?" Donald asked.

I didn't like to. It looked so… untouchable. I couldn't imagine myself defiling that seal, especially not if it was an antique.

"How much did you pay for it?"

Donald shrugged. "It doesn't matter," he said. "I just wanted you to know that I love you. And that I'm sorry."

"I love you too." I had already forgotten what we had been arguing about. I looked at the perfume again. Was it my imagination or were there tiny bubbles rising through the liquid now? "But I can't open this. If it's an antique we should keep it safe. Besides, the perfume might not be any good after all this time, and I'd hate to spoil such a lovely present."

"It's not a present if you don't use it." There was that edge in his voice again, the one I hated because it made me so fearful. "It's just a bit of bloody coloured glass. Do whatever you want with it, I don't care."

So I cracked the seal, if only to avoid another scene. I gripped the stopper and twisted, feeling the wax crumbling beneath my fingers. A fragment dug its way beneath my thumbnail but I ignored it in my attempt to get the bottle open quickly so I could defuse the brewing situation.

The stopper came out easily. I don't know why, but I was disappointed when there was no pop. Instead the ground glass slid out with a curiously slimy, lifeless sound.

I loved biochemistry in school, and it was only natural that I should make a career of it lecturing to university students. In those lessons, so far in the past now, we were always told to take a deep breath before sniffing the contents of a test tube in case we'd made chlorine or something else noxious and toxic. For some reason I felt the need to do the same now, drawing clean air into my lungs before bringing the mouth of the bottle to my nostrils.

The scent was surprisingly sweet, but not overwhelmingly so. There was an undertone of something that I couldn't make out, but it did something to take the edge off the sickliness and turn it into something quite…

Wonderful.

I exhaled so I could take a deep breath of the pure, unadulterated essence. Oh God, it was lovely!

I turned to my husband, unable to conceal the pleasure on my face. His angry features melted at the sight of my joy, and as I flung my arms around him I could feel the tension within him easing at my touch.

"I love it." I said. "And I love you."

"Well, that's good to hear." He was smiling now, at last. "Because I want you to wear it when we go out this evening."

He'd booked a table somewhere expensive. I told him we couldn't afford such an extravagance, but he was having none of it.

"We don't go out as often as we should," he said. "You can wear your blue velvet dress to go with the perfume."

"I'm not bringing the bottle with me!" I giggled.

But somehow I found myself slipping it into my handbag before we left the house.

We've always loved eating at Carlo's, which makes it all the more of a shame that we'll probably never go there again. I couldn't. It would just be too embarrassing after what happened.

The trouble started almost as soon as we got there. The main dining area is huge, as you might expect from such a popular eatery situated right in the middle of the city. I always prefer to be seated off to the side, somewhere a little more intimate and away from the main hubbub of business dinners, birthday parties and family outings. This time, however, the only empty table for two was located right in the middle of the main dining area.

"This will be fine." Donald smiled at the waitress and then at me. It was one of his 'don't embarrass me' looks that successfully warned me off objecting. I still should have, I realise that now, but that's an easy thing to say in hindsight, isn't it?

Carlo's is mainly Italian food but, in keeping with a lot of metropolitan eateries, there's a little bit of everything to maximise their clientele. I perused the menu while Donald ordered a medium-priced bottle of Sauvignon Blanc.

"Still or sparkling water for the table, sir?"

The waiter's pen was poised over his writing tablet. I can still hear the words because I wonder even now if the catastrophe might have been avoided if we'd gone for something bottled. But Donald didn't believe in paying for water in a restaurant.

"Tap water's fine," he said, and thus he sealed our doom for the evening.

We ordered our meals. The wine came, was tasted and found to be satisfactory – I don't really know why Donald still insists on doing that – and the waiter poured a generous amount into our glasses. Then the tap water arrived in a litre-sized carafe. It looked normal enough as it cascaded into our tumblers. Donald ignored it, as he always does, and concentrated on the wine. I was halfway through my starter of garlic mussels before I realised how thirsty I was. I picked up my water glass, and chanced to look at it before I took a sip.

At first I thought I was seeing events that had to be taking place over on the other side of the room. Movements and flickerings distorted by the water so that it looked as if misshapen people were coming and going, rather than the undoubtedly normal people I would see when I put the glass down.

Just for fun, I lowered my drink to see what the people really looked like.

And found myself staring at empty space.

Not entirely empty, of course. There were two recently-vacated tables, and a pair of damask curtains beyond, drawn to keep out the night, but this little slice of stillness in the otherwise bustling restaurant was not what I had been expecting.

I raised my glass.

Numerous tiny shapes swirled and squirmed in the water.

Was it the pattern on the glass itself? I ran my fingers over its engraved surface.

The tiny wriggling forms seemed to follow my fingertips as my skin made contact with the glass, converging on the trails of warmth I left behind.

"Are you all right?" By now Donald had noticed I was frowning.

I showed him my glass. "Does this water look all right to you?"

He put down his fork and peered at it, then gave me a sour look. "Seems fine to me. What d'you think's the matter with it?"

"There's something in there." I held the glass up again, aware that the remainder of my starter must be getting cold. Looking more closely, I could see the tiny swirls were not just fragments of black. Each possessed a tiny bulbous head and a tail ribbed with hairs, or possibly spines. Once again they were coalescing where my fingers were conveying warmth to the water.

I called the waiter over and explained that the water he had given us was tainted. He apologised profusely and went to get a replacement carafe while Donald looked unimpressed.

"That water looked fine to me," he said.

"Then maybe you need your eyes looking at," I spat back, more harshly than I intended.

The waiter returned in record time with a new jug of water and fresh glasses, apologising all the while as he filled them. I thanked him, ignoring Donald's grimace. I took another bite of my shellfish. The food had now lost much of its temperature and consequently its edge. In fact, it tasted so bland I was eager to wash the taste away.

There were more of those things in my new glass of water, only these were bigger.

This time I gasped, attracting the attention of surrounding diners.

Donald gripped my wrist. "For heaven's sake what's the matter?"

"The water…" Suddenly I found myself overwhelmed by an intense nausea. It was difficult to speak. "…the water still has those things in it."

Donald reached over and picked up my glass. As he held it up to the light I could see the creatures clustering at the points where his skin made contact. "Can't you see them?"

Donald shook his head. The creatures swayed with the movement. Were they watching his face? "I can't see anything. Perhaps you're ill."

"I'm not." I actually wasn't sure, but I wasn't going to let him have the satisfaction. As I spoke the creatures moved in my direction for a second before settling back around his fingertips. Were they responding to my voice? "I'm fine. It's the water that's bad."

"Then have mine instead. I've already had a sip and it tastes fine." Donald swapped glasses, placing his in front of me. I looked down to see liquid that was black with the squirming, crawling things.

It was a reflex action, but I still felt embarrassed when I realised I had knocked the glass to the floor.

Other diners were starting to raise their concerns now, in that audible mumbling that consists not so much of actual words as a generic noise of discontent that you know is being directed at you.

"Will you please calm down?" Donald was clearly uncomfortable, and appeared to be on the point of leaving.

I pointed at the water jug. Some of the tiny worm things had emerged from the water and were making their damp and sticky way up the sides of the neck. "They're in there too!" Those were the only words I could utter as I got to my feet. I looked around me. Now I could see that our table was not the only one affected. Every water jug on every table was filled with the same creatures, wriggling and squirming in their hundreds. I saw people drinking from water glasses filled with the things, oblivious of the spiny bulbous monsters that were passing from mouth to throat to stomach. I saw creatures falling from oblivious lips onto white tablecloths, struggling to reach moisture again before life faded from them.

I screamed.

"That's enough!" Over the sound of my cries I heard Donald's voice, felt Donald's hand as he led me from the table and out into the cold night air. I remember little of the taxi ride home, only that when we got there I refused a drink of any kind. I threw my handbag with the perfume in it onto my dressing table stool, fell into bed, and entered a deep sleep.

Deep, but not dreamless.

The world is water.

At first the sensation is stifling. I'm terrified I'm going to suffocate, to drown, my lungs filled with this overwhelming grey-green murk that surrounds me, that goes on and on, above and below and beyond. Seemingly never ending. Then I understand.

I do not need to breathe, at least not as I understand the term.

I float, suspended in the near-darkness of an emerald ocean. Whether I am lying down or standing upright I cannot tell. All that exists is this universe of dull, numbing fluid.

A universe filled with quiet sounds.

They are all around me, noises as of the movement of colossal rocks gently colliding, cushioned by the pressure of the vast ocean that surrounds it. The water around me remains still, however, which causes me to think.

Is something even greater in bulk than the rocks clambering over them to make that noise?

I look up. I look down. I listen.

Whatever it is, it's coming closer.

I can tell because as well as those distant, thunderous sounds, I can feel the vibrations now. A steady movement of the water against me. Regular, repetitive, and spaced out.

Whatever is doing this, it must be gargantuan.

I try kicking my legs, clawing with my hands, but it is as if I am suspended in cold gelatine, and all my actions do is urge me to take a breath.

I know it will be death if I do so. I have been granted the power to watch, to observe, and if I resist or attempt to escape, my life will be snuffed out by a billion gallons of water.

Or by that which it is home to.

I am moving now, finally. Or rather I should say I am being moved, as I do not believe I have anything to do with this motion upward. My body is being propelled by the movement of the water beneath me.

And by the creature.

I am sure of that now. Whatever has been crossing this ocean floor has decided to rise, and it is taking me with it. As I am propelled upwards faster through the water, I begin to see the light of a full moon. My head breaks the surface and I realise that I have not been the prisoner of an ocean but instead of a lake, one surrounded by trees and with a street of crumbling houses along one shore.

That is all I can take in before I feel something vast pushing up from below.

The creature is near the surface now. I wince as the soles of my bare feet come into contact with a thickened, leathery, rugose skin. And still I find myself being lifted, higher and higher until the creature, or at least some small part of its gargantuan bulk, is free from the water. Finally able to move, I cling to one of the great spines that project from the creature's body, thanking whatever luck is protecting me that I did not end up impaled as the creature rushed to the surface.

The rising ceases and the creature breathes air, gulping at it with long, wet noisy gasps. It looks down on the lake, and the trees, and the houses, and the people next to them. It is the Lord of all it surveys, and I am perched atop its spiny head, a tiny observer of which I am sure, of which I hope, it is unaware.

The creature moves closer to the shore, and the massive head bends to peer more closely at those who have gathered before it. Are they here to worship? To destroy? Are they scientists, believing they can analyse this unstoppable power from an alien world? Now that we are closer, I can see the rough wooden table that has been set up behind the row of kneeling supplicants, as well as the collection of variously shaped flasks and jars that have been assembled upon it.

The head of the creature is very close to the row of individuals, now. From their bound hands and feet I guess each of them is more likely to be a sacrifice than a supplicant.

The man responsible is over on the left, standing between his row of sacrifices and the row of rundown houses. The book he has been reading from has fallen at his feet as he stares open-mouthed at the result of his summoning. I can understand his awe, and his terror, at what he now beholds. After all, the creature he has called is looking at *him*, now.

He picks the book up – it looks crumbling, ancient – and places it on the table behind his kneeling victims. The Summoned is now so close to these people that I can see the sweat on the man's face, can almost hear the panting of his anxious breath, smell the fear of those he has brought here against their will.

He mutters something in a language unintelligible to me as he pushes the first of the sacrifices forward. The young man topples and falls to the ground, his head inches from the shore, his face turned to the side, lips spitting away lake water as it laps at his face.

I feel the creature undulate beneath me as it stretches its head further, lower, bringing one of the spines it bears into contact with the neck of the hapless individual. It pauses for a moment, then drives the spine in, just a little way, but enough to penetrate the flesh.

I feel pressure building beneath me, as if the monster I am sitting on is preparing to roar. While this is happening, the summoner has come forward, a glass flask in one hand and what looks like a pair of ancient shears in the other. Just as the beast beneath me is about to release its poison into its victim, the summoner places the blades of the shears either side of the spine that has penetrated the sacrifice. Then he squeezes the handles together with all his might.

I feel the creature's pain as the spine is broken, just as I feel its sense of release as ichor spurts from the fractured stump, ichor that the summoner catches as it splashes into the flask he is now holding to collect it.

The second sacrifice is presented. It is as if the creature cannot help itself. It lunges once again, pierces a helpless female victim this time, and as another spike is broken off by the summoner, a second vessel is filled with the noxious fluid.

By the time the third offering is pushed to the water's edge, I realise that the creature beneath me is not being tricked at all. It is, in fact, responsible for what is taking place. The Summoner is as unaware of the monster's controlling influence as the sacrifices. But I know. Perhaps it is because of my proximity to this dark god that has been called forth from the depths of the lake, because of my closeness to its body without having been made one with it.

By the time the process is over, the table is covered with jars brimming with His essence. I also realise now where it is destined to end up. In a dark and dusty makeshift laboratory filled with corkscrew-necked retorts and bubbling distillation equipment, the harvested essence being allowed to collect drip by exquisitely refined drip into a tiny receptacle.

A tiny, six-sided receptacle.

Of cobalt blue glass.

There is no time for me to visualise anything more. The ritual is over. The god is pleased. And so He returns to the depths of the lake, and I go with him. Down, down we travel into the murk, my vision increasingly obscured, my hearing dulled until the only sound is the insistent thud of my heartbeat in my ears. Without thinking, I open my lips to take a breath and my mouth and nose are filled with the essence of the grave, dank and wet and rotting. The stench is overpowering as the creature's environment floods my senses and I feel my consciousness slipping away.

When I woke I found I was still fully dressed. The rain had stopped and daylight was flooding the room through a crack in the curtains. I looked for Donald but then I saw the time and realised he must have left for work. There was no way I could do the same. Despite having slept for ten hours, I felt exhausted, and when I attempted to stand my head reeled with a giddy nausea that threatened to send me toppling into my dressing table.

I sat on the edge of the bed and held my head in my hands. It was only then that I noticed it.

The smell of the lake was still in my nostrils. Its taste was still in my mouth.

This realisation brought with it a fresh bout of nausea. I almost vomited but instead I successfully fought to keep down whatever little contents my stomach might still have possessed.

With immense effort I made it into the ensuite bathroom and without thinking ran the cold tap so I could brush my teeth.

Black wriggling things squeezed out of the tap like the toothpaste I now could not bear to touch, falling into the sink and forming a squirming mass that blocked the plughole.

That time I really was sick, into the toilet, keeping my eyes shut so I could see neither what I brought up nor the nature of what I was bringing it up into. Then I closed the lid, wiped my mouth, and wondered what to do next. A shower was out of the question. Luckily the fridge was stocked with milk and soft drinks, all of which seemed to have been spared an infestation of the crawling things that presumably needed fresh water to survive. I debated bathing in diet lemonade for a moment, but when I realised the idea had caused me to begin laughing hysterically, I forced myself to calm down.

Perhaps the shop could help. The one Donald had bought the perfume from. He'd said it was in one of the arcades. All I had to do was get there. He would have taken the car but there was a bus stop on the other side of the park our house overlooked.

All I had to do was get there.

I dragged a comb through my hair so that I looked halfway presentable, and then ventured outdoors. Now I think back it must have been obvious I wasn't well – a woman in a blue velvet evening dress staggering through the leafy greenness of a city park in broad daylight? Staggering from side to side due to dehydration and her hair in a state?

I had actually managed to make it halfway across the park when it began to rain.

It rains a lot in Wales. In fact sometimes I think we're only granted about five days of sunshine every year. Usually it's the kind of misty drizzle that's annoying without being too inconvenient. This, however, was a real downpour, hammering leaves from trees, causing people to run for cover, and turning the path on which I was walking into a sheet of water.

Water in which I could once again see the creatures.

They swarmed about my feet as the rain soaked through my hair and my dress and streamed down my skin. I knew the falling rain contained the creatures too; in fact I was certain I could feel them, wriggling against my flesh, tickling the back of neck, irritating my mouth, nose and ears.

Trying to find a way in.

I fell to my knees, tearing at my clothes and at my hair, spitting all the time to stop them from getting into my mouth. When I could still feel things tickling the back of my throat I risked taking a deep breath, and then screamed as loudly as I could. To get them out, you see. The sensation was still there, though. Which meant *they* were still there.

So I screamed again.

And again.

That's where Donald found me, on my knees and soaked to the skin, screaming my head off. He'd got to work and then had second thoughts about leaving me on my own. He took me back home, helped me tidy up, and then took my straight to see Dr Wilbraham. The psychiatrist and I talked for over an hour. Actually, it was me who did most of the talking. I told him everything I've now written here, at his suggestion, and in the supposed safety of my own home.

It's raining again, and I can see them sliding down the glass. They are everywhere outside now, dripping from the eaves, squirming in rivulets down the street outside, hanging from the umbrellas of people rushing home to escape the weather, to hide inside until it stops.

I don't think it is ever going to stop. Not this time.

I've unleashed Him, you see. By opening that bottle I did something, started something. And I realise now that none of this is my fault. It was all His will. He planned it just as surely as He planned for that sorcerer to summon Him from the depths of the lake and distil His essence so it could be bottled and kept until the time was right.

The human body is seventy percent water, ionised with salts of sodium and potassium, it's true, but water nevertheless. And I can feel His power working to purify that water so He can use it. Right now, as I type this, I can feel bicarbonate ions being turned to carbon dioxide and water, sense chloride ions having electrons ripped from their valence shells to form the chlorine I'm sure I can taste on my breath. Chlorine and water. My bladder is full, and I know the urine will be excessively rich in potassium and sodium, the ions wrenched from my cells to leave nothing but the purest water. The water He needs to live, to possess us, to make us His own.

My skin feels damp, my vision is dimming, I feel dizzy. My brain is swelling, becoming oedematous from sitting in a fluid environment that is becoming increasingly foreign to it. Soon my cells will fragment, and there will be nothing left of me but the water from which I, and all organisms, arose, and to which we must all ultimately return.

Soon there will be only water.

And Him.

I never even learned His name.

Valley Interlude No.3

"You won't find them."

It was dark in the office now. The only light was that used to illuminate the manuscripts Robert had been reading from. As he turned to address the psychiatrist he had to shield his eyes in order to make out her silhouetted form against the window. Beyond, lamps lit up the empty street, blurred pools of neon that just made the surrounding shadows all the blacker, all the more concealing for whoever – or whatever – might be hiding there.

"Won't I?" The dark outline of Dr Harrison was writing something. How could she see what she was doing? "What makes you say that?"

"Not just you." Robert put the manuscript down and suppressed a shiver, "No one. They're gone from here, just like the girl Mr Jeavons left buried on the golf course, or those girls who went to that house in Aberystwyth. They're all gone."

More scratching on the desk pad. Was it her pen, or… something else?

"Where do you think they've gone, Robert?"

"I don't know." That was the truth. In fact he didn't want to think about it any more. He was still trying to recover from how what he had just read had spoken to him, had communicated to him in the same way as the other stories he had been 'told' today.

Four stories of people being – what? Transported? Abducted? Into other realms. Or possibly all into the same, nightmare dimension. One so alien and extreme, that it seemed to prey on people from this world. It was nonsense, of course, and yet the stories seemed so real, so believable when at any other time he would have dismissed the very idea as the ramblings of a madman.

Was that what he was now? Mad?

If so, did Dr Harrison have the power to keep him here? To – what was it they called it – section him?

"Robert?"

The shadow in front of the window spoke again. Had its voice changed? Was it almost imperceptibly more guttural? Or was he just being over imaginative?

One way to find out.

Robert twisted the lamp round so that its harsh light no longer fell on him but was instead projected towards the psychiatrist. She raised a hand to shield her eyes. Did he catch a glimpse of a claw with talons before it resolved into something more human?

Stop being ridiculous. She's trying to help you.

"Does it bother you that I'm in the dark over here?" Dr Harrison reached under the desk and pressed a switch. Instantly her consulting room was flooded with light. "I didn't wish to disturb you while you were obviously so engrossed with those case histories." Robert blinked, then took in the nice, normal room with the nice, normal psychiatrist who was regarding him with some concern, her pen poised above the notebook on which were written –

Were those arcane symbols?

Stop it.

Dr Harrison pointed at the discarded folders, their contents now spilled onto the carpet. "You were saying those patients would never be found, but that you didn't know where they had gone?"

Robert coughed to clear his dry throat. "That's right."

"Are you sure?"

He was, actually. He had no idea where they were now, and he had no wish to find out.

"Do think the place where they have gone has something to do with your loss of memory?"

He hadn't considered it, but that didn't make much sense. "No. All I can tell you is that everything here is starting to feel familiar."

"You mean this city? Cardiff?"

"I mean that when I read those case files I knew the places they were talking about. I'm sure I've been there, but I couldn't tell you when."

"Nevertheless, that's some progress." Dr Harrison looked pleased. "It seems it was a good idea giving you that reading material after all."

Robert wasn't so sure. When he had woken up near the bridge he had just felt disorientated. Now he felt as if he was learning things about a world he would prefer to remain ignorant of. He ran fingers through his hair and looked around Dr Harrison's consulting room. It seemed so much smaller than when he had first walked in.

"I need to get out of here." He looked at his watch. "And I need some sleep."

The psychiatrist nodded. "I think that's a good idea, too." She paused, toying with the pen and staring at whatever she had just written. "Will you be coming back here?"

Robert shook his head. "No. That would be a bad idea."

"I don't have any more cases to scare you with, if that's what you're worried about." There was the trace of a smile, but it was forced, he could tell.

"It's not that." Once again it was difficult to explain, but he determined to try. "I just get the feeling that I should keep moving, that if I spend too long in any one place, whatever it was that took my memory is going to come after more of me."

"Even though you know that's not true?"

"Isn't it?"

Again the loss of eye contact, the nervous fiddling with the pen, the handwriting that still looked as if it was less words and more symbols scrawled on the thick paper.

"Might I give you one piece of advice?"

Robert nodded. The woman's expression had changed, the mask of professionalism had slipped to reveal the human being beneath, a person who suddenly seemed almost overwhelmed with sorrow, the burdens of the world on her shoulders, pressing down so heavily even her staunch resolve could not prevent one tear from leaking out.

"Go where you feel you should. Don't try to resist. This will all work itself out. You will get your memory back and remember who you are. But be warned you may not turn out who you hope, or even want, to be. So I ask you to be prepared for that."

Robert's eyes narrowed. "Do you know who I am?"

But it was too late, the mask was back. Dr Harrison stood up and came round from behind her desk.

"I'm sorry you won't be coming back, but I do understand if you have to keep moving."

Robert got to his feet. "How much do I owe you?"

She shook her head. "First private consultation is always free, just to see how we get on with each other – didn't Mr Stokes tell you that?"

"No." Although it made sense seeing as Stokes knew Robert had no money on him. "But thank you."

"Don't mention it." The psychiatrist held her consulting rom door open for him and again, just for a second, he caught a glimpse of profound sadness in her eyes. Then it was gone. "Where will you go now?"

"Wherever my car takes me." Robert yawned. "But definitely somewhere there's a bed."

"Well don't drive too long into the night." She leaned close, and for a moment Robert thought she was going to kiss him. Instead she whispered into his ear. "Go north. Stay away from the west for as long as you can." Then she was leading him to the exit, her demeanour once again entirely professional, as if she had said nothing out of the ordinary.

But had she, really? Or had Robert imagined it? Just as he might have imagined her other tiny slips into what almost felt like another personality, one that felt more true, more real to him, than the woman who had given him those stories to read? For a moment he felt he should challenge her, but there was no certainty that she (or what was controlling her) would tell him the truth. Before he had a chance to ruminate any further, he was on the street and the door had been shut behind him. He stood there for a moment, the only human being on the now empty street, with nothing but the black-beaked street lamps for company, their cold light only serving to emphasise his loneliness. For a moment he felt moved to knock on the psychiatrist's door again, just to see another human face before he left here. But now the building was in darkness, the plate with Dr Harrison's name on a shadowy blur that could almost not be there at all, as if this part of reality, now that it was finished with him, was fading, as if he was being told to move on by more than just the instinct he felt within him.

Time to go.

When he got back to the motorway he remembered what Dr Harrison had said and turned away from the west, travelling back the way he had come. As he passed Newport once more he was just beginning to wonder if his journey would take him back to the bridge when flashing orange beacons, and a myriad road cones up ahead, indicated a diversion. According to the overhead sign the M4 was closed due to an accident.

He allowed himself a brief smile as he realised he was following his psychiatrist's advice once again by letting the route take him where it would, and was not at all surprised when he ended up travelling north. The red and white cones, flashing warnings and yellow diversion signs soon disappeared, so when Robert felt a strong urge to leave the dual carriageway and take the slip road for Abergavenny he obeyed his instincts. Several roundabouts, junctions and turns later and he was travelling down a minor road with no lighting in what felt like the middle of nowhere. He checked the fuel indicator and saw with relief that his tank was still half full. Then he yawned, blinked the tears from his eyes, and hoped that wherever he was being guided there would be a bed at the end of it. Two miles further on and he was having difficulty keeping his eyes open. He was almost at the point of falling asleep behind the wheel when he saw lights up ahead.

'The Winterman's Arms' had the welcoming look of the sixteenth century pub it no doubt was – a squat two storey stone building set just back from the roadside with a space cleared for car parking to its right. Gravel crunched as Robert pulled in and realised his was the only vehicle. He walked back to the front of the pub, keeping fingers crossed they were open. The solitary light above the creaking sign swinging in the slight breeze did little to help him make out what image had been painted on it, but the name of the place was clear enough to be seen from the road and that was what mattered.

The building was in darkness but Robert pushed at the door anyway. It opened on well-oiled hinges to reveal a welcome hive of activity within. This was more like it! Better than a gloomy art gallery or an austere doctor's office. He strode up to the bar with the intention of ordering a pint. Then he remembered he didn't have any money.

Too late. It looked as if the ruddy-faced landlord was pulling one for him anyway.

"A stranger in our midst!" The man's voice was a roar above the hubbub as he handed Robert the foaming beer. Robert glanced round nervously and was relieved to see that the pub hadn't descended into Hammer Horror-like silence and suspicious regard at his words. In fact it was almost as if the room filled with seasoned drinkers was pointedly ignoring him.

"A stranger indeed," Robert replied with a smile. "And one with no money, I'm afraid."

The landlord beamed, which was not the reaction Robert was expecting. "Then it's your lucky night, sir! Owen over there…" he indicated a man of advancing years, clothes that had probably been worn to work on a farm for forty of those, and a mouth filled with teeth that resembling the graveyard he would most likely end up buried in before long "…Owen has just won the lottery, so he's treating everyone to free drinks!" He nodded at the pint. "If you drink that one up I'll get you another."

"Actually…" It was better to get this out of the way while he was still relatively sober. "…what I really need is a room for the night. Or even just a chair I could sleep in for a few hours. I'm exhausted and that beer will knock me right out."

"Hmmm." The landlord rubbed his chin for a moment and then called across the room. "Owen! Bloke here's fallen on hard times and is about to fall over! You all right to sub him a room here!"

Robert had difficulty telling if Owen was in agreement, or even if he had heard, but he must have because the landlord was beaming once more.

"I think that'll be fine, sir. We've only got the one room – upstairs and at the back, there. Not much call for people staying here these days. Not like in the past. But you'll find it comfortable enough." All this was said while pulling three more pints for men who looked a lot like Owen but of varying ages and states of dental decay. "Have you got luggage?"

"Pardon?"

"Bags!" The landlord was having to yell. "Have you got any?"

"No!"

"Just as well." Three pints were handed over and more started to be pulled. "You'd have to bring them in yourself anyway." The landlord reached into his pocket and tossed over a key, which Robert failed to catch. It landed with a rattle on the bare boards. "Through the door at the back there, up the stairs to the very top. Bathroom's on the left."

Robert ducked down and scooped up the keys.

"Thank you!" he bellowed back. Was it getting louder in here?

"Pleasure! If it gets a bit too lively down here and you can't sleep I think there's a radio in the room. No idea if it still works but it might help to drown out this unruly lot! Now gentlemen! Patience please! We're not going to run out of beer, not tonight."

Robert left the man to it, following his directions to a scarred wooden door to the right of the bar that apparently led to the toilets. It also led to a narrow wooden staircase that was almost invisible in the cloying darkness of the vestibule in which he found himself, darkness that showed no sign of relenting as he ascended the creaking steps.

Cautiously, Robert felt his way, with hands outstretched to the rough wood-panelled walls either side. Was it his imagination, or were the stairs becoming narrower the higher he went? Another three steps yielded a break in the wall to his right. His eyes were adjusting to the gloom now, and he could see a corridor stretching ahead, the outline of a single door at the end. He took a step towards it but recoiled when he heard what sounded like muffled sobbing coming from behind the wood. Had the landlord been mistaken? Was the room already let?

Then he realised the steps continued, up to a higher floor. This wasn't his room at all. Robert took a step back and by the time he was climbing the staircase once more the sound of crying was nothing more than a memory.

The crushing narrowness of the staircase wasn't, however. Now Robert had to turn sideways to make progress. If the walls got any closer together he would have to stop or end up stuck, and the prospect of being wedged here overnight, the men below oblivious to his cries for help, had him slowing as he edged his way along. The stairs couldn't go much further, he reasoned. He had to be close to the top of the building.

He was just about to turn back (or rather, back track uncomfortably and probably dangerously in the dark) when the stairs ended at a door. The knob was loose and it took a while to grip the mechanism but Robert persisted. Despite his efforts it still seemed reluctant to open and so it was with a shove that he finally fell into the tiny attic room in which he was to spend the night.

His hand fumbled for the light switch. Robert fully expected it not to work, but the click rewarded him with feeble light cast by a single bare bulb that hung from the apex of the sloping roof. There was a bed that looked clean, and when he patted the grey blanket Robert was relieved (and a little surprised) that no cloud of dust puffed up from it. Otherwise there was a tiny desk, a wobbly-looking chair and a bedside table hardly deserving of the appellation seeing as it consisted simply of a square of plasterboard supported by a couple of bricks.

On this 'table' stood an ancient-looking radio-cassette player, its black casing splashed with flecks of paint and coated with a thin patina of dust. When Robert picked it up he noticed the twisting black cord that emerged from the player's base and snaked beneath the table and out of sight. He grimaced. If it wasn't already plugged in there was no way he felt like chasing around down there for the electric socket. It was unlikely he was going to need it, anyway. He could barely hear the sounds of the pub up here.

Except, now that he concentrated… Now his mind was off getting up here and getting in here, he could hear what was going on downstairs.

Everything that was going in downstairs.

He could hear orders for beer and more beer. He could hear discussions about the latest rugby scores, he could hear about how Tom's wife was in hospital with 'women's problems' and he was having trouble looking after the kids. How Barry Pugh had just been laid off and how it was the fault of those 'bastard English bosses' of his.

It did not sound like the kind of noise that was going to calm down anytime soon, either.

The radio would at least distract him. Robert flicked the 'On' switch.

Nothing.

He turned up the volume.

Still nothing.

He adjusted the tuning dial, running the little red marker up and down the bandwidth.

Complete and utter silence.

And was it his imagination, or was the sound of voices from below getting louder?

Perhaps the tape player worked. Robert pressed the eject button and, to his surprise, a tape popped out. It was worn and he couldn't read the handwriting on the grubby white label, but hopefully whatever music was on here would provide sufficient distraction to help him sleep.

He popped the tape back in and pressed 'Play'.

"My name is Richard Lewis Morgan. I am Welsh. And there is something horribly wrong with me."

Robert pressed 'Stop'. It wasn't music after all. Probably some radio play. Not something likely to help him sleep.

There was rhythmic thumping from below. Then someone started singing, quickly joined by what sounded like the combined drunken efforts of the entire pub.

Even talking would be preferable to that.

Robert rewound the tape and pressed 'Play' once more.

He quickly realised it wasn't a radio play, or any kind of professional broadcast.

No, what was on the tape had not been recorded for anybody's entertainment. At least, it didn't sound to have been.

It sounded more like a confession.

Learning the Language

My name is Richard Lewis Morgan. I am Welsh. And there is something horribly wrong with me.

Right now, I'm about two thirds of the way up Skirrid Fawr, or the Holy Mountain as it's known to many of the residents of the nearby town of Abergavenny. My girlfriend Natasha is just a little bit ahead of me – she's already out from under the tree cover and making her way across the long, bare, open summit of the mountain to the white stone marker at the end. I've taken this opportunity to take a breather and go over as much of all of what's happened as I can remember. My mother always told me if something is bothering you a lot, then you should think about it, say it out loud even. Things always seem more manageable if you say them out loud.

Natasha will not be coming back down the mountain.

Actually, writing that has made what I have to do a little easier. The knife in my pocket is made of stainless steel and I've owned it since I was a boy. I'm the only one to have ever used it, except for the time Reverend Watkins borrowed it to get the hymn book cupboard open in Llantryso Church. It's the only thing I have that my father gave me. Apart from my destiny, of course.

Some people call this place the Holy Mountain because when Christ was crucified God struck it in his anger, cracking the mountain in two. You can still see the fissure today, overgrown with brambles and ferns and dotted with sheep who don't mind venturing into what some presumably believe is a divine rift. Why God should have aimed his wrath at Wales rather than at Jerusalem, or Rome, no one has ever been able to explain to me. It's also claimed that once, when the devil strode across Wales, his foot came to rest on this place and thus broke off a fragment of the rock. I like that story better, but then I would. While I have never seen much evidence of God at work in this country, I know that this is a land of ancient power and even more ancient beings. My mother and father knew it, too. After all, that was how I came to learn of them in the first place.

If I move on a little I can just see Natasha ahead of me, her white jacket bobbing along the mountain top. She'll be at the marker in a bit. It was put there many years ago by the Welsh National Trust. It's what they call a triangulation or 'trig' point, to allow you to orientate yourself with other mountains in the area. Far fewer people know that it is no coincidence that these triangulation points are where they are, that they are markers of the deep seated power of each mountain, that a sacrifice to the spirit of a mountain must be made at the site of the marker. In blood.

She's nearly there, and there's no one else around. I didn't expect there to be this early on a Tuesday morning.

Time to get moving, I think.

I have already mentioned going to church in my childhood and you might therefore be forgiven for thinking that my family were Christians. Until I reached a certain age I had assumed that myself. We went every Sunday, my mother, my father, and I. I should have suspected something was wrong when I learned that my school-friends' church attendances differed from my own in one significant way. They always went to the same one, whereas my parents did their best to attend a different church every Sunday. There were so many in the area around Abergavenny that it easily took us several months to get round them all. Each Sunday the routine would be the same. Father would tell us where we were going and mother would pack a small picnic if we were going to be driving for more than an hour. We were always the first to arrive and my parents would spend the time before the service making a careful examination of the graves before securing themselves a seat at the back just prior to the service beginning. Father would be jotting things down in a small black notebook right up to the point where the vicar took his place at the front, and again afterwards before leaving the building. Each vicar, and each congregation, was always very welcoming towards my parents, presumably because they always told them they were thinking of moving to the area, and that it was important to them to see what the local church was like. If I asked if we were really moving house once we were in the car afterwards, my mother would give me a look, and ask me if I really wanted to leave that lovely house of ours.

Seeing as I've brought it up, this is as good a time as any to describe 'that lovely house of ours'. Accessed via a tiny country lane on the outskirts of town, the house where I grew up was the Victorian vicarage to the now derelict and desanctified church that adjoined it. I loved that old house, even though the sun never quite seemed to reach it, even though we often needed to have the electric lights on throughout the day, and even though for much of the year it was so cold there that I would wake to a crust of ice coating the inside of my bedroom window. It was my childhood home and I regarded it with the same affection that my parents did.

I was fortunate, I suppose, in having parents who did not need to go out to work. We were by no means well off, but I always had reasonable clothes to go to school in, and my considerable academic achievements at such a young age had already served to ostracise me from my peers. Unfashionable clothing merely served to cement my reputation as 'odd' – something which I was quite happy to encourage.

Thus it was that I was out of the house more than my parents were. My father spent most of the daylight hours in his study, a vast book-lined room in which he would lock himself for hours engrossed in whichever volume he had taken down from the woodworm-ridden shelves.

One day, my father chanced to leave his study door open and I, being a curious child who had never been told to stay out of it, found myself examining the heavy tome he himself must have been reading before being called to the telephone. I could read at least as well as any boy my age, and it was with a mixture of confusion and fascination that I tried to read the peculiar combinations of consonants, the arrangements of vowels and letters, into words that were as unpronounceable as they were unreadable.

I was in the process of turning the page when I became aware of a presence behind me. My father had returned. He did not seem unhappy with my gentle handling of the page, and so I asked him.

"Is this Welsh?"

He appeared to ponder my question for a moment before replying.

"It is," he said. "But a more ancient and darker Welsh than most who now call this land home would be aware ever existed."

"Can you read it?"

A smile. "Some," my father said. "And just a little more every day."

"Is it what you're looking for in the churches?"

The smile broadened but no answer was forthcoming. "I think your mother is looking for you," he said. "You'd better go to her."

My mother hadn't been looking for me at all, and when I returned to my father's study the door was once again locked.

I never learned to speak modern Welsh. My parents were among the many residents of the country who were unable to converse in their native tongue and so it was never an issue in our household.

The dark Welsh, however, the ancient and almost forgotten language my father had shown me in what turned out to be a quite unique volume, was another matter altogether. My education began one morning over breakfast, with my father scribbling a few letters on the back of the envelope that had housed yet another final demand for the electricity bill.

He passed the creased paper over to me. "How do you think that should sound?" he asked.

I frowned. To me it just looked like a random collection of letters that didn't belong together. But I did my best, producing something that made me sound as if I could use a powerful decongestant.

"Try again," said my father, "but try making the sound in your throat, rather than your nose."

I did as I was told. "That's better." My father was obviously pleased, and my mother flashed me an encouraging smile as she cleared the plates away.

By the end of the week I has mastered a number of new 'words' and was able to move onto my first guttural and awkwardly pronounced sentence. I remember that Saturday afternoon well, as I was made to repeat the five words over and over until I could recite the sequence of noises perfectly, and without the aid of the volume from which my father had transcribed them.

"Good," he said, eventually satisfied. "Now when we go to church tomorrow, I want you to say those words under your breath once the vicar steps into the pulpit. Very quietly, mind. No one else must hear them. Not even your mother and me. Do you understand?"

I nodded. "Why?"

His response made no sense to me at the time. "Because the ones we want to get in touch with need to be called in the right way," he said. "They won't listen to us, but they might listen to you."

"Who are they?" I wanted to know. "Are they friends?"

"We hope they will be," said my mother, resting proud hands on my shoulders. "We hope they will be very good friends indeed."

"But how will they be able to hear if I'm so quiet?"

I could see my father had to suppress a chuckle at this. "Because they have very special ears," he replied. "Ears that can only hear certain special words."

"Are they Welsh?"

Both my parents nodded in a way that suggested pride in a child who has taken a great leap forward.

"They are," said my father. "The purest Welsh there is. From the times when England did not even exist, not as anyone knows it now."

"Is Wales older than England, then?" My parents seemed in a revelatory mood and my twelve year old self was keen to exploit it.

My father seemed to be considering something for a moment and then, prompted by a nod from my mother, he spoke again.

"Wales is not just older than England, my son," he said. "There are some who believe it to be the place where life first sprang from on this planet. To be born Welsh is to be born not just privileged, but to be born into an ancestry that leads back to a time before man, before the mammals that led to the development of man."

"Before dinosaurs?"

My mother nodded. "Failed experiments of those who first came here," she said. "They cast them out to other parts of the world, where they eventually died and gave rise to fossil fragments – the only evidence of their passing."

A bit like the chat your parents try to have with you about the birds and the bees, this was all rather hard to believe.

"We did about dinosaurs in school," I said. My parents nodded. "And evolution." They nodded again. "And the Bible." Here they frowned and shook their heads.

"Throughout millennia people have tried to come up with explanations for who we are, where we came from, and where we might go after this life," my father said. "None of it is true. The truth is in the volumes in my study, and I have so much yet to decipher, so much that I need help understanding."

"You can help us," my mother explained. "You are able to say the words, and you are just young enough that your voice should be in the right frequency to reach them."

"But why in a church?" I wanted to know.

"People feel they are closer to God in a church," said my father. "In Wales, they are closer to the ancient beings that slumber beneath the earth. It is easier for Them to hear you in such places."

"And the gravestones?" My parents exchanged looks. "You're always looking for what's written on them," I said.

"It is not what's written on them that's important," my mother said, "but the way in which they have been arranged. These, too, are markers of the receptivity of one of the Ancients to our communications."

"And we believe we have found the one where we may best be heard." My father's eyes were glittering with triumph, even though he had received little in the way of confirmation that he was on the right track.

"And we're going to go there?" I asked.

"We are," said my father.

"On Sunday," said my mother.

"Tomorrow," they both said together.

You may be wondering why I was sitting in St Peter's Church in the tiny parish of Llanwenarth Citra. You may be wondering why I had not refused point blank to be involved in something that sounded at best ridiculous and at worst frankly dangerous. But I was twelve, I was shunned by school friends and had no one other than my parents to talk to. When you are that age and that alone, it's very difficult not to go along with what you've been told to do.

So there I was, sitting at the back of this small church, in between parents who were convinced that when I made some strange noises something fantastic and unworldly was going to occur. Quite what it was they hadn't told me, and now I wonder if they had actually thought that far.

The congregation ceased its sullen rendition of 'How Great Thou Art' and resumed their seats, as did we. Father had pointed out before the service began that with us present the congregation made up an odd number, which seemed to be of great significance to his mind. Now, as the vicar ascended the steps to the pulpit, my father prodded me, as if I needed reminding of my task.

Even at the last minute I hesitated, wondering if it might perhaps be better to face the wrath of my parents than whatever I might call forth from the depths of the planet.

But in the end, I did as I was told.

At first, nothing happened. The vicar, an elderly man with a few wisps of white hair crowning his otherwise gleamingly bald head, continued to address his flock with alternating words of condemnation and reassurance, the people before him nodding in agreement as he poured loathing on those whom he claimed were responsible for the general state of moral decay in the country.

Everyone assumed the rumble we heard was due to an encroaching electrical storm.

When the building began to rattle I imagine some must have thought they were to be witness to the first earthquake in Wales in a millennium. Perhaps others thought the wrath of God was about to be visited upon them.

Which, in a way, it was.

But the thing that made people panic was when the red fog descended outside the building, covering the windows and turning the feeble daylight a shade of scarlet.

"Fear not, my brethren," said the priest in the most fearful voice I had ever heard. "If we are to be judged, let us not be afraid, for our hearts are pure and minds are –"

We never got to find out what the vicar thought our minds might be like, because at that point the stained glass exploded inward and the red mist that had coalesced on its surface began to drip into the building, running down the white walls in crimson rivulets, pooling on the floor tiles and spreading towards the frightened crowd, who even now were retreating to the centre aisle in a bid to escape the creeping miasmic terror.

All eyes turned to the pulpit and widened in horror. The vicar, struck by numerous shards of splintered glass, was now slumped over, his body a rainbow of glittering colours, the predominant of which was red.

My parents stood, horrified by what I, and by turns they, seemed to have caused. They turned for the entrance, only to find that others were already ahead of them. The middle aged robust-looking lady who opened the door found herself faced with more of the red fog, which billowed in and, like superheated acid, dissolved her flesh from her bones as it made contact.

"Send it back!" My father was squeezing my shoulder so hard it hurt. "Send it back now!"

"I don't know how!" I sobbed through tears. "You didn't teach me any other words."

"Backwards," said my mother. "Say them backwards."

"It was hard enough saying them forwards," said my father, his normal reserve gone. "How is he possibly going to be able to reverse the words of summoning?"

Personally I had no idea, but I was going to try. Amidst all the screaming and the stampeding, the desperation and the panic, I climbed onto a pew and tried hard to remember the final word my father had taught me. Then I reversed the letters.

Then I spoke the word.

Nothing. Just the same screaming and madness and encroaching red death.

Never mind, there were four more words to go.

Carefully and methodically, I remembered each one, turned it around, and spoke it, using the same guttural whisper my father had showed me.

As the last croaking syllable left my lips, something happened, although it was not what I was expecting.

The world turned white.

At first I thought I had been blinded. Then, as my eyes began to adjust, I realised that I, and everything around me, was covered with ash. Tiny fragments of it floated through the air, coming to rest on the motionless bodies of those around me.

Including those of my parents.

I jumped down from the pew, stirring up a fine cloud of white powder as I did so, and waded through more of the stuff to where my parents' bodies were lying.

I reached out to touch my mother's ash-coated face, and the flesh beneath crumbled into yet more of the dust that surrounded me. I grabbed at her hand and it turned to nothing beneath my fingertips.

My father's body was the same, as was the body of everyone else in the church. A slight breeze blew through the broken windows, and reduced the shapes that still resembled human forms to powder. I took faltering steps towards the door, and made my way out into a world that I quickly realised was not my own at all.

The sky was not just the wrong colour – a strange admixture of red and gold peppered with orange pinpricks that I assumed must be stars, although a few of the large ones were obviously planets – it was the wrong shade as well, as if the sun that gave this realm light was much further away than the sun is from our earth.

The church was still there, standing behind me against this darkly glittering backdrop, and the graveyard, too. Now, however, the teetering stone markers resembled rotted teeth in the mouth of some vast and cankered beast, and I wondered if the leathery substance on which I was now standing might be its tongue.

I took a step forward and the world shook, the ground yielding a little beneath me, as if perhaps I was walking on flesh rather than earth. A sound midway between an ambulance siren and a creature screaming in distress seared my ears, and I put my hands up to cover them.

But that was not the worst.

As I looked up to the heavens, at that vista so unnatural and so alien, the sky itself parted, splitting open lengthways, and an eye more vast than the entirety of creation regarded me with curiosity.

I could feel it probing my mind, filling it with knowledge, with experience beyond my years, as if it was preparing me for something. I suddenly felt older, much older.

I realised with terror a little later on, that it was not just my mind that it had changed.

"We thought we'd lost you, too."

The nurse had a lovely Welsh accent. The doctor with her was English and I instantly disliked him. Both of them looked at me as if I was lucky to be alive, and when I looked down to see most of my body covered in bandages I could see why. I would have asked them what had happened but it took several days before I was on a sufficiently low dose of morphine that I could form sentences.

In a word, Llanwenarth Church had exploded. The ongoing investigation had postulated a leaking gas main (didn't they always?) but nothing had been proven. The building had been destroyed and nearly everyone attending church that Sunday morning had been killed.

Everyone, that is, except me.

And even I was not who everyone thought me to be.

I had mumbled my date of birth to both nurses and doctors to be rewarded with sympathetic looks and reassuring words.

"I'm sure you'll remember who you really are soon," one especially pretty nurse had said when I had insisted I had been born just over twelve years ago.

"My dear fellow…" the consultant had given me a stern look on his ward round a few days later, "…you seem to be an intelligent young chap so I'll be blunt with you. Who knows, it may serve to jolt you back into reality. However old you may think you are, by my reckoning you are at least twenty five, if not older than that. I'm sure your real date of birth will come back to you in good time, as will your real name and where you come from." He flipped through the case notes. "As for your address, our computer system has no record of a house being there. Nevertheless, I'm sure once you're up and about and out of here everything will start to come back."

"Up and about?" I croaked in a voice much deeper than the one that had quoted those unwieldy words in church days – or was it years? – ago.

The consultant nodded. "Beneath those bandages are a whole collection of minor cuts and abrasions. A couple of your wounds needed suturing and there's a nasty burn on your right arm, which is why you were on the morphine, but that's healing nicely. There's really nothing to stop you from getting out of that bed and seeing if you can remember how to walk. In fact I insist on it."

I was wheeled from my bed to the physiotherapy department two floors down by a bored-looking porter who stopped to converse with one of the young female domestic staff. It turned out he was still very sorry about going off with someone else at the nightclub last Saturday and that if only she would give him another chance he would prove how faithful he could be.

This conversation was intended to be conducted out of my earshot, but somehow I seemed to have developed an extremely acute sense of hearing. More peculiar than this, however, was my realisation about halfway through what they were saying that they had been talking in Welsh, a language that up until that moment had always been a complete mystery to me.

The porter returned, red-faced, and continued to push me towards the lifts. On the wall next to the push buttons was a list of all the floors and what was located on them, in English and Welsh.

I could understand both languages perfectly.

I was still shaking as I was wheeled into the physiotherapy department. The physiotherapist was stern, but I probably needed it. She thought my lack of coordination was because of shock which, in a way, it was. But it wasn't the result of physical trauma that caused me to totter and wobble along the walking bars, rather it was the shock of having discovered my new ability, as well as having to adapt to a body that was now several inches taller, hairier, and considerably better developed than the puny twelve year old one I seemed to have been relieved of by my experiences. It didn't take me long to get used to it, however, and soon I was considered physically fit for discharge.

The psychiatrist, however, wasn't so sure, and, after a month of counselling in an attempt to recover what she called my 'lost years' I was eternally grateful to her for arranging my discharge to a halfway house close to the hospital. It was somewhere I could 'mentally get back on my feet again' rather than being left to fend for myself, something which would inevitably have led me to living a hand-to-mouth existence on the streets of Abergavenny. Fortunately I did not have to remain within the confines of the building, and so, one sunny day shortly after I had arrived there, I made my way to where my parents' house should have been.

It was a walk of about two miles, and took me straight through Abergavenny town. As I walked, I noticed two very strange things. The road signs, all in Welsh as well as English, were now perfectly readable in both languages.

But the Welsh communicated something entirely different to me than what was written in English.

As I read the words, as I took in their meaning, I realised I was interpreting them as the Dark Welsh my father had introduced me to at my home in that increasingly distant never-land of the youth I seemed to have lost. The words spoke of a rising, of a return, of the sacrifices that must be made and of the locations at which they needed to take place. And most importantly of all they stressed the very special quality the victims had to possess. Not virgins like in the horror films, or babies like in the black magic novels my mother used to consume. Oh no, the sacrificial victims needed to bring about a reawakening of the Ancient Ones of this land only needed to possess one quality.

They had to be English.

Why have the Welsh always despised the English so? Harboured a hatred of that nation that always went beyond the friendly rivalry of a rugby match or simple neighbourly competition? Even when I was a child in school the teacher would make unpleasant jokes about the English and the children who claimed that nationality would squirm in their seats, embarrassed and not understanding why they should come in for such vilification.

The Welsh have always hated the English, and now, perhaps for the first time in millennia, I had been shown the reason why.

You need to be made to hate something before you can be made to kill it. And if that hatred is ingrained over generations it just makes it all the easier to carry out your task when the powers that put that hatred there in the first place tell you it is finally time for them to return.

By the time I arrived at the site of my parents' house I was not surprised to find no trace of it. It wasn't needed any more. For all I know it had never existed. The crumbled remains of the desanctified church were still there, although now something told me that were I to trace my steps back to Llanwenarth I would find ruins that were very similar.

It does not take much to disorientate a man and I, it seemed, had become the plaything, or perhaps more accurately, the Messiah, of the Ancient Gods of Wales. I walked back through the town, trying to ignore the road signs, trying to ignore the whispering voices in my head that were insisting, in the Dark Welsh of the ancients, that the first victim needed to be soon, that English blood needed to be spilled on the sacred Welsh soil of a nearby mountain to begin the cataclysmic chain of events that would change this land, and the world, forever.

As I stumbled back into the halfway house, my fingers pressed to my temples to try and shut out that infernal whispering, I almost cried out, screaming at the creatures in my head to stop, that there was no one I could offer them, that there was no one I knew who I could convince to come with me to their dread place of sacrifice.

There was a girl sitting in the front room, flicking through a magazine.

She had the weary, vaguely tarnished look of someone who has seen too much at too young an age. A bit like myself, actually. She looked up as I entered and gave me her best attempt at a smile.

"Hello," she said in an accent that sent a vortex of hot blood swirling through my veins. "I'm Natasha."

Writing all this down has helped, I think, although I've just gone over the account in my head and realise I'm finding it more and more difficult to determine how much of what I've written actually happened and how much is me trying to remember what happened and getting it wrong. There might be lots of things wrong, but I think I know how to make them right

There isn't much left to say. Here I am, four days later, close to the Place of Sacrifice. Natasha's reached the marker now. How white it looks, gleaming in the morning sunlight.

The Welsh sunlight.

The sunlight of my fathers, and their fathers, and of those who live beneath the mountain.

The English shall not have it, none of them.

Natasha will be the first. The first in a long line of glorious sacrifices to the spirits of this holy land on which only the Welsh are fit to tread.

Natasha will be the first, and then I shall look for others.

And if you are English, I will be looking for you.

Valley Interlude No.4

The tape came to an end. Robert stayed sitting on the edge of the dusty single bed, the only sounds the audible hissing of the blank tape left to run, blended with the noise of muffled voices from way beneath him. Eventually, he reached over and hit the eject button. The tape popped out. Its black plastic casing looked old and scuffed, and the writing on the label had been rewritten and crossed out so many times as to be indecipherable. It occurred to him that there might be more, or perhaps something different, on the other side, but no matter how much he fast forwarded, it was blank. Oddly, when he turned the cassette back over to play the original side again, that too was now somehow blank.

Most likely the volume had broken, he guessed, switching the machine off. Now all he could hear was the drone from the bar. He switched off the light and lay down but it was no use. In the pitch darkness his oversensitive hearing was determined to try and make sense of what was being said beneath him.

No, not being said.

Being sung.

Because that was what it now sounded like. The drone that he had taken for voices had resolved itself into something that peaked and troughed, both in volume and pitch, and there was a rhythm to it now as well. Irregular to the point of being irritating, it was like Chinese water torture for the ears, the beat never quite landing when you wanted it to, phrases left unresolved, notes not quite reached but neither a tone nor semitone off, more they were just ever so slightly wrong – like a tune being sung by a group of people who were both tone deaf and had no sense of rhythm at all.

It was infuriating.

Robert swung himself off the bed and switched the bedside light back on. The clock beside it told him it was gone midnight. What time did the locals go to bed here? And during midweek as well.

He was pulling his shoes on so he could go downstairs and complain when he remembered the confession he had just been listening to. The places mentioned were nearby, he knew. Was it possible that those men downstairs were involved in the same thing? Might they have the same attitude to the English?

Was he even English?

That was a good question, almost as good as how did he know that places like the Skirrid and Llanwenarth were nearby, seeing as he hadn't had the chance to look at any maps and had mainly been relying on road signs to get him this far. Never mind that, now. He wasn't going to get much further if he didn't get any sleep, and there was precious little chance of that while that noise carried on. Which gave rise to the most important question of all.

Irrespective of where he was actually from, what would they think if he went downstairs and asked them to keep it down?

There was only one way to find out.

This time, the packed bar did do the traditional horror movie thing.

Silence descended as Robert stepped into the crowded, muggy area. In fact the atmosphere in the bar had become so damp that he had trouble breathing and had to cough twice before he could get any words out.

"Everything all right, sir?" That was the landlord. Was it Robert's imagination or did he seem rather less friendly now than when Robert had arrived?

"Yes, thank you."

"Room all right?"

"Yes."

"Warm enough?"

"Yes, thanks."

There was a pause for a moment, almost as if they were expecting him to say more. When he didn't the landlord continued. "Sorry there's no radio or telly in the room."

"Oh that's okay. There was a tape recorder but..." But he shouldn't tell them he had most likely broken it, should he? But now they all seemed to be waiting for him to continue. "I had a listen and it didn't have any music."

"You listened to it, then, sir?"

"Yes."

"To what was on it?"

"Yes."

A man the size of a small bear boasting a nose so red and bulbous it would probably light up the room if the lights went dead drained the last of something from a bottle so black it was impossible to see what it contained. Then he thumped it on the bar and without turning to Robert added, "Did you listen to it all, sir?"

There was no point in lying. "I did, actually."

"And now you can't sleep, is that it? I'm not surprised. But we all agreed it was best you learned about it for yourself rather than one of us tell you."

Robert's heart missed a beat. "You all agreed?"

The landlord nodded. "That's right, sir."

"Took a vote we did," said bulbous nose.

"Unanimous it was," said the shrivelled little man next to him. "Best way, we all thought."

Robert tried to take a step back but the door to the staircase had swung shut. There were at least ten people between him and the exit, so there was nothing else he could do but say, "And are you all part of… of…"

"What he was going on about?" That was bulbous nose again. "Good God no, sir. But we thought it was important that you know, just in case you fancied a bit of a wander around some of the more out of the way parts hereabouts."

Silence fell again. No chatting, and definitely no weird singing. He could hardly ask them to keep the noise down if they weren't making any, could he?

"Where are you headed, sir?" The landlord snapped the cap off another unlabelled black bottle and handed it to bulbous nose.

"At the moment, Aberystwyth," Robert replied.

"Leaving in the morning, then?"

"That's the plan." Although leaving now was starting to look more and more tempting.

"Any particular route in mind?"

He hadn't really given it much consideration. Maybe one of them had a map he could borrow. He thought hard about the signs he'd seen. "I was thinking of maybe going over the Brecon Beacons?"

As one the population of the pub heaved a collected groan of disapproval. That plan didn't go down well with them at all.

"I suppose you could," said the landlord.

"But it can be dangerous," said bulbous nose before taking another suck from his bottle.

"Dangerous for the wrong kind of person," said his friend at the bar. "If you know what I mean."

Mumbled assent indicated that the rest of the pub knew, even if Robert didn't.

"I'm not English, if that's what you mean."

The words came out before Robert had a chance to stop them. Even as he left the sentence hanging in the sudden silence he had no idea if it was true or not. He still had no idea where he was from. And now he had said that they were going to ask him, weren't they?

But they didn't. In fact some of them started laughing.

"No, sir," said the little man at the bar. "That's not what we mean."

Robert had no idea what to do next so he just stood there with his eyebrows raised in expectation of an explanation. Eventually, once the laughter died down, he got one from the landlord.

"I'm sorry, sir, and doubly so because of course you've just listened to that tape. No, what we mean is that some people just can't help getting into all sorts of trouble. They act as magnets for it, if you like. And those mountains aren't the sort of land to get lost in if you are such a person."

Robert tried to make sense of this. "A stranger, you mean?"

"Could be a stranger, but rest assured you can just as easily be born here, live all your life here, and still wander along the wrong path at the wrong time of year and…"

"And what?"

"And never come back," said bulbous nose.

"Never be found again," added his shrivelled companion.

"Mind you," said a voice from behind him. "The last people we know of that the mountains took, they were strangers. Here on some sort of holiday, I think."

"Celebrating a birthday," corrected the landlord.

"My mistake, you're quite right, a birthday."

Robert turned to see an older gentleman behind him dressed in worn herringbone tweeds that were fraying at the sleeves.

"We did our best to warn them, didn't we?" he said. His words produced murmurs of assent. "As much as we are allowed to warn people, at any rate."

"What do you mean?"

The tweedy man smiled. "Can't tell them what's going to happen to them. It's not allowed."

"Not allowed?" Robert looked around him. "Not allowed by who?"

"By whom, don't you mean?" said bulbous nose, setting off another barrage of laughter.

"Never mind by whom," said the man in tweed. "You'll find that out in good time if you're meant to."

"So you can't tell me what will happen to me if I travel over the mountains?"

"That's right, sir." Two chairs were being pulled up now, one for Robert and one for the man in tweed. Bulbous nose brought over two of the black bottles. Robert sniffed at the neck and then took a sip. It was fruity and surprisingly strong. He resolved not to swig at it despite the temptation as the man continued. "I can't tell you what will happen to you, but I can tell you what happened to them."

Everyone in the place seemed to be waiting to hear. Robert, resigned to the fact that he wasn't going to get any sleep for the next couple of hours at least, took one more swig from the bottle and relished the sweet burning sensation slip down his throat as he made himself comfortable and prepared to listen to the story.

Somewhere, Beneath a Maze of Sky

Lost.

Mark Williams took a deep breath of the chill mid-morning mountain air, and looked around him. Beneath sky the colour of dirty fog the land stretched out in all directions. The rock-pocked, bracken peppered, scrubby-grassed land that offered no clues as to which way either he or the four people with him should go.

Definitely lost.

Mark coughed, and his head pounded with the hangover from last night's revelries. He rubbed his arms and wished he'd gone to the pub wearing something warmer than just a T-shirt with a loose jacket over it. But then he hadn't expected to wake up on a desolate Welsh hillside with four other people in a similar state of post-inebriated disorientation, birthday night frolics or not.

It was the cold that had woken him, as it did all of them, eventually. The biting, picking wind nudging at them, an insistent reminder that if they didn't start moving soon they could quite easily die of exposure.

Awareness of pain had come soon afterwards, of course. That special, pounding, overwhelming hangover horror reserved for those who drink too much, party too hard, and never learn from their mistakes. That grim and nauseating reminder of the price of such hedonism, a price that can bleed into much of the following day. And, if one is lucky, only as far as that.

Mark had opened his eyes only for the harsh sunlight of the Welsh morning to pierce his vision and make his headache even worse. Forcing himself to his feet, he heard something crunch as he did so.

The others were lying nearby, all of them in similar states of semi-wakefulness and suffering the after-effects of last night's ingestion of absurd quantities of alcohol. Even Tamsin, Mark's girlfriend of the past six months, had proved herself no lightweight once the tequila slammers had started to be passed round. Now she was sitting up and hugging her knees, her eyes as red as her shoulder-length hair, her face even paler than usual.

Tamsin's friend Julie was a couple of yards away, leaning against a boulder the colour of granite, and redecorating it with her own stomach contents as Jeff, who had failed in his numerous attempts to chat her up last night, held her long black hair out of her face. Jeff looked just as ill, and was obviously biting back the urge to throw up himself. At least he'd be warm in that woolly jumper, Mark thought, before turning his attention to the birthday boy.

Simon Reynolds was in the worst state of all, which was hardly surprising, considering how much alcohol he had consumed. Once his eye-hand coordination had begun to fail him, he had been fed yet more. Of course, sitting him in the wheelchair someone had thought to bring along from the local hospital, and then plastering his arms to the support rests with yet more materials obtained from the fracture clinic under false pretences, had also helped to reduce Simon to little more than a receptacle for whatever people wanted to feed him. Provided it fitted down the funnel that had been jammed into his mouth, of course.

Simon was in exactly the same state this morning.

Mark rubbed his eyes and promised himself that once the world stopped spinning he would go and help Simon out of all that. A quick check with the others had revealed that Charlie, Simon's brother, was not among their group. Mark winced as another wave of nausea threatened to cause him to topple over. No doubt Charlie was behind all of this. Just wait until they got hold of him.

No one knew where they were.

Once Julie stopped throwing up she pointed to something near Mark's feet.

"What's that?" is what she probably said, although the words actually came out minus a few important consonants.

Mark looked down. On the ground close to where he had woken up was a brown paper package, damp from the dew but, apart from getting a bit crushed from where he must have stepped on it, looking otherwise intact.

"It's probably from Charlie," Jeff added as he tried to stop Julie from stepping in the mess she had made. Despite her temporarily weakened state she was still strong enough to push him away. She might possibly have told him to fuck off as well, but her language still wasn't that intelligible.

"Probably," Mark managed to grunt as he bent down to pick it up.

When you feel as if you have consumed the better part of an off-licence, it is often inadvisable to consider performing such an act as bending over, and Mark quickly found himself on the ground again. Once he felt able to, he rolled himself off the envelope he had once again managed to crush against the unyielding terrain. Then he picked it up and tried to focus on the words scrawled in black marker pen on the front.

"It *is* from Charlie," he said eventually, after managing to work out that the phrase was 'Simon's Saviours' and not some incomprehensible gibberish. The package had been taped shut with deliberate and, in view of the state in which those for whom it was intended would be in when they found it, sadistic intent. Mark picked at the layers of sticky plastic, resisting the urge to tear it open despite Tamsin suggesting it.

"I might damage something important," he said.

"You mean more than you have by falling on it?" said Jeff, who was finally giving Julie a wide berth. He looked at a loss now his role as protector had been effectively removed.

"Shut up." Mark wasn't in the mood to placate anybody, but he *was* very keen to get back into the warm. Fortunately, his fingernails weren't as badly bitten as Tamsin's, as vomit-stained slippery as Julie's, or as sealed in plaster of Paris as still-comatose Simon's. With a bit of concentration and a lot of ignoring of his headache Mark soon had the package open.

Tiny shards of brittle black plastic fell to his feet as he withdrew the white sheet of paper he found inside.

"'To Simon's Saviours'," he read out, his voice still quavering from the after-effects of drink. "'At first we thought it would be fun to leave Simon on the hillside by himself and see how long it took before he started to panic from all that ghost nonsense we heard those locals talking about in the pub. But we thought that would be unfair, and so he has the four of you to help him stay calm and get home. You all look like sporty types, and I'm sure at least one of you must have done some orienteering. So that's what the compass is for. The pub, where we're all waiting for you with food, drink, and plenty of pain killers, is due south. All you have to do is get Simon back home and make his twenty first birthday party a real occasion for him to remember. Best of luck, Charlie.'"

Jeff looked at Simon's still-unresponsive body. "I think it's already been enough of a birthday for him to remember," he said.

Mark nodded.

Julie wiped her mouth. "Is that the only other thing that's in there, then?" she said. "A compass?"

Mark tipped out what was left in the envelope.

Several pieces of plastic and a little metal pointer fell into his left palm.

"Oh… fuck." That was Tamsin.

"Must have happened when I trod on it," said Mark. "Sorry."

"Sorry?" said Jeff. "Sorry? How the hell are we supposed to get back now, you stupid bastard?"

"Shut up, Jeff," said Julie. "It's not his fault."

"It's not my fault we're stuck out here, either." Jeff was still too hungover to panic effectively, so instead he just stood and shivered on the spot. "How the hell did the rest of them get us out here without us knowing?"

"We were really drunk last night," said Tamsin. "I mean *really* drunk. In fact I don't think I've ever been that out of it."

"Me neither," said Julie. "And look at Simon. You'd think they drugged him or something."

The four of them fell silent at that.

"You don't think…" said Jeff.

"Don't be stupid," said Mark.

"…that as well as plaster of Paris and that wheelchair…"

"Oh… fuck," Tamsin said again.

"Why not?" That was Julie. "If you can sneak equipment out of a hospital then why not a few sedatives as well? Isn't Charlie a medical student, Mark?"

"I don't know him that well," said Mark as he looked at the others. "And I'm guessing no one else here does, either?"

There was a groan from behind them.

"Has no one thought to get that plaster of Paris off him?" said Julie, looking at the two other men.

Jeff looked bewildered and picked up a rock twice the size of his clenched fist.

"Be careful," said Mark, "you might hurt him."

Jeff proffered him the rock. "You do it, then."

I suppose I asked for that, Mark thought, as he took the rock from Jeff and approached the slowly wakening Simon. The near-comatose birthday boy managed a scream that became a dry heave as Mark brought the rock down, shattering the grubby white plaster that encased both of the man's arms.

Simon's legs were a different matter.

"They're wrapped in wire," Mark said after a cursory inspection. "And what looks like a padlock."

"Does anyone have the key on them?" said Julie, once again looking to the others.

"I bet we don't," said Jeff, turning out his own pockets. "I bet part of the joke is that we have to get Simon back to the pub with him still in the wheelchair."

"Bloody marvellous." Mark leaned over and said, none too gently, "Do you hear that, Simon? Your brother is a bloody psycho!"

Simon, still lacking the ability to speak, or, it would seem, to focus, responded by trying to throw up again.

"So what do we do now?" said Julie.

"We try to come up with answers rather than question after question," said Mark, none too kindly.

"That's not very nice, Mark," said Tamsin.

"Well in case it's escaped your notice, we're not in a very nice situation," Mark snapped. He instantly felt bad for doing so and said sorry, but the others were already looking away from him.

"Does this terrain look familiar to anyone?" Tamsin asked. The resounding silence suggested not.

Jeff rubbed his chin. "Maybe we should split up."

"Oh yes," said Julie, a flare of panic in her eyes. "That should increase our chances of all dying of exposure very nicely."

Jeff looked hurt. "I was thinking if we all set out in different directions it would increase our chance of finding help for the rest of us."

"We should probably stick together, especially after what those blokes said." said Mark.

"They were talking crap," Julie said in between coughs. "Just trying to scare us. But never mind that. If we split up what are we going to do about Simon? Draw straws to see who gets to push him?"

There was no answer to that, or at least none that anyone wished to voice.

"Well how about a bit of basic orienteering?" Tamsin was looking at her watch. "It's just after ten. Where's the sun?"

Four faces looked up.

Thick grey cloud stared back.

"I vote we go that way," said Jeff, pointing to the least rocky-looking terrain.

"Any particular reason?" Julie's face seemed to be stuck in a permanent sneer.

Jeff stood to one side to reveal a group of small stones. With a little bit of imagination it almost looked as if they formed an arrow.

"Oh don't be daft." Julie gave a loud, drawn-out, overly dramatic sigh.

"It's good enough for me," said Mark, taking the handles of Simon's wheelchair and pointing his friend in that direction. "We'll take it in half hour turns with him – fair?"

Julie looked as if she was about to object but a scowl from the others silenced her. The wind had picked up and it looked as if it might rain. The one thing they needed to do now was get moving.

"It's getting harder to push this." They had been walking for nearly an hour before Mark started complaining.

"Probably because we've been going uphill," Julie replied, "in case you hadn't noticed." It was the first thing she'd said since they'd set off.

Mark hadn't, but now, as he looked around him, he realised that as well as developing an incline the landscape had begun to change as well. The short, bristly grass had got longer and damper, and it was in danger of getting tangled in the wheels of Simon's chair. The wind had picked up, and seemed to be even more blustery back down the path. Mark glanced behind him and thought he saw someone wearing a long grey coat that was blowing in the breeze. But when he looked again it had vanished.

"You all right, Mark?"

Mark nodded to Julie. "I'm just thinking maybe this direction wasn't such a good idea."

"Or maybe it was." Jeff was pointing to the hill ahead of them. "Once we get to the top of that we should have a fantastic view. With any luck we'll be able to see the best way down."

Mark wasn't convinced. He looked at his watch. Someone should have taken over from him ten minutes ago. Simon was still out for the count. Mark wondered how much he must have drunk to still be in such a state.

There was a shout from up ahead.

Mark looked up to see that Tamsin had run on and was now at the brow of the hill. She was waving to them but whether it was a 'hurry up' wave or a 'go back' wave no one could tell. It was only when they all got there that they could see what she was trying to say.

The land had come to an end.

A hundred foot sheer drop gave way to a shale-streaked valley running at right angles below. The other side had to be at least fifty feet away.

The only way across was the bridge.

"That doesn't look very safe." Julie was eyeing the fraying rope handholds. At least all the wooden slats that formed the walkway were intact, even if the closest ones looked weathered.

"If you think I'm pushing Simon across that you're mad," said Mark. Jeff laid an experimental foot on the first slat. It creaked ominously, but held his weight.

"It might be okay," he said, "and let's face it, this is the first sign of civilisation we've come across. Who knows where it might lead?"

"More of the same?" said Julie with little enthusiasm.

"No." Tamsin was shielding her eyes now, trying to get a better view of the far side. "I think that's a wall over there. A wall with a gate in it."

"Then what are we waiting for?" Jeff took another step and the bridge gave another creak. "One at a time, yeah?" he added.

The others showed no inclination to follow as Jeff began to make his way across. For ten long minutes the only sounds were the whistling of the chill breeze as it made its way down the valley, and the sounds of the ropes and slats protesting at Jeff's weight.

Finally, he reached the other side and tried the gate.

"It's jammed!"

His words were hardly understandable in the wind. Mark cupped his hands around his mouth so he could be better understood. "What?"

"The gate," came the reply. "I need help to open it!"

"You go," Julie nudged Mark.

"And we'll push Simon across, will we?" said Tamsin with a snort as she set foot on the bridge. The wind was picking up now, and the whole structure had begun to sway. Was it Mark's imagination or were the creaks louder and more numerous as Tamsin crossed?

"Fuck this," said Julie, once Tamsin was safely on the other side. "I'm not staying here."

Whether it was because Julie was in too much of a hurry, or perhaps it was just plain bad luck, but when she was about two thirds of the way across, there was a sickening crunch as her left foot shot through a piece of rotted wood.

"Jesus Christ!" Julie gripped the right rope hold with both hands as her leg slid through up to the knee. When she tried to pull herself up splintered wood dug into her skin, making it bleed. Julie looked from Mark at one end to Jeff and Tamsin at the other.

"I'm stuck," she shouted.

From the far side, Jeff stepped back onto the bridge. It gave a sickening lurch as he did so.

"Jeff, don't!" Mark cried. "You'll bring the whole thing down!"

Jeff withdrew and the swaying bridge calmed a little. Julie looked horrified at his retreat and tried again to pull herself out.

The rest of the slat gave way.

Julie screamed as she fell through the gap in the bridge, her legs flailing, fingers locked around the frayed rope hold.

"For God's sake help me!" she screamed.

Jeff stripped off his jacket and shirt tied them together. They added Tamsin's coat to the improvised lifeline but it still wasn't long enough reach the hanging girl.

Mark could see Jeff say something to Tamsin before he took down his jeans and tied it to the improvised safety line by one leg.

Now it was just long enough.

"It'll never hold," Julie screamed.

"You've just got to use it to lever yourself up," Jeff shouted back. "Let go of the rope with one hand first and see if you can grab it."

Julie tried twice to reach the safety line. On the third attempt she started to cry. "I can't do it!"

"Yes you can," now Jeff was leaning out as far as he could, with, Tamsin holding onto his left arm as he flung the line of tied together clothes at Julie with his right.

Finally, the girl managed to grab it.

"Good!" said Jeff. "That's very good! Now try and pull yourself up!"

Julie, her face streaked with tears, released her hold on the rope bridge altogether and grabbed at the clothes line with both hands.

As she started to climb over it the knots began to unravel.

"Hurry, Julie!" Tamsin screamed. Her friend had just managed to climb over the first coat when the knot in Jeff's jeans came undone and Julie slid backwards. She tried to grab at the wooden slats, the rope, anything, but it was too late. She slipped through the gaping hole in the bridge, slipped through the air for what seemed like an age, and then hit the rocks below, spattering them with red as her body landed with a horrible crunch.

First Mark could hear nothing but Tamsin's screams as Jeff looked on in disbelief. As the world shrank round him, he realised he could hear a mumbling voice close by.

Simon.

He was still dazed from whatever he must have been dosed with at the party, but at least he was conscious. And he was trying to tell Mark something.

"…failed the test," was what Mark thought he said.

"What?" Mark crouched down beside his companion. "What did you say?"

The words, hardly more than a whisper, came again. "She… failed the test… bad… luck…"

Mark took hold of Simon's shoulders and shook him. "What are you talking about? Do you know where we are?"

His questions were rewarded with a slow nod. "Dad told me the story when I was little… haunted… the unlucky… no chance…"

And that was all. Simon's head slumped forward and he resisted all Mark's further attempts to rouse him. Worry that was close to panic began to claw at Mark's insides. What had Simon meant? Mark looked down at Julie's bloodstained corpse, at the bridge that had killed her because she had literally put a foot wrong. He glanced behind him and immediately wished he hadn't.

Standing against the skyline was the figure he had seen before. Even though it was further away, somehow his impression of it was clearer, so much so that he could now tell that the grey flapping thing it wore was less a coat and more a sort of cloak with a hood attached that obscured the figure's face.

"Hey!"

The figure vanished as soon as Mark called out. His thoughts were interrupted by a clang from the other side of the bridge. He looked up to see that Jeff and Tamsin were no longer there. They must have managed to get the gate open and passed through into whatever lay on the other side.

Getting rid of the unlucky.

Cold terror took Mark's spine in its shadowy embrace. What was on the other side of that gate? A reward for the 'lucky'?

No.

Not if it was something to do with rooting out the unfit, the unlucky, the unsuitable. For that surely there had to be more tests.

Oh, Christ.

"Simon," Mark spoke to him gently even though he was most likely deaf to the world. "Simon, I'm going to have to leave you here for a bit. I have to go and get the others. They don't know what they're getting themselves into. I have to bring them back before it's too late."

His companion said nothing. A pang of guilt made Mark wrap his own coat around Simon's comatose body before he took a step onto the bridge.

There was nothing to suggest which slats might crumble and which were sturdy, and it took several experimental taps with his toe before Mark was able to negotiate a safe route across. This only served to amaze him all the more that Jeff and Tamsin had got across unscathed. Just lucky, he thought. He hoped their luck would hold out.

When he got to the other side he found himself faced by the gate.

It was eight feet of solid rusted metal set into a stone wall of the same height. It was difficult to see where the wall ended but Mark guessed it surrounded the compound that the gate gave access to. He also guessed that the heavy iron catch that opened the door would be missing from the other side.

He took one last look back at Simon before turning it.

The figure was standing behind his friend.

"Simon!"

No answer.

"Simon! Behind you!"

Still no answer. As Mark watched in horror, the grey outline laid a hand on Simon's shoulder, a hand with fingernails so unnaturally long and black they looked more like claws.

Tamsin and Jeff must have managed to free the catch from the surrounding rust as it shifted quite easily. As Mark shouted again he took a step back against the gate. Now it shifted easily and he all but fell through the opening.

As it clanged shut in his wake he heard a terrible scream from the other side of the bridge.

"Simon!" Mark hammered on the rusted iron but his attempts made little sound, as if the metal itself was sucking away the energy from his fists. Eventually, the heels of his hands turning purple from the bruising, he was forced to give up and turn round.

Inside was like nothing he had ever seen.

Whatever the place was, it was obvious it had been lying derelict for a long time. The crude criss-crossed wire fencing that was as high as the walls, and had obviously been intended to convert the compound into a kind of maze, had blown down in places. Elsewhere the rain had caused much of the meshwork to rust and come apart, the incessant wind helping to tear great holes in it. The ground had probably once been hard-packed earth, or rock, or a mixture of both. Now thick, yellow, jaundiced grass ran rampant, partially obscuring the strange rusting creations that lay scattered at regular intervals within the enclosure. Standing at the gate, Mark could see the devices varied greatly both in size and in design. Each resembled the kind of medieval war machines Mark remembered being taught about in school. There were catapults, crossbows, and others that he couldn't quite fathom the exact workings of, but which consisted of enough taught wire and lethal-looking projectiles that their function was obvious. In the far wall on the other side of the enclosure, Mark could just make out another gate that he guessed must be the way out.

Tamsin was lying just to Mark's left.

At first Mark thought she was just stunned. Then he saw the rusty iron arrow that had pierced the left side of her throat and exited through the back of her neck. As he pulled her body forward, her skin icy to the touch, he could see that her back was soaked with blood. He made a noise that was somewhere between a sob and a cough as he laid his dead girlfriend's body back against the grass and closed her eyes.

Then he looked around for what had killed her.

He didn't have to search far. Three feet away lay a contraption that consisted of an automated crossbow bolt, primed to fire when the gate was opened. Mark noted that the chamber that fed bolts into the mechanism was now empty. Tamsin must have been the recipient of the final arrow in the chamber. And, Mark guessed, when the device was operating normally, it probably didn't fire every time the gate was opened. Only if you were unlucky, he thought, if Simon's garbled words held any truth to them.

Mark took a step forward and waited, expecting some other death trap to be activated by his movement. When nothing happened he let out a sigh of relief before wondering where Jeff was.

As Mark searched the area before him and his eyes began to look beyond the rancid, crawling vegetation, he realised that not all the browned structures protruding from it were rusting metal.

Many of them were bones.

It was impossible to tell how many bodies lay there. As Mark crept along, avoiding fences and listening for clicks and creaks, he saw broken thigh bones and fragments of shoulder blades. Now and then the remains of a broken skull peeped at him from the undergrowth, sometimes with an arrow protruding from an eye socket. One bore an ancient-looking helmet, green with verdigris and fused to the bone by its long stay in the damp soil.

He was a third of the way to the exit gate when he found his friend.

Jeff seemed to have stepped on a device that had been designed to fold a man in half backwards, but because the machine was old and was not working properly, it had instead managed to bend him far enough to crack his spine but not kill him.

The loss of blood from the hole in his side had done that.

Mark pictured Jeff staggering across this hideous battleground, already wounded from something Mark himself was yet to encounter, and then stumbling into this rusting Venus flytrap. At least he wouldn't have felt much, Mark thought, not below the waist, anyway.

Mark shivered. So far he had been lucky. The traps he had encountered had either been too worn to work, had decided not to work, or had been set off by his now-dead friends.

But how long would his luck last?

He was now halfway to the exit gate. Before him lay a long stretch of fencing, blown down by the incessant winds. Rather than go around it Mark walked straight across, noticing the bed of tiny rusted iron spikes lying just beneath the meshwork as he did so.

Once he was over that, Mark found himself facing a stretch of filthy water. He could have gone round it, but the gate was just there, on the other side. All he needed was the guts, or more specifically the luck, to be able to make it across. The question was, how deep was it? He looked around for something to prod the water with.

The only close object suited to the task was a weathered human thigh bone.

It came out of the ground with a moist sucking noise. Mark grimaced as he crouched by the water's edge and, holding the end of the bone by thumb and forefinger, lowered it into the water.

There was a hissing sound, and the bone began to dissolve.

Mark could have cried. What the hell was this? How could there be acid here, acid that was still working in a place that looked as if it hadn't been used in years?

There was a scratching sound at the entry gate, as if someone was scraping a sharp knife against the weathered metal.

Or claws.

Something was coming after him. Something that felt enough time had been granted to those fated to run this macabre gauntlet. Now the chase was on.

Mark looked around him, at the twisted, rusting traps, at the bodies of his dead friends, and then back towards the gate. He could probably make it if he took a running jump at it.

Probably.

It was starting to get dark. That made no sense. Mark looked at his watch. According to the dial it was a little after lunchtime. But as the sky began to turn the colour of old blood Mark wondered if he was even still in the world he knew. He backed up to the rotting fence he had just crossed. He knew full well that to jump and fall short would mean the end of him, but there was no other way. A gust of wind blew behind him as if to urge him on. Mark nodded thanks to the elements as his legs began to pound, as his heart began to beat even faster, as he took a deep breath and propelled himself over the pool of acid.

And then he was at the gate. Mark leaned his weight against the heavy steel and sobbed with relief. It was nearly over. Whatever this place was, he would soon be free of it. He took one last look around.

There was something else in the compound with him.

Something grey and clawed and ancient.

Something that was pulling back the cowl that concealed its face.

Mark caught a glimpse of skin stretched so tight over jutting skull bones that in places it had perforated to reveal emptiness beneath, of a lipless mouth that chattered in excitement, and of eyes filled with hate and a terrible hunger.

Without any further hesitation Mark slid back the bolt and stepped outside.

It was in the few seconds in which he took that step that he realised he had seen other gates at other sites around the wall. He had been so focused on this one he hadn't noticed them before. Despite managing to avoid all the traps that had been set, as Mark Williams plunged to his death in the chasm several hundred feet below he realised he hadn't quite been lucky enough.

Valley Interlude No.5

Dust.

That was the first sensation that came to him – that his mouth and nostrils were clogged with the stuff, powdery, acrid and dry. Robert coughed and sneezed in rapid succession. Then he shivered. Finally he opened his eyes.

He was cold because of the breeze that was blowing through the wide open doorway of the building he must have fallen asleep in. It was also unnaturally bright, as if someone had left all the lights on.

Robert tried to move his head, only to discover that his right cheek appeared to be stuck to the wood of the table on which he must have collapsed from exhaustion after hearing that last story. He snorted. At least they could have been decent enough to help him upstairs. He placed his palms flat on the sticky surface and gently peeled himself free. As he straightened up, it quickly became apparent why nobody had helped upstairs.

It was because there was no upstairs.

In fact, very little of the pub seemed to have been left standing by whatever giant claw must have reached down during the night and scooped away most of the walls, possibly taking all vestiges of life with it.

"Hello?"

There was no answer, save for the banging of the door in the wind, and the song of a blackbird that had come to inspect the scene.

Robert ran his fingers through his hair. As he regained consciousness and took in more of his surroundings he realised something was very wrong here. The floorboards were gone, replaced by grass and strewn with rubble that looked as if it had been there for years. The table, and the chair he was sitting on, were the only pieces of furniture. There were no bottles, no glasses, and no pub to speak of. If he wasn't there to vouch for it, the scant tumbledown remains of the building in which he now found himself could have been mistaken for the ruins of a witch's cottage.

What made him think of that?

It was the stories, of course, all the stories he had been told. It wasn't surprising they were starting to get to him. But the pub last night, that couldn't have been his imagination, could it? And the story – had he dreamt it?

Stay away from the west for as long as you can.

That was what Dr Harrison had told him. But now he'd received a warning not to go over the mountains. He knew he was unlikely to end up on foot far from the road.

But all it would take was for the car to break down in a deserted place and…

That settled it. He wasn't going anywhere near the mountains. He'd take the heads of the valleys road, get back onto the motorway and make his way to Aberystwyth from there.

A sudden panic gripped him. The pub, its rooms, its furniture, even its clientele had all vanished. Would his car be where he left it?

It was. The car park was now an overgrown tangle of brambles and scrub but fortunately he had parked close to the road. After a little encouragement the engine started. Despite what must have been an uncomfortable night propped up against a table, he felt curiously well rested and by the time he was back on the main road he felt almost like his old self again, albeit one still without a memory of who that old self might be or where he had come from.

Which just made where he was going all the more important.

It took him two hours to get through what in the past had been among the most industrial areas of the country. As he drove past what had once been hives of activity he could feel the terraced houses, the potholed streets, the empty factories, all with their stories to tell.

"I'm sorry," he felt moved to say out loud when he was not yet halfway through, due to their insistence. "I'm sorry but I can't listen to all of you. Not now, I don't have the time. Maybe I will one day, and if I can, you know I will."

That seemed to calm them a little and he was back on the motorway heading west before he began to think about what had just happened.

Houses that had once belonged to those now lost and the lonely, disenfranchised and destitute, had spoken to him.

Streets whose histories were streaked with tears and blood had pleaded with him.

Buildings that now lay empty and abandoned but which had once been frenetic with the energy and vitality of industry and production had begged him to stay and listen to their stories.

And he, possessed by some unearthly power that for now he couldn't begin to understand, had promised that, granted time and the stamina to do so, he would.

What was happening to him?

Now he was approaching Swansea. His destination lay further ahead but something was telling him to turn off here. Despite efforts to the contrary, before Robert realised it he had left the motorway and was heading towards the city. The compulsion continued as shopping centres and retail parks began to herald the start of Swansea proper. The car kept moving until he found himself pulling up in a narrow side street. But still, he knew this wasn't where the next story lay.

He left the car and started walking, eventually coming to a busier road. A park lay opposite. Was that where he was supposed to go?

No.

What about the hospital that was up ahead on the right?

No. It was what lay before that.

The church.

The sign outside announced with pride how it had been built in the late 1400s and had survived numerous bombings of the area during both world wars. Rather less ostentatious were the timings of the daily services. Finally, pinned at the very bottom of the wooden frame, was a paper notice announcing this week's timetable for the various groups that used the church as a meeting place. When Robert reached out and held the paper to stop it flapping in the breeze he felt something akin to an electric shock.

This was where the story waited.

The Church With Bleeding Windows

There was blood everywhere.

It had splashed across the front two rows of pews, soaking the hymn books and turning them into red raw bricks of coagulating clot. It dribbled in broken rivulets down the pine walls of the pulpit so that the place from which God's Word might be communicated now resembled a speaking platform in Hell. It had drenched the gleaming eagle's head of the brass lectern, and now crimson drops were falling from the bird's jutting beak, adding to the spreading scarlet pool beneath.

The vicar's body was in the aisle.

His head lay elsewhere.

That was all Martin knew because that was all Martin could see from his hiding place in the choir stalls. Beside him, his sister Alice knelt in shivering silence. He had no idea where everyone else was.

He also had no idea what had killed the vicar.

He had seen it. That hadn't helped.

"Has it gone?" Alice was trembling. Martin didn't blame her.

"I've no idea." How could he? The thing could be hiding anywhere. It was so small it could probably squeeze into any confined space, could hide in any patch of shadow. For all he knew it was clinging to the roof beams above them right at this moment.

Martin quickly glanced up to check.

Nothing.

Just the nice, normal kind of high vaulted ceiling you might find in a church that had been sitting on this spot for the last five hundred years or so.

"Where are the others?" Though she was next to him, Alice sounded miles away.

"I don't know." Everyone had scattered after the attack. Martin hadn't heard the ancient, creaking door open so it was safe to assume they were all still in here somewhere.

Alice's group.

Or rather, the Reverend Cyrus Protheroe's group. The one he held every Thursday night. A kind of drop in thing, offering social support for people in the community who suffered from 'dependence problems' and needed somewhere to talk.

Six of them had attended the meeting this evening.

Plus Martin, who had only come along because Alice said she wasn't going otherwise. And she needed this, possibly more than any of them. More than two years on heroin and god knew what else before that, now she was finally clean. The rehab centre had offered her follow-up after her discharge, but the first appointment wasn't for weeks. And Alice needed close follow up. Very close follow up indeed.

That was why Martin had agreed to come along with her. It hadn't surprised him that the group had been small, made up of a couple of ex-smokers, someone with alcohol problems and somebody else trying to stay off the cocaine (it wasn't working), as well as one furtive-looking guy who wouldn't admit what his vices were, although the tattoos suggested to Martin that he had been in prison. They had sat in a circle, Martin included so he could hold Alice's hand, and talked for an hour, before Reverend Protheroe had made them all promise they would return next week. Then he had led them across the church to the exit.

None of them got that far.

Something had leapt from the shadows and attached itself (Martin could think of no better word) to the vicar's head. The lighting in the church was bad and it quickly became impossible to distinguish between the blood spraying from the man's neck and the thing that seemed to be trying to burrow into it. After that they had scattered.

Martin checked his phone for the umpteenth time.

Still no signal.

"We've got to get out of here," said the voice from beside him.

"I know." Alice would be coping with this less well than he was, so Martin bit back his desire to tell her to stop stating the bloody obvious. "I can't see anything between us and the door…" *just the entire length of the aisle and what's left of Reverend Protheroe that we'll have to climb over* "…so I think we should try to get over there."

"No!" Fingers clutched at his arm. Martin had already prepared himself for the fact that Alice might be too terrified to move, and that he might have to carry her. Then he realised she was pointing at something.

Someone.

Martin remembered her name. Cath. She looked in her mid-fifties but was probably younger, her skin wizened and creased by the cumulative effect of smoking forty cigarettes a day from the age of fifteen. She claimed she had quit two months ago. Martin hadn't been so sure. He had been sitting next to her in the group and the smell of stale tobacco had been pretty overpowering.

Cath was making her way along the back wall towards the exit. She probably thought she was being quiet, but from where he was hiding Martin could hear the crackle of every breath she took.

Now she was twisting the handle, and trying with all her might to pull the door open. It wouldn't budge.

She had just stopped for a breather when the thing struck.

It might have been following her, or perhaps it had simply crawled down the aisle from where it had been feeding on Reverend Protheroe. All Martin knew was that one minute Cath was on the verge of freedom, the next a shadowy shape had leapt onto her chest. He heard a fit of strangled coughing augmented by a scream that was all the more terrifying because it was so feeble, so desperately gasped by what little strength her failing lungs were able to muster. After a brief fight, Cath fell to the floor with a feathery silence that just made the sound of the thing crunching its way through her ribcage all the more horrible.

And then the others were rushing to her aid.

Martin saw the remaining members of the group run to help as the monster began to burrow into Cath's chest. Jane, the twenty five year old cocaine addict, began hitting the thing as hard as she could with the wooden tip of a broom she had found. Kevin the alcoholic divorcee had taken one of the heavy brass candlesticks from the side chapel and trying to knock the thing off the bleeding, wheezing woman. Meanwhile Dave, the man with probable prison tattoos, tore a poster from the green baize-covered noticeboard behind them. He rolled it into a tube, set fire to one end with his lighter, and thrust it at the creature.

Martin had to go and help. "Will you be all right here?"

Alice shook her head and grabbed his hand. "I'm coming with you."

They got to their feet and made their way from the choir stalls. By the time they got to the door it looked as if Dave's tactic was working. In the light of the flickering flame, Martin got his first good look at what had been terrorising them.

He had been expecting an animal, perhaps an inner city fox gone crazy, or a cat escaped from some secret animal testing facility. What he found himself looking at was much weirder.

A small heap of what resembled butcher's offal sat on Cath's chest.

At first Martin assumed that her killer (for Cath had ceased moving) had gone, somehow escaped without the others noticing. Either that or it was invisible. Then Dave thrust his improvised torch at it once more.

The heap of offal moved.

Alice screamed, distracting the others.

Seizing its chance to escape, the creature slid from the gaping, empty cavity that had once contained Cath's lungs and trachea, shot across the tiled floor, hit the door, and then slid off into the shadows to the right.

"Come on!" Jane leapt for the exit and tugged at the heavy wrought-iron handle. To no avail. "Why the fuck won't it open?"

"Probably because this is an inner city area and if you don't keep places locked everything gets nicked while there's a group going on." Kevin went and took hold of Jane's shaking hand, guiding it to her side.

"You mean we're locked in?" Alice was squeezing Martin's wrist so hard it hurt. He ignored it.

"It looks that way," he said.

Dave looked up from his search of the headless body in the aisle. "No keys on him."

"Ok." Martin tried to think. "Why don't we all move to the other side of the church, as far away as possible from where that thing went, so we can work out what we do next."

No one argued. They were too all busy checking their phones again. Still no signal.

"What the fuck is it?" Jane still had the broom.

"It looked like something out of a lab," said Kevin, hefting his candlestick. "You know, one of those experiments gone mental."

"Too right." Dave no longer had a weapon and looked ill at ease. "Christ knows what they're cooking up in the basements of those factories."

But it was Alice who silenced them. Alice with her tiny fearful whisper as they got to the other side of the church and huddled in a chill corner.

"It's the devil," she said. "We've sinned and the devil's come for us. We don't deserve to live after the lives we've led, and this is how we're going to be punished."

That kept them quiet while they all wondered what the thing really was. It seemed highly unlikely any of them were going to guess. Not in the entirety of their rapidly diminishing lifetimes.

If Gladys Jenkins hadn't already been dying of an undiagnosed cancer of the gall bladder, it's likely nothing would have happened. If she hadn't been over zealous in cleaning behind the organ pipes at St Gwilym's church it's also likely nothing would have happened. But she was and she did, and that, in essence, is why we have a story to tell.

Gladys was new to Swansea. She had only recently moved from her home in Abergavenny to be closer to her only son, Dennis, who had recently undergone a messy divorce (to those blissfully inexperienced in this particular aspect of the legal system, be assured that there is no other kind). The fact that Dennis had done all he could to persuade her not to come had been gleefully ignored by a woman who had always believed she knew what was best for her son, and that right then that meant having his mother close by.

But upon her arrival her son had suddenly found himself to be, in his own words 'incredibly busy right now', and consequently Gladys had quickly found herself at a loss for something to do. But, having been a solid and some would say unyielding member of her church back in Gwent, she had quickly availed herself of the local minister and explained that she would be delighted to give his dusty old church a spring clean. The Reverend Cyrus Protheroe had, not for the first time in his life, raised his eyes heavenwards to thank the Lord for this latest offering of Someone Willing to Do God's Work For Nothing.

"If it's not too much trouble," he had replied to her kind offer, "that would be great."

It wasn't too much trouble, not at all. And so it was that Gladys had spent the best part of that week dusting, scrubbing, polishing and generally making the inside of the little church near the park gleam as if it had been furnished anew. Finally, with the pine pulpit sparkling, the brass lectern gleaming, and the pews positively glowing in their new Mr Sheen-induced radiance, Gladys had turned her remarkable reserves of energy elsewhere.

The space behind the organ pipes was narrow, but not too narrow for a seventy-four year old spry widow to fit into, dusters and all. It was when she was giving the back wall a good going over with the vacuum cleaner that she dislodged some chunks of plaster, which, in turn, after due rumbling and the collapse of a couple of loosened bricks, revealed, at about chest height, a cavity the size of a large earthenware jar.

Which is exactly what was sitting within it.

Gladys reached in and took the container from its resting place, dislodging more dust and fragments of plaster as she did so. Tiny spiders ran to take shelter in the cracked cement between the brickwork whilst larger wriggling things plopped onto the floor and vanished between the floorboards.

Gladys did not notice any of them. She was too busy grimacing at the pot, with its clay seal and its strange writing – more like scratches – around the rim, and oh, such a lot of dust sticking to it that she couldn't possibly show it to the Reverend without first giving it a bit of a clean.

Unfortunately, the pot never got to have what would undoubtedly have been a jolly good scrubbing, because as Gladys tried to back out of the gap between the organ pipes and the wall, one of the wriggling things that still remained in the cavity managed to drop onto her hand and, momentarily startled, she lost her grip on the urn and dropped it.

The clay pot had lasted centuries in its protective cavity. In the hands of Gladys Jenkins it lasted only moments. It hit the floor and shattered. Gladys peered down but it was too dark to see the contents which, at that stage, just happened to be too invisible to be seen by anyone.

That was not to last for long, however.

Invisible claws tore at Gladys' clothes, razor sharp talons ripped into the skin on the right side of her abdomen, and... *something*... burrowed its way past her ascending colon, slipped to the right of her pancreas, found what it was looking for, and proceeded to feast on the aggressively malignant tumour that had arisen in Gladys' gall bladder and common bile duct. Finally, its job done, the creature departed, leaving the ragged, disembowelled carcass of Gladys Jenkins jammed behind the organ pipes, which is where it remained, the icy atmosphere of a Welsh church in February and a significant lack of curious souls during the course of the afternoon meaning it was yet to be discovered.

The creature did not know that Gladys was dead; it had not been designed to think, it had been designed to do, and keep on doing.

Until someone told it to stop.

But only if they knew how.

"Smoke?" Dave had taken out a half-empty packet of cigarettes and was offering them around.

Martin shook his head. "I don't think you're supposed to smoke in here, mate."

"Oh yeah?" Jane had already lit hers and was puffing away as if her life depended on it. "Well you're not supposed to pull vicar's heads off in here either but someone went and did that, didn't they?"

"Something." Kevin's correction earned him a glare. "Something killed Cyrus and Cath."

"Or somethings." Martin was staring at where Cath's attacker had disappeared.

"What?" Jane spat.

"Well I know it's dark, but wasn't what attacked the vicar smaller? Hardly anything at all in fact." Martin looked round for support.

Kevin nodded. "I know what you mean. I thought it was a rat until it started biting so deep that…"

"Don't think about it." Martin waved smoke away from his face. "And the thing we saw on Cath's chest was bigger, wasn't it? Probably the size of –"

"A cat!" Jane had finished her cigarette and was looking in Dave's direction for another one. "There's a rat monster and a cat monster in here with us! Jesus Christ!"

"Or a monster that's got bigger." Dave had put the cigarettes away and seemed to have no intention of taking them out again, which earned him a scowl from Jane. "After all, it's had something to eat now, hasn't it? Two things in fact."

"So it will be bigger that a cat now." Alice's whisper came from behind Martin.

"Fucking hell," said Dave to nobody in particular, "I *knew* it was aliens! Fucking alien bastards that want to eat our livers!"

"No." Martin was still thinking. "It doesn't want our livers, but it does want different bits of us. I wonder why?"

"Don't be stupid," said Jane. "It's just gone for the easiest bit to bite down on."

"No." Kevin was shaking his head. "Martin's right. I saw it. That thing climbed up the vicar to get to his throat, but with Cath, it stopped at her chest."

"Maybe it needs different bits?" Martin was stamping his feet against the chill. "Maybe it's trying to build itself into a human being?"

"Fucking body snatchers!" Dave's words echoed around them. "I'm still sticking with aliens, oh yes I am, thank you very much."

"If it's building a body why didn't it take more? There should have been enough between both of them to make somebody halfway decent, shouldn't there?"

Jane was right. "It didn't even take good bits, at least not from Cath." Martin scratched his head. "Her lungs were the only part it seemed to want, and I would have guessed they'd be the very worst bit of her."

"So it's a shit judge of organs, so what?" Dave was edging towards the south transept. "I'm off to look for the keys. Anyone fancy coming with me?"

Jane skipped to his side. "I will." She took his arm. "Especially if you give me another fag."

"I'll give you what for in a minute girl." Despite his threat Dave had the packet out and was letting her take one. "The rest of you coming, then?"

"Best try the vestry." Kevin pointed ahead. "I think it's up there on the right. There's some sort of room there, anyway, I saw it on the way to the meeting."

Martin nodded. "Sounds fair. Let's all stick together and if anyone sees anything, shout."

"We're hardly likely to keep it to ourselves, are we?" Somehow Jane had already almost finished her second cigarette. She stubbed out the butt and they moved off, alert for every breath of sound, every flicker of movement.

Cath's lungs, and something in the vicar's throat.

It still bothered Martin. He had seen that pulsating thing, and it hadn't been eating that woman's lungs. It looked more as if it had been adding them to itself.

Which was ridiculous. Why on Earth would it want to do that?

*

On the opposite side of the church, behind a sarcophagus that allegedly housed the body of a thirteenth century knight, the creature was resting. This was probably the last time it would need to do so as it reorganised the new organs it had accrued. The bigger its corporeal body, the stronger it became. Soon it would have sufficient strength to keep moving indefinitely, to once again fulfil its purpose after having been locked away for so many years.

For buried deep within that rapidly increasing mass of seething diseased tissue resided a demon, conjured into being by a well-meaning alchemist at some point during the 1600s. Even the demon wasn't sure when, and the alchemist is no longer around to tell us, suffice to say that if it had ever turned up on the demon equivalent of a TV antiques show, whoever was appraising it would have been very impressed at its rarity, right before it gobbled them up and added their flesh to its own.

Unfortunately for all concerned, the well-meaning alchemist of sixteen hundred and whatever it was had got things a bit wrong. His intention had been to bring into being a spirit capable of curing disease, of gently, definitively and, most important of all, *painlessly* extracting the 'evil humours' (as the spell in the even older book that dated to well before sixteen hundred and something had described them) from the affected individual, leaving them healthy, smiling, and without the slightest sense that the diseased organ in question had been effectively ripped from them by invisible claws the size of grappling hooks. Which, of course, is what actually ended up happening.

The alchemist had immediately become extremely unpopular. In fact he would have been burned as a witch were it not for the fact that the local magistrate was suffering from an acute absence of his cirrhotic liver (too much port), the local sheriff had succumbed to a sudden lack of his entire gastrointestinal tract (a radical but extremely efficient way of dealing with tapeworm) and the local constable was running around screaming and clutching the red raw area where his genitals had once resided. This one was nothing to do with the demon. The constable's wife had caught him in the hayloft with the local witchfinder and had failed to be convinced by the so-called 'learned gentleman' in question – talking at an awkward angle it must be said – that the behaviour between the two men was in fact due to Lucifer having taken up residence within their sheep, Lolly, who was standing nearby. It also hadn't helped that she had been just about to give the very same Lolly a once over with the sheep shears but had been distracted by the unnatural noises coming from the barn.

So, as you can see, there wasn't really anyone left to torture, behead or burn the alchemist, which was actually a jolly good thing because he was the only one who had any idea how to stop the demon he himself had conjured. He mouthed the words from another page on the spell book and the creature was irresistibly attracted to the earthenware pot he had prepared for it, symbols inscribed into the still-drying clay and all. The demon cast off the diseased body it had begun building for itself, shrank to the size of a fist, and slipped into its new custom-made prison. The alchemist sealed the lid with a mixture of earth, blood, wax, and something so unmentionable it cannot even be reproduced in a story of this nature. The book hadn't said anything about holy ground being necessary to keep the demon imprisoned, but the alchemist thought it a good idea anyway. A few words and a bag of gold to the men engaged in rebuilding the south-facing wall of their local church, and the alchemist went off with the plan of enjoying a stress-free life elsewhere. He didn't, by the way. In fact he ended up causing quite a bit of trouble throughout Wales, but we shall leave that for another time. Meanwhile, as the years (and the religious movements that held sway over the country) came and went, the demon waited patiently to be let out. Plague, fire, and even world wars passed and the creature remained secure where it had been placed.

Until Gladys Jenkins came along with her dusters.

It *was* the vestry, and it didn't have any keys.

"So where the bloody hell are they, then?"

"Maybe the monster ate them."

Jane looked unimpressed by Dave's attempt at humour. "Where else is there to look?"

Martin closed the desk drawer he had been searching with one hand while Alice held onto the other. "He must have hidden them somewhere."

Jane addressed him as she might a child that Martin would immediately have felt sorry for. "That's what we've been doing, isn't it? Looking for them?"

"I don't mean here." He jerked a thumb towards the doorway where Kevin stood on guard. "I mean out there. Maybe he had some special place he put them that only he knew."

"In that case we're fucked." Dave sat on the lone swivel chair and spun himself round.

"Not necessarily," said Martin. "After all, we were with Mr Protheroe for almost the whole evening, weren't we?"

"Oh my God, that's right." Jane was nodding. "He met us all outside the church, didn't he? We saw him unlock the door. Christ, he even made some comment about 'keeping out the draughts' as he closed it behind him."

"He must have locked it as well."

"I don't remember him locking it," said Dave.

"That's funny." Jane didn't sound amused. "I figured you of all people would notice that sort of thing."

Dave got to his feet. "What do you mean by that?"

"Shut up the pair of you." Martin slammed the drawer shut and went to the vestry door. He laid a hand on Kevin's shoulder. "Kevin, do you remember the vicar locking the door behind him when we came in here?"

The man in the doorway didn't move.

"Kevin?"

Silence.

"Mate, are you all right?" Dave had a hand on Kevin's other shoulder now, which was just enough pressure to cause the man to teeter backwards and topple over.

To reveal the disordered mass of lungs, gall bladder and larynx that was busy adding Kevin's diseased alcohol-ridden liver to its bulk.

"Run! Now! Or we'll be trapped!" Martin ignored the vomiting noises coming from Jane in the corner and pulled Alice over the mess in the doorway. Dave followed, then went back to get Jane. He dragged the retching girl out of the room. They were edging away when the creature finished what it was doing and looked around for its next task.

Which apparently was the cocaine rotted tissue at the back of Jane's nose.

The girl screamed as the mass of sticky diseased internal organs launched itself at her face. She tugged at it helplessly as the demon thrust invisible claws into her mouth to get at the unhealthy tissues of her soft palate. Her screams took on a higher pitch as it found them and tore them free.

The creature dropped to the ground with a plop while Jane tried to stem the blood spraying from what had once been her face. The monster was looking around for who to cure next while Dave grabbed Jane from behind and pressed a cloth he had found in the vestry to the gaping hole where her nose and upper lip used to be. The white sheet quickly soaked through to red as Dave dragged her away. By the time Dave had caught up with Martin and Alice, Jane was dead.

"Fucking thing!" Dave laid Jane's body on the flagstones with surprising gentleness, then joined Martin and Alice as they backed towards the altar.

As the creature came round the corner and into the light of the choir, the three of them gazed at it in disbelief. The mixture of cartilage and pipes it was using to get around made a slippery scratching sound on the stone, while the bulk of its body consisted of two blackened lungs on top of which sat Kevin's fatty liver. Stuck to front of it was part of Jane's face.

"That's the stupidest fucking monster I've ever seen."

"How many monsters have you seen, Dave?" Martin agreed with him but didn't know what else to say.

"More than my fair share of human ones, that's for sure, but never mind that. What are we gonna do?"

The creature was rearing now, as much as it could, anyway. As it did, they could see there was something else surrounding the mixture of lumped together organs. Something larger, with long, tapering claws that, if viewed at the right angle, was almost corporeal.

"Have you got anything wrong with you?"

Dave blinked at Martin. "You what?"

Martin was nodding at the creature. "I think it takes the bit of you that's diseased."

"You mean it likes to eat cancer?"

"Cancer, infection, bad tissue. Anything."

"But the vicar didn't have anything wrong with him," said Alice.

"Not that we knew, and perhaps not that even he knew. But I bet he had something wrong with his… whatever bit that is that's lodged in there between the liver and the lungs."

"Well I'm fit as a fiddle." Dave flexed his biceps as if that was somehow proof. "Are you saying it won't touch me?"

"I'm not saying anything. But I'm guessing that's the case."

"Right." Dave took a step forward as Martin and Alice took one back. "I've had enough of this." Another step forward. "Come on then, Mr Monster." The creature swung its 'head' towards the sound of his approach. "Let's see how you deal with someone who can defend himself."

He was only five feet away when the creature leapt and began tearing at him, at his skin.

His tattooed skin.

That appeared to cover most of his body judging by the rips in his clothing that were opening up everywhere.

"Fucking run!" Dave was holding it off but it was a struggle. "I'll keep the fucker busy for as long as I can."

"Where can we run to?" Martin didn't know what else to do, where else to go.

"Maybe he hid the key near the door," said Alice. "Maybe it's under the rug or something obvious."

It was worth a shot.

"I said run!" Dave was almost bent backwards now as invisible claws tore strips of skin from his arms and chest.

Martin grabbed Alice's hand and together the two of them hurried through the choir and down the aisle, sidestepping Protheroe's body and reaching the door as Dave's screams echoed behind them.

The key was wedged behind the charity collection box to the left of the door.

"It's coming!"

Martin turned to see the creature, now wrapped in colourful strips of Dave, making its undulating way through the choir, like a giant Technicolor leech.

He slid the key in the lock and almost fainted with relief as the key turned.

"Hurry!"

The creature was almost upon them as Martin pulled the door open, pushed Alice through, and then slammed it shut. Angry wet slurping sounds suggested the creature was too bulky to slide underneath.

"You'd better lock it."

Martin had no intention of doing anything else. He even tested the door just to make sure.

"Come on," he said. "Let's get to a police station."

"Couldn't we just phone them?"

"They'll think it's a prank, and we need to convince them it isn't before that thing gets out. God knows what it could do, or what size it could grow to, in a city this big."

Alice nodded.

It only took a quarter of an hour for them to locate the appropriate authorities, but it was time enough for the creature to have squeezed itself down the church's only toilet, and accessed the sewage system.

Which just happened to be connected to the hospital close by.

Valley Interlude No.6

Robert recoiled from the sign and looked around him. How long had it taken for that story to enter his mind? Nobody was staring, nobody had stopped, and definitely nobody was asking him if he was all right because he had been staring off into space for the better part of half an hour.

He checked his watch.

He had been standing outside the church of St Gwilym's in Swansea for two minutes at the most.

He rubbed his eyes and took a step back. The blare of a car horn reminded him how close he was to the street. Up ahead he could see the hospital again, the one where presumably that demon creature was right now trying to enter. Perhaps if he went down into the sewers he might even see it.

He shook his head as he regarded the manhole cover to his left. He tried telling himself it was because he didn't have a crowbar to lever it up, but himself was having none of it. Robert didn't want to go down there because Robert didn't want to come face to face with whatever might be lurking beneath the streets.

Or perhaps it was already in the hospital? It could be hiding in the ventilation ducts right now, just as such creatures always seemed to do in monster movies, crawling along in search of new food, growing and growing until they became unstoppable.

For a moment he debated going over to the hospital to warn those inside. Then he remembered that they might just have a psychiatric unit, one where he could potentially find himself spending the rest of his days if he told them everything he had learned since coming to Wales.

Because it was starting to feel more like that, now. With every story he was told, whether by the random people he met, or the stories that just wanted to tell themselves, each one felt like information he was being made aware of, information that was meant to fit into a cohesive whole, like a kind of unofficial gazetteer of the weirdness that lurked just beneath the country's seeming normality.

And would that be the format from now on? Had being told those initial stories primed some part of him so that now all he needed to do was look at something and it would tell him its tale?

His gaze drifted back to the hospital. He went to take a step towards it but something stopped him.

No, that wasn't where he was supposed to go next.

Where, then? Back the way he had come?

No.

His heart began to beat faster as he realised he was incapable of moving from the spot he now seemed to be rooted to.

Not the hospital, not the street, not back to his car.

Once realisation dawned, Robert cursed himself for his stupidity. The building he was standing outside had not finished what it needed to tell him. More had happened there than the release of a sixteenth century alchemical demon. Something had happened prior to that, to one of the congregation.

No, not the congregation. Robert closed his eyes to concentrate.

Not the congregation, the staff.

The organist.

Something had happened to the organist and they had been forced to leave. But that was not the terrible thing that had happened to them.

The terrible thing had come afterwards.

What Others Hear

The world is thinner in some places.

Occasionally we may encounter signs that warn us of these locations, where reality is brittle and all that we understand has the consistency of little more than tissue paper. Often, however, there is nothing obvious, and we have to rely on the instinct we have developed through millions of years of evolution, the instinct that tells us to beware, to stay away, to leave well alone, even though the so-called higher parts of our brains can conceive of no logical reason why we might feel this way. Sometimes we are so distracted by the woes and hardships of everyday life that our instincts become dulled, our minds so occupied with the mundane that we fail to realise the dangers we are exposing ourselves to. But we ignore such warnings at our peril.

Where a land steeped in myth meets an ocean witness to more tragedy than the human mind can bear, our world is especially thin. The barriers have been worn away by the incessant play of illogical horrors, of fates unexplained, of desperate longing at the unfairness of life. It should come as no surprise that in such places the waves have a song to sing, a song that is heard by the surrounding hills as they wait for that which slumbers beneath them to awaken, a song that will not be finished until time itself ends. If the light is at just the right angle, and one looks carefully, one might see patterns in the troubled waters, and in the sand, too – unnatural configurations that change every day, symbols and messages left for races long gone, and with only the merest trace memory of how to interpret them inherited by those who believe they are now the dominant species on this planet.

In these special places those whom society might kindly describe as being of a sensitive disposition need to take special care, lest the assault on their already finely-tuned senses should be too much for them, driving them into an abyss of madness from which there is little chance of return.

In some places, the sensitive must take special care.

And there are some places they should never go.

William Martin came to the seaside town of Llanroath to convalesce.

He chose it for a number of reasons. One was that he had spent many summers on the coast of South Wales as a boy, the trips to the Gower peninsula and to Carmarthenshire with his parents still amongst his fondest memories, and he hoped he might find some comfort from a part of the world that was, for the most part, familiar to him. Second, Llanroath was small, tiny in fact, and as he attributed his recent breakdown in part to the pressures of big city life he felt a break from it would also do him some good. Third, and perhaps the most decisive, Llanroath had a church in need of an organist. While he was aware that it had been in part his employment in a similar role at St Gwilym's Church in Swansea that had driven him to his current state of malady, he could not be without music. Besides, it was more the administrative and political aspects of the post, not to mention some of the dreadful children he had been required to teach and their even more dreadful parents, that he cited as the true cause of his breakdown. The works of Bach, Mendelssohn and Vierne hardly deserved to have the accusatory finger pointed at them as being the cause of his temporary insanity.

"You should probably take a break from the music completely for a while, anyway," his psychiatrist Dr Montague had instructed.

His ENT consultant had told him the very opposite.

"There's no real way of curing tinnitus," Mr Ramply-Watson had explained, his blue eyes bright beneath the circular examination mirror strapped to his forehead. Martin had always wondered which doctors actually wore that alien-looking thing and now he knew. "What you have to do is find ways of either blocking it out or blending it in with everyday sounds. It may sound strange, but even though your exposure to loud music was most likely the cause of the problem in the first place it's probably going to be the best palliative for your condition as well."

Of course it had been difficult to believe. Not so much the part about palliation: Martin had always considered his music to be a panacea, a welcome salve for the wounds of everyday life. It was more the fact that it had been the cause of the constant and persistent ringing in his ears from which he now suffered in the first place. Surely such a condition was the province of machine operators and heavy metal music fanatics?

"You have a demonstrable degree of deafness," the specialist had said, pointing to lines on the audiogram printout that meant nothing to

Martin. "And from your history I can determine no risk factors other than the fact that for much of your life you have listened to far more music than the average human being, some of it no doubt louder than is strictly safe. I agree that it's rare for someone to suffer deafness from the kind of music you say you listen to, but it's always possible that your auditory nerves are more sensitive than others, and that they are more prone to damage than one might normally expect." Mr Ramply-Watson had put down his pen and given Martin a hard stare, "Either way, the fact of the matter is that you have partial hearing loss and that is the most likely cause of your tinnitus. I don't think a hearing aid is going to do much good, but there are other treatments available and we can explore those. In the meantime background music will probably help. As long as it's not too loud."

As is sometimes the nature of the medical profession, especially of those in different specialties, Dr Montague the psychiatrist had objected to this, but not as vehemently as Mr Ramply-Watson had proposed it. After all, aggression tends not to be part of the nature of a doctor of mental health, but he did voice his concerns in slightly louder tones than usual.

"It could be the music that was the cause of your breakdown in the first place," he said as Martin shifted uncomfortably in his chair. "Not necessarily the listening to it, but the constant requirements of your job, the need to perform perfectly those intricate five-part organ sonatas you told me about, the constant complaints from parents who felt you weren't doing your job properly, the pupils themselves who either refused or were unable to rise to your very exacting standards. Your auditory hallucinations, your feelings of frustration and low self-esteem, all of these have most likely arisen from your everyday working practice. Take a break." The psychiatrist had crossed his legs at this point. Perhaps, Martin had thought, it was his way of emphasising a point. "Take a break and get away from it all, somewhere you can feel safe. The medication I've prescribed will help with the worst of your symptoms, but it's the change of environment that will do you the world of good."

The change of environment.

William Martin arrived in Llanroath early on a Wednesday evening, the bus that took him south from Carmarthen railway station having been delayed by an accident just two miles from his destination. It was a hot day, even for late May, and it was with breathless relief that he was finally able to escape the baked air and step down onto the deserted main street. It wasn't yet dark, and the clouds in the twilit sky above him were like black ink in blue water. The bus pulled away, leaving him alone, the susurration of the gentle breeze sufficient to block out the tinnitus that was threatening to return, now he no longer had the sound of the vehicle's engine to keep it at bay.

Martin put down his case and rubbed his temples. To his left the street disappeared into darkness. Further on was a hill the silhouette of which he could just make out, as well as the crooked crenellations of the ruined castle that he guessed must be perched at its summit. To his right the street led to a T-junction running perpendicular, and on the other side of this T stood the pub where he had booked a room.

The Rugged Cross was tiny and ancient, and so was the cramped attic room in which Martin found himself after being guided up two flights of creaking stairs of reasonable width, and then up a third staircase that had to be the narrowest ever contrived by an architect. The landlord's name was Meillir Harris. He seemed pleasant enough as he apologised, explaining that the tavern's other rooms were occupied at present, but that as soon as a larger one became available, Martin would be moved. Martin thanked the man, who seemed as relieved to leave the room as Martin was to finally have space to move within it. The sloping roof mean that he could only stand up straight if he stood in the very middle, and the single bed with its unwelcoming-looking grey blanket creaked when he sat down. A minuscule window set just below the apex of the roof gave him a view, but he would have to wait until tomorrow to see what it was. Right now, the splintered wooden frame enclosed merely darkness made all the blacker by the light of the bare bulb that hung from the ceiling. Opposite the bed, which filled one side of the room, a rickety wooden bureau provided space for Martin to unpack. The three drawers were lined with newspaper yellow with age and tinged with dots of mould, and so it surprised him to read the date on one of the spread out pages as being just last month.

The matchbox-sized bathroom was two floors down and Martin witnessed not a soul as he made his way there and back again. He had not eaten since lunchtime but found his appetite lacking after the events of the rest of the day, and so he decided to make an early night of it.

There was nowhere to plug in his white noise generator.

The thorough search Martin performed of the entire room failed to yield a single plug socket, and so the device he had been provided by the hospital's ENT department went back into its box as Martin's anxiety rose a few notches.

How was he going to stop the ringing sounds now?

They were always worse at night. Everything was always worse at night. It was in the unyielding darkness that he had finally had his breakdown as the whispering, piercing noises that had plagued him for weeks finally resolved themselves into whispered words he could not ignore. While Dr Montague had assured him the medication he was on would keep the voices at bay, the thought of a night alone with nothing but silence terrified him.

Once Martin knew he was too scared to undress and get into bed, and that if he were to stay in that room his symptoms of mounting panic would only worsen, he realised there was only one alternative.

Despite the lateness of the hour, he would explore the town.

The landlord was calling last orders as Martin passed through the tiny bar. The two customers refused to be distracted from their cloudy beer, and even the landlord seemed unconcerned by behaviour that must surely have looked strange to him.

The main street was deserted, and the light breeze made just enough sound to distract Martin from the noises that were beginning to build inside his head. It wouldn't last, though, and Martin knew that soon the tinny whispering would become loud enough to upset him.

Where could he go?

The moon was out now, and the silhouette he had first mistaken for a castle was now bathed in silver, revealing the crenellations to belong to a bell tower, the crooked walls to be merely the angle at which the little church was positioned on the hill, much closer to the village than Martin had imagined.

There was a light on inside.

His mind made up, and with the night still warm, Martin set off up the main street, the lamps seeming to flicker in time with the whispering inside his head as he passed. Soon the buildings and the lights were gone and the road had narrowed to a single track lane. A cloud passed over the upper half of the moon, like a mask attempting to cloak a damaged mind, and Martin found himself groping in semi-darkness, his only guide the dull glow from the church.

By trial and error and several collisions with damp undergrowth, Martin discovered that the road curved round to the right and, as it crested a hill, ended at the low stone wall of the cemetery. As if to reward his efforts, the moon suddenly divested itself of its coverings and he was allowed a metallic-grey view of the cold, unyielding building before him.

The gate in the stone wall swung open at his touch. In the darkness of the lane Martin had walked as fast as he could. Now he could see where he was going, his footsteps were more cautious, perhaps because whatever might be watching would now also be able to see him. He made his way along the gravel path that led to the door. The church was bigger than he had expected. It looked fourteenth century and had probably been built at a time when its congregation would have numbered over a hundred from the local farming and seafaring communities. Martin approached the door with a mixture of trepidation and indecision. What was he going to say to whomever he found inside? Would there be anyone in there? Was leaving a light on in the local church a custom in these parts? A traditional guiding of the lost soul to the sanctity and protection of the Lord?

Or could there be some other reason?

Martin scarcely had time to consider this when he realised that now there was no light within the church. The dull glow that had guided him after the moon's temporary abandonment had vanished.

The vibrations within his head were starting to make themselves known again now that he had stopped walking, the silence of the evening the perfect canvas for their delicate, insidious brushstrokes of paranoia. Martin ignored what he thought he could hear and rattled the door handle, emboldened by the presumed absence of anyone within.

It took a little struggling, and for a moment he thought the door was locked, but eventually it creaked open to reveal a panoply of pews awash with ethereal silver-tinged shades of ruby, emerald and sapphire from the moonlight's passage through the stained glass of the windows opposite.

Martin took a step inside and the door banged shut behind him. It made him jump but, once he appreciated that it had failed to arouse the interest of anyone who might be in the building with him, he proceeded in a slightly more relaxed state up the aisle to where he could see the organ, positioned to the left of the altar.

It looked open.

He could see the manuals, two of them, arranged in stepwise fashion, the protective wooden shutter that one would normally expect to be locked over them slid back to also reveal the organ stops that were arranged in two corresponding rows above the two sets of keyboards.

The sounds in his head were more piercing now, like wire being scratched across steel, the grating tones resolving themselves into words that told him how useless he was, how worthless, how he could never succeed in anything. He would never have thought the word 'failure' could sound so abrasive until he began to hear it inside his own head.

There was only one cure.

Martin located the brown power switch in its circular plastic moulding and flipped it upward.

A sound like a dragon taking a breath filled the room as the organ's working mechanism filled with air, preparing to breathe pure music through the pipes that stood proud above him. All it would take was the merest touch of his fingertips, both to make the instrument before him sing, and to make the voices stop.

He sat himself on the polished wooden stool and was about to begin playing when something made him hesitate.

Made him look to his right.

Made him see the picture above the altar.

It should have been comforting, that painting. At least, Martin assumed that must have been the intention, depicting as it did Jesus Christ at the time of his crucifixion, the arms outspread, the face bloodied by the crown of thorns, the single nail through both feet pinning them to what was probably cypress wood, or so some scholars believed.

It wasn't comforting, though. It wasn't comforting at all.

It was positively hideous.

As Martin stared at that picture he realised it wasn't so much the image of the Christ figure itself that was disturbing, but what surrounded it. Now he could see that what had initially looked like a murky fog done in unsavoury shades of charcoal grey and muddy brown actually served to conceal horrors that seemed to lurk deeper within. Martin tried hard, but he could not quite make out the shapes that he felt were crawling just beneath the paint.

But he was sure they were there.

He shook his head and looked again. It was easier to see them now, those things with tiny segmented bodies and multi-jointed limbs that seemed absurdly, supernaturally long as they plucked at the skin of the dying man on the cross.

As he watched, one of them turned and looked at him.

And spoke.

It was too much of a coincidence for it to be anything else. The high-pitched whine that pierced Martin's left ear had him clutching his skull in pain. The noise that now filled his head began to vary, as if the pointed tip of one of those insectoid claws was being dragged across his eardrum. It was all Martin could do to reach the organ stops with his right hand and blindly draw as many of them as he could before playing the first thing that came to mind.

The Bach fugue was not meant to be performed with such an inappropriate combination of pipes as he had selected, but it served to blot the worst of the ringing in his ears. Within a few bars Martin was able to open his eyes, and within a few more the scratching on the inner wall of his skull had subsided. Another line of music and a modulation from G Minor to D Minor, and Martin realised the only thing he could now hear was the music. He relaxed but didn't stop playing. How silly he had been, how foolish, letting his tinnitus get the better of him to the extent that he had started hallucinating like that.

Without taking his fingers from the keys, Martin looked to his right to reassure himself that the picture above the altar was nothing more than the sort of image one might find in any ordinary country church.

What he saw made him scream.

The painting was bleeding.

Tiny pinpricks of dark red were erupting from the murk surrounding the crucified figure. As they coalesced they began to run down the painting, trickling over the pale form of Christ and adding crimson rivulets to the tortured body on the cross.

Martin took his fingers from the keys and swung himself off the organ stool to get a better view. Almost immediately the whining, scraping, screaming sounds were back, and this time they were much, much worse, as if the organ music had inflicted some terrible torture on the things he thought he had seen, as if it was their bodies that had broken and burst and bled as a result of his playing.

Martin tried to get back on the stool but now the noise was so bad all he could do was clutch his head and sway from side to side as the creatures screamed, as the creatures cursed him.

As the creatures swore revenge.

The nearest hospital was Glangwili General in Carmarthen, and so Martin was taken there after being discovered early the next morning collapsed in front of the altar. The doctor who saw him in the emergency department diagnosed a combination of lack of sleep, stress, and most importantly a lack of attention to his treatments and medications as having caused the episode, and Martin was discharged with the promise that he would keep any nocturnal wanderings to a minimum.

It was another baking hot day and the taxi that drove him back to Llanroath had all its windows open. Martin welcomed the breeze as the depot injection he had been given at the hospital began to do its work.

"Don't forget you've been given it," the doctor had warned. "Taking your regular medication on top of this could prove disastrous. It should last for five days and then you should start on the tablets again. And find somewhere to plug in that white noise machine!"

Back at The Rugged Cross Martin was met by the landlord and his wife, Llinos, both of whom looked worried.

"I'll be fine," Martin reassured them. "But if it's at all possible I'd like a different room."

"Of course," said Mrs Harris, taking his arm and leading him into the snug. "Meillir will sort that out for you, won't you, Meillir?"

Her husband nodded as she sat Martin down and asked him what he would like for breakfast. Martin shook his head, explaining that he was still feeling queasy from the medication he'd been given.

"Well you have to have something," the woman replied, looking shocked. "How about some lovely eggs? And tea with lots of sugar – that should have you back on your feet in no time."

Before Martin could object she had disappeared into the back. He rubbed his eyes, stretched his arms, and looked around him at the empty seats and polished wooden tables.

He frowned. Surely if the pub was as full as Mr Harris had claimed there should have been one or two late eaters? Or at least the evidence of their presence in the form of greasy plates, toast crumbs and coffee rings on the tables?

Martin took a breath and the tang of stale beer assailed his nostrils. In the background, the pleasant clatter of Harris and his wife going about their morning duties helped to keep what little noise there was inside his head at bay. Llinos had sat him in sunshine, and now it was beginning to hurt his eyes. He was about to move when she returned, bearing a plateful of food he knew he could never hope to consume.

"Just have as much of it as you can," she said in reaction to his shocked expression. "It'll do you good."

Martin regarded the mixture of greying scrambled eggs and crumbling rust-coloured black pudding.

"I'll try," he promised, wondering how he could turn attention away from the unappetising pile before him. Then he remembered the slip of paper in his wallet on which he had scribbled the details of who he was supposed to report to when he arrived. "Can you tell me where this is?" he said, taking it out and showing it to her.

Llinos Harris frowned as she peered at Martin's cramped handwriting. "Take a right out of here and keep going," she said. "You can't miss it. I don't know how happy he'll be to see you, though."

Martin frowned. "Why not?"

Llinos nodded at the paper again. "That's the vicar's place," she said. "And it was the vicar that found you."

Llanroath vicarage was the grandest building in the village. Set back in its own grounds, the Victorian redbrick could have passed for the old village school. Or, Martin thought as he approached it, the old village hospital; the kind of place where you were locked away until someone came to claim you.

If anyone ever did.

Stop thinking like that, Martin told himself as he rang the bell and waited in the drizzling rain.

Fortunately he was not left waiting, or worrying, for long.

"Are you feeling better, now?" the Reverend Idris Clements asked as he showed Martin into his study. With his stocky build and balding, bullet-shaped head that betrayed the scars of what Martin hoped were sporting injuries and nothing more serious, the vicar looked more suited to the role of a rugby international prop forward than the pastor of a small Welsh village. He motioned Martin to sit and then dropped himself into a swivel chair that creaked alarmingly as his bulk made contact with it.

"I am, thank you," Martin replied. "Although I have to say I am rather embarrassed, especially as I've come here to be your new organist."

"Have you now?" The vicar grinned and there was a glint in his eye. "So what exactly were you doing? Getting a bit of practice in before you came to see me?"

Martin could feel his heart pounding against his chest. "Actually," he said, "there are probably a few things I should explain about myself."

The vicar was very understanding which, when Martin thought about it later, was hardly surprising. Of course, he only mentioned his medical diagnoses and omitted the bit about the hallucinations he'd had last night.

Clements steepled his fingers. "And music stops these… voices, does it?" he said.

Martin nodded. "Lots of types of sound will, but I'm sure you can understand why the organ works best."

The vicar nodded while reaching into his right hand desk drawer. He took out a small bunch of keys and tossed them over. "These should get you into the church and the organ whenever you feel the need to play," he said. "I can't explain why you were able to get into the church so late the other night, nor why the organ had been left open." He gave Martin a beatific smile. "Perhaps the Lord had something to do with it," he said.

Clements rose to indicate their meeting was over, and Martin followed him into the hallway.

And gasped as he saw the picture hanging there.

There was nothing in what was depicted that shocked him. It was a landscape painting, probably of somewhere local, depicting rolling hills curling around a sandy beach. No, it was not what was depicted.

It was the style of the picture.

The whole thing had been rendered in the same murky colours as the background of the painting of Christ in the church. The mountains had not been coloured the vibrant emerald of a summer's day, but rather the muddy, unappetising green of midwinter. The sand was the colour of old flesh, washed out and dying. But the strangest thing was that it was obviously meant to depict a view through a window while a storm was raging. The sky was so clogged with thick grey clouds that the heavy raindrops looked filthy against the glass, and Martin could almost feel the wind rattling the pane of the picture's frame.

"That's quite an… odd picture," Martin said, trying to find a word that wasn't too damning.

"Local artist," said Clements. "Or rather he was. You probably saw the painting he did for us behind the altar up at the church."

Martin nodded. Was it his imagination or was something moving in the murk of those black waves? Something just below the surface but yearning to break through, yearning to drag itself onto that flaccid corpse of a beach and feast on the necrotic tissue of the land.

Nonsense.

"It's a bit… grim," he said.

"I suspect he was influenced by the weather," Clements chuckled. "It does rain rather a lot here." He took a step back and cocked his head sideways. "It's called 'The Land in Anger'." He gestured at the picture. "All this roiling, swirly stuff is apparently intended to signify that whatever lives beneath the soil could one day break through if sufficiently angered."

Martin raised his eyebrows. "What's it doing in your house?" he said.

Clements shrugged. "An artist, down on his luck – what else could I do when he came calling? I bought it from him as an act of charity and gave him a commission to repaint the figure you can see behind the altar. I thought it might help his state of mine but, alas, it was not to be."

Martin didn't like the sound of that. "I'm guessing he's no longer with us?" he said.

Clements shook his head. "Despite our best efforts," he replied as he showed Martin out. "And I wouldn't want the same thing to happen to you so please, if you feel I can be of any help at all, do not hesitate to get in touch."

Martin nodded. "I promise I will," he said.

"Remember you can use the organ at any time. And if your head gives you trouble, I've been told it often helps if you write things down," the vicar gave Martin a knowing look. "I believe it is said to have a purging effect."

Martin's new room was slightly bigger, and the window that looked out over the street gave him a view of the church tower that should have reassured him but which instead he found disconcerting. His fear of what he imagined he had seen there was stronger than any comfort the building could offer.

The ringing in his ears had dulled for now. But for the occasional piercing whine he could live with it, and his white noise generator, plugged in and by the bedside, was off for the moment. He had not brought any means of playing music as he had been warned this in itself could be damaging.

So Martin sat in the near-silence, the only sounds the gentle scraping in his head occasionally blocked out by a vehicle passing by. On the table in front of him sat the blank exercise book he had purchased from the village newsagent's on his way back from the vicarage. His pen was yet to violate the sheer white of the paper and his thoughts were already turning to another walk, perhaps even another visit to the church – anything rather than this gaunt, maddening isolation that was meant to be recuperative but instead stood a chance of driving him more insane than the city life that had caused him to come here.

It began to rain, the heavy, filthy drops that struck the glass reminding him of the painting at the vicarage. Before he knew it, the sounds in his head were beginning to worsen as well – scraping, clawing, whining, constantly changing as if they were trying to make themselves understood.

And then he did understand.

Not everything, but enough for him to realise they weren't like the voices he had heard during his breakdown, or even during what had happened in the church last night. They had a different timbre, a different urgency, and, most important of all, they didn't seem to be trying to destroy his self-confidence. In fact the few words he could make out were strange.

Very strange indeed.

Martin picked up his pen and began to write, if only to see if it might help. He was putting nonsense on the page – he knew that, but it didn't stop him, and as he wrote the words down the voices in his head gave him new ones. Before he realised it he had filled a page with odd combinations of letters. A few of which were familiar, most of which were unrecognisable.

And then the voices went away.

Just as it stopped raining.

Martin put down his pen, took a deep breath, and realised he felt much better. Perhaps the vicar had been right after all. He grabbed his jacket and left for the church, intending to confront the altar painting while he was still in his current state of wellbeing.

The way looked very different in the grey light of day, and as he approached the building Martin felt some of his anxiety beginning to creep back. His head was still refreshingly empty of noise, however, and this spurred him on, through the lychgate, along the path and into the building.

The picture was still there, but it looked much less threatening now. It was still as disturbing as an image of a man crucified against a murky background could be, but today Martin could not see any evidence of shapes lurking close to the body, and of course there was no blood.

Blood which had flowed in response to his playing.

Martin licked his lips and looked at the wooden cover of the organ console. It had been replaced and locked after the events of last night.

Of course he had the keys now, he thought, fingering them in his jacket pocket. It would only take a minute to play something, to run through a few bars of a Bach cantata and keep his eye on the picture to prove to himself that what he had seen was just the product of his tired, overworked and unhappy mind.

He unlocked the console cover, slid it back, and flicked on the power switch.

After he had drawn stops that would allow for a soft, reassuring timbre, Martin paused, his fingertips hovering over the keyboard. He took one more look at the picture, decided what he was going to play, and began.

For the first couple of minutes he didn't dare look away from the instrument, allowing the music to calm him, the repetitive lines of the fugue overlying each other, mingling and taking on new variations that were so familiar to him he could have played the piece in his sleep.

It was nearly over before Martin realised he was too scared to look up.

He finished the piece, and selected stops that would produce a more bombastic sound, as if his playing might act as a shield for what awaited him behind the altar.

He managed two pages of Bach's Fantasia in G Minor before he forced himself to turn his head to the right.

At first it was difficult to see what had happened. It was as if the entire wall behind the altar had been replaced by a black void, an empty nothingness from which not even light could escape. As Martin continued to play he realised the space below the stained glass window wasn't black at all.

It was red.

Deep red.

And now there were things coming out of it.

Martin watched in horror, his fingers still playing of their own accord, as the surface of the slick crimson was broken by multi-jointed thread-like appendages as red as the scarlet pool from which they were arising. Searching for purchase, some quickly found the grey stone on either side, while others met with the polished tiled floor, scrabbling as they attempted to lever out whatever bloated, unholy bodies were still concealed within the ghastly place from which they were attempting to escape.

Were they real? Hallucination? An effect of the drugs he had been given in the hospital? Or would they actually look even more terrifying if he hadn't been given the medication?

As more of the spider-like limbs appeared, and thread-like antennae began to probe the new, strange atmosphere, Martin realised that deliberation was not going to save him.

He slid himself off the organ stool and ran, down the aisle and out through the doors, closing them behind him in case they offered some barrier to what was coming after him.

When he turned round, the world had changed.

The sky had darkened and, worse, reddened to the point where it was almost as if he were looking up from the surface of an alien planet.

Clouds that resembled amoebae crawled across the heavens, enveloping stars and leaving trails of black dust behind them.

The cemetery was still there, as was the road, and Martin tore towards it, turning right and heading for the sea, where he could see a few scant traces of normal blue sky on the horizon.

The road ended and became a dirt track which soon also faded away. Martin turned to see that the path he had just fled along had now vanished, and that the landscape looked different, barren, unearthly.

He clutched his temples. This could not be happening! It had to be inside his head! He turned toward the sea, towards the cliffs he knew towered there.

A lone figure was standing at the cliff's edge. As Martin got closer he realised he recognised who it was.

Idris Clements.

"You don't look too well, my boy." The vicar extended a hand as Martin approached. "You don't look too well at all."

Martin, his hands clutched to his temples, fell to his knees as he reached the man in black. He looked up to see red flooding across the sky, obliterating the last vestiges of blue. The unhealthy burnt-looking sun that now hung in the alien heaven bathed everything with pallid light, lending the landscape a sickly ochre hue that made Martin feel nauseous.

"What's happening?" he asked.

Clements shook his head. "Nothing," he replied. "Nothing to me, anyway. What might be happening to you, of course, could be an entirely different story."

Martin narrowed his eyes as the pounding in his head worsened and the light surrounding him seemed so ugly as to be almost malefic. "What do you mean?" he croaked.

"So many of them come," said Clements. "And so many of them die. All of them, eventually." He indicated the waves tearing at the rocks below. "And all of them down there."

Martin looked at the water, at the way it swirled beneath the unnatural light of the new sun, creating patterns that he could almost believe were intentional.

"They are," said Clements, as if reading his thoughts. "Or at least I believe them to be. Just another method of communication we no longer understand, like the things you, and others, have heard and seen."

Martin shook his head. "But what I could hear was just part of an illness," he said. "An imbalance of brain chemicals and electrical impulses."

"And what do you think caused those imbalances in the first place?" Clements gestured around him. "There are myths about the creatures that live beneath these hills, that slumber out there in salt water that is far deeper than anyone could ever know. But there are other myths as well, stories of the servants of these old ones who are the very opposite in terms of size. They are as tiny as their masters are vast, and are perfectly capable of crawling along nerve fibres and sending their own messages to them."

In the changing world around him the vicar was the only constant, and now Martin hung onto that desperately. "How do you know so much about them?" He looked at Clements in disbelief. "And you being a man of God!"

Clements smiled. "I'm a man who likes to be on the winning side," he replied. "Two thousand years ago it was Christianity. Two million years ago it was beings much older even than that, and very soon they will rise again. I haven't decided which side to take yet," he added. "I'm just trying, in the fashion of the true scholar of theological matters, to gather as much information about them as possible. Which is where people like you come in."

"What do you mean, people like me?" Martin said, having to shout to be heard above the roaring of the blood-tinged surf.

"Sensitive people come here," Clements said. "They are both drawn to this place and are receptive to the things here that the less gifted amongst us are unaware of. They see and they hear, but they don't understand. That poor artist fellow was one. I tried to help channel what was revealed to him in the hope he might be able to make some sense of it, but it all became too much for him. His legacy remains, however, for the scholars amongst us to try and interpret, just as your crude attempts at describing your experiences in that notebook will be added to the increasing body of documentation about those that slumber beneath these hills."

"I can hear them again!" Martin was shaking now. "I can hear them, but not out here, not out in this world." He clutched at his temples. "The world has changed but I can still hear them inside my head," he moaned. "They make scratching sounds, clicks and squawks. How can I make them stop? How can I get them to realise that I don't understand them? That I'm not a part of this world they're showing me? And that I never will be?"

"Perhaps not 'never'," said Clements. "Perhaps all it might take is a leap of faith."

He looked down into the swirling scarlet foam below. Martin followed his gaze.

"It's the only way, you know," said Clements. "I've seen too many like you. Once it's gone this far there is only one way to stop the madness, if madness it is, rather than truth."

He helped the organist to his feet.

"That's the problem with you sensitive types," he said. "You're the only ones who can see, the only ones who can communicate, and yet it's just all too much for your minds to deal with."

Martin peered over Clements' shoulder at the vast lobulated creature towering behind him, its multifaceted eyes focused on Martin, one huge serrated claw poised to take him in its grasp.

"Whatever it is you're looking at," Clements said, "it can't see me. I haven't revealed myself to it. But you have. And there's only one way out. Unless you wish to wait for its friends to catch up with it. They want to meet you too."

That was it. That was enough. Martin took a single, deep breath, thrust himself forward into the air, and then he was gone. The waves swallowed him and left not a trace.

And on a lonely Welsh hillside beneath a sky that now threatened rain, a solitary figure made their way back to where it, and others like it, lived, to await the coming of others sensitive to the ancient horror that lurked beneath the seemingly silent landscape. Other who would be able to see, and hear, and unwittingly break down barriers that were already so thin as to be almost absent.

Almost.

Valley Interlude No.7

Robert was back in his car, driving north and feeling increasingly detached from the world around him.

He was feeling strange because he had no memory of getting into his car, let alone starting the engine or making his way out of Swansea. Yet here he was, on the coast road heading once again towards Aberystwyth.

As he neared his destination, the same questions kept coming back. He still had no idea of his name or where he was from, but he knew that the answer lay up ahead, and that he was being guided by a force that must have been watching over him, and maybe even controlling him, ever since he had woken at the suspension bridge.

But what did it all mean? Had he been born here? Was this where he had grown up? Was this even the real Wales? Was it instead perhaps a fantasy, a simulacrum, a world of his mind's own building? Worse than that, was it a prison he had created for himself, a labyrinth of his own imagination from which there was, and never could be, any escape? Each road turning back on itself, every path spiralling back, every word of advice he had been offered, every direction he had been given, would they change anything?

He kept his attention on the road ahead, his surroundings brought into sharper focus by his thoughts. Not green hedges but prison walls. Not towering pine trees but watchtowers, not mountains up ahead but the ends of the earth, the end of his world. Very definite limits beyond which he could not travel because his imagination was not capable of venturing there.

He glanced in the rear view mirror. The country lane behind looked much like the country lane ahead. He guessed that either would take him to the same place. He kept his foot on the accelerator. Even if he was trapped, he refused to stay in the same place, and that had to count for something.

Didn't it?

He took one hand from the wheel and pinched his eyes. It felt like weeks since he had found himself beside the bridge, and yet he barely remembered the passing of two days. But the sheer volume of the stories he had been told felt almost overwhelming.

He looked to his left. In the far distance the sun was setting, casting a bronze glow over the calm ocean and lending the sky an otherworldly hue that reminded him of the other dimension he had been allowed to glimpse by the most recent story.

The road ahead was empty and the sunset was beautiful. He allowed himself another glance across the landscape, bare but for grass likely kept short by the sheep he had seen dotted here and there. Nothing but grass and sea and sunset.

Except there was something, up ahead.

It was sufficiently distant from the road that it had to be right on the cliff edge, and as Robert's car passed it he could see the outline of a great old house, now gleaming bronze in the dying light. As he took in its grandeur he felt himself gripped by another tale demanding to be heard.

Better pull over, he thought.

But before he could even turn the wheel the story was upon him.

The Devil in the Details

There are many unforgiving things in this world.

The sea along the West Wales coast can be particularly harsh – brutal even – when the weather is bad and the waters have a mind to be unfriendly. Frothing waves the height of the oaks that pepper the fields further inland lash at unyielding rock, scooping away shale and tearing at the land, pulling a little of it away with every hammering of merciless salt water. It is a slow process, this erosion of the earth, but the sea does not mind – it has all eternity in which to complete its task.

Cloaked now in the darkness of midnight, only the stars and the full moon above are witness to the onslaught that is currently being wrought upon a sheer cliff of wet rock the colour of charcoal that rises for over a hundred feet above the crashing waves below. It is a clear night, and the noise the sea makes can only barely be heard by those within the house that is perched just a few hundred yards from the cliff's edge.

The house, three storeys and eighteen rooms of gothic splendour, used to be further inland, but the relentless work of the waves below has brought the cliff's edge a little bit closer than when the house was originally built nearly two hundred years ago. In fact, there is now nothing beyond the west wing but a few hundred yards of weather-beaten emptiness where nothing but wild grass grows, and nothing but wild creatures venture.

Beyond that is the yawning emptiness of the night sky above and the vast and insatiable appetite of the black sea below.

The unkempt state of the grounds does not concern the owner of the house. Nor, on this night, does it concern those he has invited to share it with him. For tonight is special. Those stars are in an alignment unseen for many years; that moon has achieved the exact and appropriate state of fullness and is at just the right angle above the house in which a meeting is currently taking place. The storm clouds are yet to gather, but if all goes to plan they will come at the utterance of a single word, providing the requisite preparations have been made, the correct incantations spoken with appropriate pronouncement and accentuation, the correct symbols inscribed upon the floors and walls in the correct mixture of animal's and children's blood.

And then of course there is the sacrifice.

Since the new owner moved in a year ago a number of alterations have been made to the house, the most obvious of which is the roof. The clustered columns, crumbling spires and tiles of the middle section have been removed and replaced by an altogether different structure. Apparently there was some discussion regarding these alterations in view of the building's listed status, but a generous cheque to the objecting parties, and an accident befalling the member of the Welsh Assembly who would not be bought off, has meant that now the main part of the building's roof consists of a dome of highly polished glass. It is multi-paned in an array of different colours and hues, all constructed according to diagrams in the ancient texts the current owner keeps concealed in his secret library. To the casual observer, of whom since the building has been renovated there have been a total of none who have lived to tell the tale, the dome might be explained away as an observatory, an architectural quirk, or a place of prayer.

It is this last that is closest to the truth.

If anyone were to venture close to the house during the hours of darkness (a most unwise thing to do, as I am sure you realise by now) that dome would usually be difficult to make out. It would simply appear as a humped silhouette against the backdrop of night, as if the house had grown a tumour or was trying to cast off a body foreign to its design and construction.

Tonight, however, there are lights burning within the dome, the flaming torches casting pools of orange light that reflect off the stained glass, painting this unholy rooftop chamber with an astounding panoply of flickering colours. Again, the positioning of the sconces has been as a result of precise and painstaking mathematical calculation. Nothing has been left to chance. The owner is all too aware that the slightest mistake could result in catastrophe. He has already lost two disciples through experimentation gone awry, and while their bodies reside in a private asylum near Swansea, he knows their minds will never be recovered as they have become the property of beings no sane man would ever be able to behold.

Tonight, however, he is confident that he will succeed. That with which he wishes to converse knows nothing of forgiveness, or mercy.

Indeed it understands little of human affairs and has little interest in them, except when the opportunity arises to acquire souls. Then it becomes interested. It becomes very interested indeed.

A deal is shortly to be made, the repercussions of which will not be fully realised by those present until it is too late for any of them.

There are many unforgiving things in this world, but the things that exist outside of our normal perceptions are the most unforgiving of all.

Maxwell Chantry's eyes glittered in the light cast from the flaming torches. His face, obscured by a cowl of scarlet velvet that was featureless except for two eye holes, bore an expression of triumph none of the thirteen assembled in the sanctification chamber could see as he raised the ceremonial blade. His gaze drifted for a moment to the heavy iron rings set into each corner of the granite block before him. The naked girl lying on the stone was unrestrained, a requirement of the ritual, as was everything else that had been arranged for tonight, but Chantry still felt a pang of concern that the soporific mixture he had administered to her half an hour before might stop working. Then the worry was gone. If the drugs did wear off, he had also hypnotised the girl into such a state of submissive acquiescence that before she realised what was happening it would be all over. For her, anyway.

As the chanting of words unheard by mortal ears in centuries reached a climax, Chantry gripped the ivory hilt of the curved, cruel-looking blade. As he did so, the intricately arranged emeralds and rubies that had been set into the bone of the handle amidst rituals of their own dug unforgivingly into the flesh of his palm. Chantry spread his arms wide, threw his head back, and uttered the final words of the ritual, his breath hot against the silk lining of his mask, before looking down once again at the girl.

Her eyes were closed but he knew they were blue behind those pale lids. Her tiny lips, pursed slightly in her relaxed state, bore not a hint of makeup, nor did the rest of her face. Her long, flame red hair spilled over and down the stone behind her head, the tresses resembling streaks of blood in the shadowy firelight.

And now it was time for the real blood to flow.

Chantry brought the blade down with the surety of a man for whom such an act was the culmination of years of planning. The blade pierced the girl's creamy skin on the right side of her belly, just under the midpoint of the border of her ribs. Chantry aimed the knife upwards so the polished steel pierced the girl's liver, the part of the body traditionally regarded by the ancient Greeks to be the seat of the darkest emotions.

They weren't entirely wrong, either, thought Chantry as he withdrew the blade and waited as a crimson flow began to flood from the wound. For a moment nothing else happened. Chantry was on the verge of closing his eyes and praying for aid to a different demon in the pantheon, despite the dangers, when, all at once, the girl's blood began to change. Before the awed expressions of those gathered in the room, the blood that had been spilled lifted into the air. At the same time its state began to alter. No longer liquid, the blood was now changing to a rust-coloured smoke that rose above the body of the girl, hanging in the air just inches from Chantry's face. As it started to swirl and coalesce, the smoke began to take on a shape that filled Chantry with a mixture of gleeful anticipation and appalling dread.

The figure was cross-legged, the muscles in its limbs so well defined that the apparition might have been an anatomical specimen. Long claws extended from both fingers and toes, curling in a way that was even crueller than the blade Chantry still held. The face was still little more than a nebulous cloud, the rudiments of horns forming from the substance that was still spilling from the dying girl.

The dying girl whose eyes suddenly opened.

Who saw the thing floating above her.

Who took a deep, impossible breath and uttered a long, drawn out and even more impossible scream.

The work of years took just seconds to dispel. Even as the girl drew breath the apparition started to shimmer, to lose its form, the delicately charged particles that made it possible for the demon to appear in this dimension already repelling each other and returning to their normal state.

Chantry could feel his insides turning to water as everything he had been working for vanished in little more than a puff of smoke. He relaxed his grip on the knife and it fell to the altar with a clatter.

The girl, still bleeding but very much alive, reached for the blade and sat up. She took one last look at the form floating above her, even more monstrous now that it was becoming distorted as a result of the ritual's failure, before, with a howl of insane agony, she began to attack her own face. The honed blade swiftly reduced her beautiful features to a red raw mess, and by the time Chantry had wrested the blade from her the girl was unrecognisable. Low moans bubbled from the bloody and ragged hole that was her mouth as Chantry pushed the blade in again, into her heart this time. He made sure she was dead before pulling the cowl from his head and taking several large gasps for air. The tears on his cheeks were not for the bloodied mess that lay before him, rather they were tears of rage and frustration at his failed experiment. He threw the knife to the floor before his horrified coven and made sure to regain his composure before he spoke.

"The stars will remain the same for some time yet," he said eventually. "We may still succeed."

"I need a virgin."

Dr Patrick Masters put down his scalpel, turned his attention away from the writhing figure on the makeshift wooden operating table, and regarded the man who had just barged into his private domain with an air of disdain.

"At a risk of stating the obvious," he replied as Chantry peered through the dim gloom of the subterranean chamber in which the surgeon was conducting some very private business, "Aren't you wasting your time looking for one in Swansea?"

Chantry coughed. The smell in the crumbling brick-lined room was as strong as the rudimentary gas lighting was weak. "How on Earth can you see to actually do anything in here?" he said.

The mutilated thing on the table groaned. Masters picked up a relatively clean-looking gauze swab, poured something noxious and soporific onto it from a large bottle of ribbed brown glass, and held it over what was left of the subject's face for ten seconds.

"He won't be bothering us any more," said Masters once the convulsions had ceased. "But to answer your question, this particular case doesn't call for the most precise of techniques. In fact the individual who provided me with the necessary funds for this particular assignment stipulated that I should produce the desired modifications with as little finesse as possible. Before I finally did away with the fellow altogether, of course."

"Of course." Chantry held a silk handkerchief scented with Hugo Boss to his nose. He had suspected it might come in handy when he had discovered Masters' current whereabouts. "Now, could we possibly discuss some business in more salubrious surroundings?"

Masters peeled off his latex gloves, undid the cord on the stout red rubber apron that had protected his black waistcoat, and rolled down the sleeves of his tailored white shirt, fastening each cuff with a link in the shape of a tiny gold scalpel blade.

"Seeing as the business you wish to discuss is hardly likely to be in any way legal," he said, taking his suit jacket from a twisted iron hook in the wall just behind him, "I would have thought this an ideal place in which to consider any requests you have that I might cater for."

"True," said Chantry from behind his handkerchief. "But the smell."

"Ah, yes." Masters looked back at the body on the table. "The poor fellow claimed he didn't have the guts to have an affair with the wife of my client. Fortunately I was able to prove him wrong before he expired. *Un*fortunately he ended up making rather a mess of himself when confronted with the proof. Nevertheless, I have no intention of being seen in public with a possible employer, so I am afraid it's here or nowhere at all." He gave Chantry a mirthless grin. "So for both our sakes hurry up and tell me exactly what it is you actually want me to do."

"Exactly what I told you just now," Chantry replied, hoping the after shave would retain its potency for a few more minutes. "A virgin."

Masters rolled his eyes. "And if you're going to persist in inviting witty remarks that I really rather consider beneath me, I see no reason why we should continue this conversation."

The doctor made to push past but Chantry stopped him. "I need you to make one for me." He said.

Masters stopped, a gleam of interest in his eye. "Go on."

Chantry spread his hands. "What else is there to say? I have need of a virgin for a certain… ritual; and as you quite rightly surmised, I am not in a position to simply find one roaming the streets of a major city in South Wales. I do, however, have a willing volunteer who is familiar with what I require and is willing to take the risks the procedure entails for the quite fabulous rewards that may be hers. There's just one problem."

"I see." Masters rubbed his chin. "Well obviously I'd need to take a look at her, to determine whether or not reconstruction of the area was possible without major grafting of tissue from elsewhere…"

"But you can do it?" For the first time Chantry's voice held a tone of desperation that did not go unnoticed by the surgeon.

"I can do it," Masters replied. "But are you sure that's what you need?"

"What do you mean?"

"Well," Masters narrowed his eyes. "Ritual. Virgin. And you have that house out in Pembrokeshire that you turned into some kind of observatory despite it being several hundred years old and having listed status. I can guess what you're up to, and I had always assumed that the virgin in these sorts of things was meant to be as much symbolic as anatomically correct. Do you really think that stitching a bit of epidermal tissue over a natural orifice that isn't really meant to have it there anyway is going to be acceptable to whatever no doubt dreadful thing you're intending to conjure up?"

Chantry shrugged. "I only have a little time in which to complete that which I wish to achieve," he said. "All I need is for you to do what I am asking. I'm happy to pay whatever fee you quote, and as a sign of good faith I'll arrange for a box of your favourite Monte Cristo cigars and two cases of Perrier-Jouet champagne to be delivered to your address tomorrow morning."

"I no longer smoke," said Masters with a self-satisfied grin, "but make it three cases and we have a deal."

The house of Maxwell Chantry, two days later.

The stars are still right, the moon is a little less full, but not to the extent that it should affect the proceedings.

The same room, the same time, the same ritual.

The girl on the altar is once again naked, is once again drugged. She is somewhat older than the previous victim and with the years of her greatest beauty behind her, she has agreed to participate in Chantry's ritual in the hope she might be able to recapture her lost youth. It is but one of many claims Chantry has made in order to convince her to submit, both to the ritual itself and the ministrations of Dr Masters' scalpel beforehand.

Chantry is wearing the same red silken cowl, is gripping the same, cruel, curved dagger.

He speaks the words of power once more. The words that should conjure the mighty demon he wishes to do his bidding.

The knife flashes down.

The blood begins to flow.

And flow.

Soon the chill granite is covered in it. The sacrifice moans softly as her pale body gives up the last of her life essence to the unyielding stone.

Maxwell Chantry takes a step back, raises his eyes heavenwards, and waits.

And waits.

"It didn't work."

Dr Patrick Masters switched off the blowtorch and lifted the eye guard.

"How did you get in?" he asked.

Chantry waved a rusty-looking key. "The owner of a disused slaughterhouse can be tracked down, you know, and paid off. Even on a Sunday."

Behind them, the middle-aged man hanging naked from the meat hook begged for his life once more. Masters tore a piece of heavy silver packing tape from the roll he had used to bind the man's hands and feet and applied it to his victim's mouth.

"That should keep you quiet for the moment," he said. "Of course that's what you should have done in court, isn't it?" He looked at Chantry. "My employer would have got six years if it hadn't been for a very accommodating young lady who was able to provide him with an appropriate alibi. Or should I say, a very inappropriate one."

Dr Masters chuckled at what was obviously a private joke. He put the blowtorch down. "I'm guessing you have yet to find success with that ritual of yours?"

Chantry nodded. "Nothing appeared," he said. "Not a sausage."

"Ah, now, if you want sausages," Masters pointed to his latest victim and then to a large metal box on the other side of the room. A conveyor belt led into one side and on the other was a receptacle obviously intended for whatever unfortunate creature the machine was capable of grinding to a pulp. "If you wait a little while I might be able to help you there." The victim in the corner began to wriggle more than ever. "Oh stop that," Masters gave him a prod with the soldering iron. "That was just a joke."

"In case I haven't made myself clear," Chantry said, looking distinctly uncomfortable in the presence of all this torture that wasn't sexy or intended for the conjuring up of higher powers. "Your surgery didn't work."

"Nonsense," said Masters, picking up a hideous-looking automated corkscrew device and switching on its motor. He allowed it a few experimental, and very noisy, spins, before turning it off again. "The surgery was as good as could be expected under the circumstances. I warned you it probably wasn't going to be sufficient. Which does make me wonder what on Earth you're doing here."

"I have one night left," said Chantry. "Tonight."

Masters took a long, slim, rocket-shaped piece of shining metal from the table. By adjusting a screw on the right hand side spikes emerged from it before the entire thing split in half and opened up like the jaws of a crocodile.

"And what do you suggest I do about that?" Masters asked, applying a little bit of oil to the ratcheting mechanism.

"I have another willing volunteer," said Chantry.

Masters raised an eyebrow. "Really?"

"Yes."

"*Really*?"

Chantry's shoulders slumped. "Not really, no. To be honest this time I was wondering if you genuinely might be able to rustle one up for me, or you might perhaps know someone who could."

Masters would have rubbed his chin in thought but his hands were quite bloody and he didn't want to take his gloves off. Nevertheless he put on a very thoughtful expression before looking over at his victim again.

"I don't suppose you're a virgin, are you?" he said.

The gagged figure nodded as best it could for someone suspended in mid-air.

"I'm sorry but I don't believe you." Masters turned to Chantry. "He couldn't lie in court but he's very happy to make up any old bollocks now that his old bollocks are in danger of coming into contact with some of my friends here."

"Can you help me?"

Patrick Masters held up the rocket-shaped device.

"I have a lot to get through this afternoon," he said. "In fact I am just about to see how far this can go up my friend's bottom over there. I'll try and see what I can do but I'm not going to promise anything."

"Thank you." Chantry's display of gratitude was almost pathetic.

"Don't thank me," said Masters, applying a hefty quantity of lubrication to the shining silver. "Pay me. A lot. After all, you wouldn't want to find yourself on the other end of this, would you?"

Chantry left to several different and equally unpleasant noises, the likes of which he hoped never to hear again.

The virgin was delivered early that evening, along with an invoice that, Chantry noted, included the time Masters had wasted talking when he could have been getting on with torturing his Sunday afternoon victim.

She was a pretty little thing, Chantry thought, as a delivery man who must have been eight feet tall carried her into the drawing room and laid her on a divan upholstered in ruby velvet. He signed the forms and gave the man a healthy tip for his trouble (and to try and give a spark of life to the man's cold dead eyes). Once the two of them were alone, Chantry turned his attention to his prize.

She was naked beneath the grey blanket she had been wrapped in. Her wrists and ankles had been bound with what looked like red ribbon. Her blonde hair had been styled in ringlets and fell to her shoulders. He had no idea what colour her eyes were, as they were closed.

All his attempts to wake her were unsuccessful.

Chantry checked her pulse. To his relief it was good and strong. A drug, then? Perhaps Masters had used something similar to Chantry's own recipe. He hoped so. The victim would have to be at least partly awake for the ritual to be a success. It occurred to Chantry that perhaps he should check to ensure his cargo was… intact, but he knew it was unnecessary. The order had been satisfied upon a gentleman's agreement, and Chantry could tell from the educated, creative and overly sadistic way in which Masters had tortured his victims that the doctor was most definitely a gentleman of the old school. He could trust him.

Couldn't he?

A little later that night, Chantry stood in his observatory, appropriately robed and garbed, his disciples gathered, the girl naked and prostrate on the altar before him. He held the jewel-encrusted knife in his right hand and, while no one was looking, he crossed the fingers of his left. He figured he was allowed to be superstitious because, after all, he knew that such things existed.

Once again the moon shone through the multi-faceted glass dome, spattering the proceedings with spots of different coloured light. Once again Chantry brought the knife blade down, piercing the liver of the barely conscious young woman.

Blood began to flow.

Upwards.

Chantry held his breath as a figure began to form in the air above him. As the blood drained from her body, so the form hovering over her became more substantial. First came a skeleton of blood red bone, followed by the creation of muscles, tendons and blood vessels around it. Finally came skin, as red as the rest of the tissues.

No, not finally.

Finally came the red suit, the red shirt, and the red tie.

To Chantry, Satan also appeared to be a bit chubbier than he expected. And had rather less hair. Nevertheless he bowed his head, spread his arms wide in obeisance, and paid homage to the deity he had summoned.

"Master!"

The blood red man seemed unimpressed.

"Master," Chantry tried again. "We who are humbly gathered here greet you and await your bidding."

There was an awkward silence that lasted about a minute. Perhaps, thought Chantry, the devil's tongue was still being formed. Eventually, the figure spoke. With quite a strong Welsh accent.

"Oh you do, do you? And what do you expect in return?"

Chantry, his head still bowed, thought it best to be honest under the circumstances. "Power, oh Master. Power and the wicked delights of this world, and the next."

The figure sniffed. "Yes," it said. "That's what I thought you might want. Well, I'm afraid you're going to end up disappointed."

Before he knew what he was doing, Chantry stopped averting his eyes and looked at what was speaking to him.

With a pang of horror, he realised he recognised him.

"You're not the devil!" he spluttered.

"Did I ever say I was?" came the reply.

"But you're… you're…"

"Say it," said the figure. "Say my name. The name you gave to those bully boys of yours so they could bump me off and you could do what you wanted to this place." Now it was the figure's turn to spread his arms wide. "Say the name of Arfon Prys-Jones, the Welsh Assembly member you had killed to further your own meagre ambition."

For the moment Chantry's tongue seemed to have failed him, and so he remained silent while the figure continued.

"You really should research those whom you intend to do away with, Chantry," said the satanic incarnation of Arfon Prys-Jones. "We black magicians aren't such an insular lot. A few discreet enquiries would have revealed that having someone like me killed is the very worst thing you could do. I do not forgive, Chantry – ever. When my wife decided to find solace in the arms of another man after my death, I arranged for Dr Masters to teach him a lesson. In fact I believe you were witness to some of it. Even that nasty business with the blowtorch and that witness you paid to lie in court about what happened to me wasn't a good enough hint that I was after you."

"But… the ritual," Chantry spluttered, looking around him. "All my work. It wasn't designed to… bring you back."

Arfon Prys-Jones, black magician, late of the Welsh Assembly, recently endowed of a much greater power than could be bestowed by regional government, smiled very unpleasantly.

"Three women," he began. "Three women sacrificed during the cycle of the full moon on the grounds which I myself had intended to acquire for the purpose of praising His Most Mighty Unholiness. It didn't matter if they were virgins. All that did matter was that the last would be bound in the treated tendons of one who had killed for me."

Chantry gulped. "You mean…?"

Prys-Jones' grin grew even broader. "I am afraid Dr Patrick Masters will never get to drink all that champagne you sent him," he said. "But if I were you, I wouldn't be worrying about that. In fact in a little while, you won't be worrying about anything at all."

Behind Maxwell Chantry, there was a shuffling noise as his ex-disciples began to close in on him.

"I'm glad to see they know which side their bread is buttered," said the more powerful of the two black magicians in the room. "I'm sure by the time they've finished with you I'll need to have this room redecorated. But then you always did have terrible taste, didn't you, Maxwell?"

Chantry fell to his knees.

"Forgive me," he begged, as disciples that had become monsters used fingers that had become talons to tear at his flesh.

"I'm afraid I can't do that," came the tired reply. "There are many unforgiving things in this world, Maxwell. Unfortunately for you, I happen to be one of them."

Valley Interlude No.8

Ridiculous.

To suggest that what had just passed through his mind was currently taking place, or rather that the climax of it was, in that house over there, right now?

And yet somehow Robert knew that was what was happening.

Prove it, then. Go over there and see.

He was sitting in his car, parked at the side of the road. The sun was still setting, the time taken for the story to tell itself just moments and yet it had felt like so much longer. The house was still there, slightly darker now, a black beast of a silhouette outlined against the encroaching darkness.

If you hurry you'll likely be able to see the demon with a big mouthful of Maxwell Chantry.

For some reason the thought appealed, perhaps because it would be proof that this wasn't all in his imagination. Robert flipped the lever on the car door and got out. It closed noiselessly behind him.

The first thing he noticed was how still it was. Despite his proximity to the sea there wasn't the slightest hint of breeze. He took a step onto the grass verge. It wasn't long before he arrived at the driveway to Maxwell Chantry's house.

The problem occurred when he tried to step onto it.

It was like colliding with an invisible screen. Not so much made of glass, more like a gentler, slightly more yielding, infinitely tougher plastic. Robert put his hands up. There it was again – a barrier between him and the house, preventing him from proceeding any further in that direction.

He returned to the car and tried walking directly across the landscape, aiming diagonally towards the house.

Blocked again.

He changed direction to avoid the house and instead walk straight towards the cliffs.

Once again, no luck.

Something didn't want him going in that direction, no doubt the same something that had guided him since he awoke on the bridge. Robert shrugged. He had allowed himself to be brought this far, and he had a feeling he was nearing the end. In a way it was a relief to have the guidance. He went back to the car.

Or rather, he went back to where the car had been.

Because now it was gone.

He wasn't going mad and he hadn't come back to the wrong place. It was a straight road cutting through and essentially featureless part of the landscape. The car had vanished, as if it had been scooped away while his back was turned.

Walking, then.

He tried going back the way he had driven, just to test a theory. Sure enough, any effort to go in that direction was met once again by the steady hand of whatever giant invisible being wanted him to go the opposite way. Robert turned round. The open road stretched ahead. Despite the lateness of the hour he didn't feel cold. Nevertheless he set off at a brisk pace, hoping that wherever he was destined he reached it before nightfall.

After he had walked for what felt like ten minutes, he began to wonder exactly how far away nightfall was. The sun didn't seem to have moved an inch, still hanging just above the horizon and illuminating the way he was headed with a dusky bronze glow. It was just light enough for him to check the time by.

His watch had stopped, at a far earlier hour than it obviously was now.

Or later.

He dismissed the ridiculous thought. At the same time, however, he began to wonder. Had time, that thing he felt he had been struggling against ever since he woke up, been slowing as he had neared his destination, to the point where now he was so close it had reached a standstill? And not just time but the world itself. It wasn't simply that there was no breeze blowing. He couldn't hear the sea even though he knew it was just beyond his line of sight to his left, and there were no birds, no sounds of nocturnal animals preparing to come out for the night, nothing. The last time he had seen another car was…

He couldn't remember having seen another car on this road.

Keep walking.

It was all he could do. That and breathe the air he was still gratefully receiving.

That conjured another thought. Could that be it? Was he part of some alien experiment? Had he been kidnapped and transported to a simulation? Was he even now on some experiment asteroid station strapped to a table and having images beamed into his head as part of the research for some invasion plan?

Too many stories.

He knew that was what was really conjuring these thoughts – having listened to all the tales he had been told. If he thought about it too much he could almost feel them starting to weigh heavily on his brain, bearing down like the black dog of depression, pressing harder and harder, testing the solidity of his emotional foundations. He knew there had to be a breaking point. The question was, would his mind reach it before he reached the end?

The surface beneath his feet felt strange. He looked down. While he had been lost in thought he had crossed the road and was now walking over the heath, moving away from the sea. Ahead lay a forest, the ancient oaks tipped gold by the unmoving sun.

It will still be dark in there.

But it wasn't, at least not dark enough for him to not find the path that led through to a broad patch of well-manicured ground. Up ahead lay another building, larger and grander than Maxwell Chantry's house, and before it, over to his left, a smaller one, built in a cruciform arrangement from what looked to be the same ancient weathered stone as the main building, which he presumed was his destination.

It turned out it wasn't, as he found himself headed toward the little church and, in particular, the tiny graveyard that lay before it. Even before he reached the teetering tombstones and the ragged ivy-encrusted place of worship they belonged to, Robert could hear the whispering in his head. He suddenly felt weary, to the extent that when he reached the graveyard he felt compelled to sit. The view afforded him, resplendent in that seemingly eternal sunset, took in the graves, the church, and the big building further ahead.

Because they were what the next story was about.

Forgive Us Not Our Trespasses

"You'll feel better once we get there."

Laura Martin shifted uncomfortably in the Audi's passenger seat and continued to stare out of the window. She knew her husband Alex would be expecting a smile in return for his failed attempt at a reassuring comment, but all she could manage right at that moment was a murmur of acknowledgement.

"And once we've checked into the room we can do whatever we want."

No, more likely it would be whatever *Alex* wanted, she thought, and she knew what that would mean. She dug her nails into her palms and tried to ignore the ache between her legs from where the doctor's instruments had been only an hour ago. It did little to distract her from the discomfort, so she pressed her cheek against the chill glass, and gazed at the rain-washed landscape, trying hard not to feel as battered and lonely as the few twisted stunted trees she could see dotting the sodden brown fields to her left.

It was two years since they had married, on a similarly grim November day. Alex had suggested they tie the knot in Dubai where he had found himself working for the summer months but Laura had insisted, more for her family than for her, that she wanted to get married in the UK. They could have waited another year, but Alex was keen to push things forward, as neither of them were getting any younger, he had reminded her; if they wanted to start a family they needed to get on with it.

Laura closed her eyes at the misery of the past year. She had never been that bothered about having children, and had never experienced the same maternal cravings as many of her friends. So when, after a year of following all the guidelines and advice from their GP about how best to go about conceiving, they had been met with a distinct lack of success, she had been quite happy to resign herself to the fact that a family was simply something she wasn't destined to either enjoy or endure.

But not Alex.

It had quickly become apparent that for her husband the most important thing was to sire offspring, and he had refused to let the matter lie, clutching at every possible piece of advice from the most specialised of textbooks to the health columns of the cheapest gossip magazines. He had undergone all the tests his specialist had to offer, and was found to be in perfect health. She could still remember with a shudder the day he had received all the results, clutching the piece of paper and telling her how his scans were all clear, how his sperm count wasn't just normal but high, and how the levels of male hormone in his bloodstream were so impressive it was wonder she wasn't pregnant just by him looking in her direction.

Which was the point at which his expression had almost imperceptibly hardened, at which he had taken a deep breath, and at which a new and worrying determination had entered his eye.

The problem, therefore, had to be with her.

Now she would need tests, scans, probes, instruments inserted to check everything. After all, she loved him didn't she? And she wanted children as desperately as he did.

Didn't she?

And because she loved him, or thought she did, and because the idea of children, while not setting her alight, did seem to be quite nice, she had agreed to attend the appointment Alex had organised with a specialist through his company's private health plan.

That had been the start of a protracted, distressing and at times agonising period which had finally come to an end this afternoon when Dr Michaelson, after a final examination 'just to make absolutely sure nothing had been missed' peered at them over the top of his half-moon spectacles and announced that Laura's tests were all normal as well.

"The next step would be to try assisted conception techniques," he had explained, describing how they would go about harvesting Laura's eggs to allow in vitro fertilisation and then reimplantation. "But that could turn out to be very expensive. If I were you I would just keep trying. But we're here if you need us."

So that was what their second wedding anniversary was going to consist of. Keeping trying. Admittedly keeping trying in the beautiful surroundings of Llanyrtyd Court Hotel in the depths of West Wales, but right now, and particularly after that last excruciating speculum examination, the last thing Laura wanted to do was have sex.

And Alex's hand on her thigh when she had failed to turn to look at him had left her in no doubt as to what was on his mind, even though he was doing his best to put her at ease.

As the car sped through the rain-washed country lanes to one of the most romantic country getaways in the country, Laura sat next to her successful young husband and realised she had never felt so miserable in her life.

Until they actually got there.

In finer weather, and with a sunnier disposition on her part, Laura figured Llanyrtyd Court Hotel probably looked every inch the elegant country retreat. However, with storm clouds looming both overhead and in her heart, the granite grey manor house they were approaching looked more like a prison than a place to relax. The Audi bumped and splashed its way along the narrow gravelled drive before Alex brought it to a halt in the one remaining parking space in front of the building.

"Are you all right?" her husband asked as he fished their cases from the boot.

Laura looked at the black clouds threatening to burst over the fir-tree rimmed horizon before lowering her gaze to the croquet lawn that, until the recent storms, had probably been immaculate. Now numerous pools of grey water half-drowned many of the croquet hoops, and the weather must have distorted them as well – a couple of the more distant ones seemed to have been crushed together and almost resembled twisted fingertips reaching heavenwards from the murk.

"I'm fine," she said, feeling anything but. It was only four o'clock but it was already getting dark. God, she hated this time of year.

The pretty young receptionist's name was Jemma and her flirtatious smile annoyed Laura as Alex was asked to sign the visitor's book.

"You're in room 133," she said with a cheeky wink. "That's the 'Angel' room. Lovely four poster that's got."

"Tried it out have you," said Alex in a tone he thought was charming but which Laura found distasteful in the extreme. The girl giggled but said nothing as she handed him the key. Alex passed it to Laura, who needed nudging to take it from him.

"I can't very well carry the bags and open the door, can I?" he said, the first hints of exasperation beginning to creep into his voice. Laura shrugged and led the way up the richly carpeted main staircase and along corridors where every other hanging was a mirror, each seemingly designed to make Laura's reflection look increasingly weary whenever she glanced at it.

By the time they reached their room she realised that she wasn't going to be able to tolerate any kind of physical contact just then. She was in too much pain, too much discomfort, and was just too upset. As soon as the key had been slid into the lock and the door pushed open she rushed past their elegant sleeping accommodation and into the bathroom where she slid the bolt across and slid to the floor behind the locked door, thankful to be alone for the first time in what felt like months.

"I'll put the bags by the window so you can unpack them later," she eventually heard Alex say. "You take your time and just come out when you're feeling better."

Which could quite conceivably be never she thought as she dabbed at her eyes with toilet tissue.

A shower, unpacking, and an argument managed to waste the hours until dinner. They sat in the hotel's restaurant in restrained silence, neither wishing to upset the other any further. To Laura's relief they were almost alone, and the only other couple there looked well into their seventies. She took as long as possible over her coffee but she needn't have worried – by then Alex had drunk too much to do anything other than pass out when they got back to the room. As she pulled the covers over herself and tried to ignore his snores, she wondered if the caffeine and her worries would permit her any sleep at all.

She was woken at 2am.

At first she thought Alex had been responsible. But as she lay there, her ears straining in the darkness to locate the source of the sound, she realised that it wasn't coming from beside her. For a moment the only noise was that of her husband's deep rhythmic breathing, and then it came again – a low groaning.

That was the only way she could describe it. No matter how hard she listened in the almost stifling atmosphere of the room, she found herself unable to decide if someone young or old had made the noise, or even if it was human. One thing, however, was certain.

It was coming from just outside their room.

Laura clutched the sheet and wondered what to do. Every single film she had ever seen where this happened had taught her that the one thing not to do under such circumstances was go and see what the matter is, as only trouble can lie that way. Trouble, or worse.

She told herself not to be so stupid. This was real life – not a film. Most likely it was some old sophisticate, the worse for too much crème de menthe, staggering back to his or her room, and from the sound of that bump it seemed unlikely they were going to make it.

A minute passed and there were no further noises, but rather than being comforted by this Laura realised she was now worrying that there may be someone lying drunk outside their bedroom. Or worse, they might have had a heart attack.

At that she pulled back the bedclothes. The staff were hardly likely to patrol the corridors regularly at night and it could be hours before anyone found whoever it was, by which time they could be dead.

She pulled on a black satin robe that offered little warmth but at least was ankle length and, taking one last look at her comatose husband, turned the handle and left the room.

There was no one in the corridor.

Not that it was very easy to see, thought Laura, as she peered either way into the gloom. They obviously turned the lights down at night, either to save power or out of some misguided sense that they were providing an authentic old-fashioned atmosphere.

She was about to go back into the room when she heard a shuffling noise further down to her right. She took a few steps and realised the carpet of the corridor was far chillier beneath her bare feet than that of the bedroom.

"Are you okay down there?"

Despite keeping her voice down, she was shocked at how her words broke the stillness. There was no reply from the end of the corridor.

But there was more shuffling.

Now the sensible part of her was saying that investigating the sound might be a silly idea, but the image of some poor old soul, perhaps in the throes of a seizure, remained prominent in her mind, and Laura knew she would never be able to forgive herself if they learned over breakfast that someone had died in the hotel during the night.

She took another couple of steps forward.

"Hello?"

Now she could see something, or at least she thought she could. Perhaps it had been there all along, but it was only now that her eyes had adjusted sufficiently to the insidious darkness for it to become apparent.

Crouched next to a coffin-shaped grandfather clock was a tiny figure.

Laura relaxed. Some little kid must have got lost in the winding passageways. What was the betting it wouldn't be able to remember its name or room number and that she would have to take it down to reception, snivelling and crying? If it would deign to come with her at all, of course.

"Are you lost?" she said, approaching the figure slowly and trying her best not to upset it even more.

The figure groaned again and lurched from its hiding place.

Laura frowned. Was the child hurt? Or perhaps disabled?

Still in silhouette it began to hobble towards her, its staggering gait resembling that of a malformed dwarf. It was only when the twisted humpbacked thing came into the light, spread its stumpy arms as far as its misshapen shoulders would allow, and a single word issued from its misaligned lips that she turned and ran, the shock of what she had seen causing her to lose all her reserve in an instant, her only desire to get as far away from the thing as possible.

"For the last time there is *nothing* there!"

Alex was irritable if woken in the middle of the night at the best of times, but being woken by a screaming tearful Laura had severely discomfited him, and her insistence that there was 'something horrible in the corridor' had only added to his sense of confusion as he had pulled open their bedroom door. He had spent a moment locating the light switch outside their room before taking a good look around. Apart from the curious items of antique furniture that often seem to make their home in such establishments (the grandfather clock Laura had seen being one such) he declared the passageway to be empty. Not that he was having any luck convincing Laura of that.

"I did see something!" she said from the safety of their room.

"Well whatever it was it's gone now," said Alex, coming back inside and joining her on the bed, seeming to take note as he did so that her knuckles were white from clutching the thick duvet cover. "And anyway, surely you mean someone rather than something?"

Laura knew from his tone that either way he didn't believe her.

"I don't know what it was," she said.

"Well, what did it look like?"

The last thing Laura wanted to do was describe it, but the damned thing was going to be in her thoughts all night anyway, so she did her best to tell him what she had seen.

"I don't know if it was a dwarf or a child or… something else," she said when she had finished.

"Well I don't know what you could possibly mean by something else," said Alex, "and I don't think you do either. You were probably dreaming."

Oh, that was just typical.

"You always have to come up with an explanation don't you?" she said with more of a sneer than she actually intended.

"Only because it's the most likely reason for what you think you saw," he said, taking her hand. "And, we've been through so much in the last few months that it's surprising you haven't had some sort of anxiety dream based around the thought of children long before now. Come on – the best thing you can do is get some sleep and try to forget about it."

As he switched off the light and resumed his enviably deep slumber, Laura marvelled at how some people were able to make the most difficult thing in the world sound like the simplest of tasks. But of course she hadn't told him the whole story. She had been about to but his dismissal of the events had led her to think he was hardly likely to be more believing if she delivered the final, and most terrifying, part of her tale.

Just before she had slammed the bedroom door shut the thing had spoken to her.

Laura clutched the sheet and wiped away tears as the word came to her again now, uttered in that pained, guttural monotone, pleading and at the same time filled with menace. She knew her tears were partly in frustration at Alex's disbelief and partly because she was still in a state of shock. But most of all she knew they were tears of terror. Because as she had escaped back to the relative safety of their bedroom she knew the thing had wanted to come with her, that it had wanted her to respond to the attempted embrace of those outstretched stumpy arms, that it had wanted her to take it with her. All because of that one word.

"Mummy."

"Sorry about last night."

Laura managed a weak smile across the breakfast table the next morning as her husband did his best to croak an apology. She couldn't be angry with Alex, looking so grey from his hangover, especially as she had really been the one who started things yesterday. Of course the fact that he had felt too ill to make any advances on her this morning had probably added to her sense of relief more than she realised.

"That's okay," she said, carefully avoiding the marmalade so she could take his hand. "Let's go for a walk this morning, shall we? You look as if you could do with some air."

It had rained again during the night but the sun was out, meaning that at least they could see where the worst patches of mud were as they strolled. The grounds were extensive, and the house was well out of sight when Alex pointed ahead of them and said,

"Is that a church?"

Laura thought it unlikely, but it was difficult to think what else the squat grey tower poking above the trees ahead of them could belong to.

"Sometimes these places had a church on the grounds for the family and the staff," she said. "But if it is one it's probably not used now."

Sure enough, as they made their way through the glade of skeletal trees, they soon came upon a crumbling stone building, its roof intact but at the point of caving in. A thick growth of green mildew over the windows made it difficult to work out what the images rendered by the stained glass in the weathered stone were actually meant to depict.

"You'd think someone would try and clean them," said Alex with a grimace.

Laura suppressed a shudder.

"Maybe they prefer to keep whatever's in the glass covered up," she said, and then immediately wished she hadn't. She ignored her husband's perplexed look and tried the heavy iron ring set into the door, fully expecting it not to budge. It wasn't exactly easy, but with a little persuasion it turned and the door opened a little, but not much. No matter how much Laura pushed the gap refused to widen and she realised they would have to squeeze through to get inside. She let go of the handle to find her hand was covered with rusty brown powder.

"Stop thinking it's blood," said Alex, handing her his handkerchief, "because I know you are."

She remained silent as she rubbed what was probably just the dirt of years from her fingertips, refusing to rise to his taunting. Instead, despite his barked protestations, she slipped through the gap in the open doorway, and was inside before he had a chance to stop her.

The damp filth clotting the windows leant the darkened church interior an eerie green glow, and Laura was glad that when Alex grudgingly followed he didn't close the door behind them, or they would have had difficulty finding their way around.

The pews were still there, although most were in far too great a state of disrepair to support a person's weight. Laura reckoned that, when it was in use, the tiny church could have sat around twenty in all, although today any expectant congregation would have found itself facing a crumbling pulpit whose wooden steps had long since disintegrated. The altar was the simplest of stone slabs at the front of the building, and any attempts at decoration had either long since been removed or eaten away.

They were about to leave when a beam of sunlight found its way through a gap in the mossy growth covering the window and illuminated the left hand wall. So, Laura thought, the church hadn't been entirely stripped of its ecclesiastical décor. Here was the Lord's Prayer, or rather the Pater Noster, the Latin text painted in an elegant gold script several inches high on a narrow panel of black wood that reached to the ceiling.

"Now that's interesting," said Alex, his face looking something other than pissed off for the first time that morning.

"Go on then," said Laura as he failed to elucidate. "What's grabbed your attention?"

"The lapsed Catholic in me, I'm afraid." He pointed to the sixth line down. " '*Et non dimitte nobis debita nostra*'. That's not right."

"Well you've lost me," she said. "We didn't do Latin at my comprehensive in Salford."

"They've put that 'non' in by mistake. What's up there reads 'Forgive us *not* our trespasses'. You would have thought someone would have spotted that."

"True," Laura nodded. "Especially if you did. Is any of the rest of it different?"

Alex shook his head.

"Difficult to tell, but I don't think so."

He stepped forward to take a closer look. There was a heavy rattling as he almost fell. He cursed, leaning heavily against the nearest pew before looking down to see what had tripped him up. It was so dark that before the phrase 'there might be rats and spiders' had a chance to issue from Laura's lips he was feeling about on the floor. There was more rattling as Alex picked up the trophy that he turned to proudly present to her.

It was a length of rusted steel chain – the kind that might be used to keep heavy gates securely locked. Only this was much longer and was interrupted at regular intervals along its length by steel rings the width of a tennis ball.

"Looks like they had trouble getting people to stay and listen to the sermons," said Alex with a grin, yanking on the chain to reveal that it had been secured at intervals to the back of the pew in front of him.

"Alex put it down," said Laura. "That's not funny."

"I can't think what else this sort of thing might have been used for," he said. "Don't they look like shackles to you?"

She jumped as the crash they made when he dropped them reverberated throughout the building.

"And look at the marks here," he said, pointing to a set of regular gouges in the wood of the pew next to him. "Doesn't that look as if someone has tried to escape? Were they were so desperate to get out of here it was a case of either claw their way to freedom or die of boredom?"

No, she thought. Not boredom. Whatever those scratches might mean she was sure they weren't made by anyone who was bored.

"We should get out of here," she said, grabbing his arm.

"I did try to tell you we shouldn't have come in here in the first place," he said as she pulled him to the exit. What little sunlight there was vanished as they squeezed their way out, leaving Laura desperately glad that they were out of there.

It wasn't until they were outside that she realised how foetid the atmosphere had been in the church, and she was still taking deep gulping breaths of clean air when Alex called out,

"It's got a funny graveyard as well!"

She followed the sound of his voice, coming round the side of the building to find him leaning against one side of a rectangular enclosure fashioned from now rusting ironwork. Within, set at regular intervals in ground as unkempt and overgrown as that outside it, stood a set of tiny headstones.

"Graves of the family who lived here, presumably," said Alex, as Laura tried to make out the names rendered in Gothic lettering on the lichen-spattered grey stone. The rickety gate fell inwards with a crash at her touch.

"For God's sake be careful!" he hissed. "We don't want to be paying for any damages."

"'Margaret Bridsoe, a tiny gift from God now returned – aged four years'," she read before moving to the next. "'Samuel Bridsoe, taken before his time – aged six years'," said the next.

Alex tried to tell her to stop, but it was no use. It didn't take long for Laura to read every stone before looking at him with an expression that suggested she had a worse hangover than he did.

"There must be twenty children buried here," she said. "None of them over the age of six. Some of them died almost as soon as they were born. And according to the inscriptions they're all from the same family."

"Maybe it was yellow fever or something like that," said Alex. "What are the dates?"

"There aren't any," she replied. "Just a name and an age and the kind of 'It was God's will' type of comment that I'm amazed the parents could stand to keep having inscribed."

"At least it clears up that this must have been the family's church," said Alex, looking back at the squat stone building. With the glare of the sunlight gleaming off it the building almost seemed to be defying his gaze. "I suppose it wasn't uncommon for very rich types to have a church built in the grounds of their stately home so that their spiritual needs were taken care of."

"Doesn't look as if it did them much good, does it?" said Laura, wiping away a tear as she couldn't help but think about all that false hope, all that endured suffering that must have come from seeing child after child die. And of what? She would probably never know. And she was actually quite glad about that.

*

That night she was torn from her slumber once more, only this time it wasn't a sound that was responsible for the burning, tearing sensation deep in her throat that had her spluttering and pushing away the bedclothes in an attempt to relieve the awful constriction clawing at her lungs.

This time it was an odour.

No, she thought as she sat up in bed, staring in disbelief at her husband's still-sleeping form, not an odour. The overpowering acrid stench that had assailed her nostrils had faded a little now, but it was still there, stinging her mucous membranes and making her bite back the nausea. It was a stink she could remember only vaguely, when as a little girl she had, for a short time, attended a huge Victorian primary school where the wooden-floored corridors had received a daily rinsing with carbolic. That was what had woken her – that overpoweringly disinfectant smell that reminded her of being very small and very afraid.

And she realised she was just as afraid now.

She pulled back the bedclothes, coughing again to rid herself of the irritation that lingered at the back of her throat, and made her way to the door. She took one last look back at Alex before opening it.

The smell was much worse in the corridor, but that wasn't what caused an icy chill to grip her deep inside.

Her surroundings had completely altered.

Rather than the well-furnished passageway of the night before, Laura found herself standing on bare wooden floor tiles. The walls were painted a pale grey and were devoid of decoration. The light was just as dim as when she had ventured out previously, but now, rather than coming from ornate faux Victorian replicas, it emanated from bare cobweb-encrusted and somehow more genuine-looking gas lamps set at regular intervals in the ceiling. Laura raised her hand to her mouth to stop herself from screaming, and tried to get back into the bedroom.

The door was locked.

That was ridiculous! The bloody thing used a mortise lock and the key was on the dressing table. Even if Alex had woken in the short time she had been out here he wouldn't have been able to make it over there and then to the door and besides, why would he? Despite that, she raised a fist to hammer on the door.

Which was now made of reinforced steel.

She had to be still asleep, she thought. That was the only explanation for what was happening. All she had to do was concentrate and she would wake up.

There came a scream from the far end of the corridor.

Laura clutched her nightgown around her and cowered by the door that no longer led to safety. What should she do? Even if this was a dream, didn't they say that if you died in a dream you died in real life? She closed her eyes tightly and willed herself to wake up.

There was another scream.

Followed by voices.

The clearer of the two was that of a man whose authoritative tone suggested he was in charge of what was taking place, and he was answered by a woman who sounded no less stern. Both were far enough away that when Laura opened her eyes and realised that for now there was to be no escape from this particularly vivid fantasy, she began to pad down the corridor towards them.

She was surprised when the corridor opened onto a landing exactly the same way as it did in the hotel. The balcony with mahogany railings was the same too, and as she crouched behind them, Laura was able to view what was happening downstairs.

Or rather, what had just finished happening, as a nurse wheeled a whimpering figure away into the darkness. She presumed the poor individual had just been subjected to treatment on the operating table that dominated the harshly lit area. Laura barely had time to take in the black and white chequered floor tiles, exactly the same as the hotel's, the plethora of antiquated surgical equipment laid out on trolleys of gleaming steel, and of course the operating table itself, the one that looked as if it had been transported from another era, before a deep voice boomed from the shadows.

"Just one more tonight, I think, and then we shall be done."

Laura edged a little closer to the top of the stairs to see an imposing-looking man in a three-quarter length Victorian frock coat of emerald velvet, the front of which had been protected from the man's recent activity by an apron stained with streaks of red. He was currently washing the blood from his hands in an earthenware bowl, the water within it freshly poured from the steaming jug close by. He dried his hands with a towel and moved the apron aside to consult a gold pocket watch.

"Did you say one more, Doctor?"

The nurse had returned and looked as severe, if not more so, than the surgeon, who snapped the pocket watch closed and gave her a brisk nod.

"It is late," he said, "but there is so much work for us still to do, and even though we may tire at times, our bodies may ache and our minds grow weary, we know that our souls may rest easy in the knowledge that we are doing our Lord's work. Bring one more."

Laura's heart skipped a beat as the nurse nodded and made for the staircase.

"Not one of *those* cases," said the surgeon. The nurse stopped. "Something less challenging. It is after all past midnight and I am tired. Fetch something from the rooms at the rear."

Laura allowed herself to breathe again as the nurse walked off in the direction where the hotel's dining room would one day be, and turned her attention back to the man in the frock coat.

She couldn't see what colour his eyes were, but they glittered as they examined the clean instruments that had been laid out for his last case of the night. His lean face was a study in concentration as he threaded three sets of sutures onto fresh needles, and the operating light gleamed off his head of curling black hair as he turned away from her to lay a fresh sterile sheet on the operating table. What kind of patient was going to be brought in here next, Laura wondered. Judging by the man's dress she was watching a scene from the nineteenth century, and from what she could remember there weren't many operations that could be performed because anaesthetic agents were yet to be invented. The most they might be able to manage would be lancing an abscess.

Or an amputation.

Without anaesthetic.

As she heard two sets of footsteps approaching, Laura suddenly realised she had no wish to watch what was about to take place, but now she was unable to tear herself away. She gripped the wooden balcony rail in horror as the last kind of patient she had expected to see in a place like this was brought in.

The little girl couldn't have been more than four years old and walked with a pronounced limp. A grey cloth had been tied around her eyes, presumably so that the sight of the operating theatre equipment wouldn't distress her. The nurse helped her onto the table where the child waited surprisingly patiently as the surgeon dripped something onto a square of white muslin.

"Am I really going to see an angel?" the little girl said as the doctor approached her, the medicated swab gripped in his now gloved right hand.

"You might do," said the nurse in what was probably the kindest voice she could manage. "You might see all kinds of things if you're very, very good."

The little girl opened her mouth again, but if she did say anything else, the sound was muffled as the swab was held over her face until she stopped struggling.

"Antalgic gait left lower limb," said the surgeon as the nurse painstakingly wrote his dictation in a large leather-bound ledger, "caused by varus deformity of the hip. Incision to be made over the origin of the adductor magnus muscle."

Laura had presumed that no anaesthetic would be used for the operation, and as the first incision was made she had to press her hands over her ears as she realised that she had been right.

It made a change for Alex to be awake before her, even if it was because he was shaking her to stop her screaming.

"You'll wake everyone in the hotel," he hissed.

She looked over at the clock before pulling herself free from his arms and getting out of bed.

"Now where are you going?" he asked.

"It's nearly dawn and I can't sleep," she said, searching through her clothes.

"Well I don't feel that tired either," said Alex in a tone that made her insides curdle. "So why don't you come back here and we can find some other way to keep ourselves occupied?"

"I had a horrible dream, Alex," she said by way of response. "A horrible… nightmare, and I need to clear my head." She began pulling on a pair of black woollen leggings. "You go back to sleep and I'll see you at breakfast."

She saw his face assume the expression that always precluded a tirade, but she never heard the outburst that followed as she had already shut the door behind her and was making her way down the corridor.

The nice normal hotel corridor.

Laura left the building making as little noise as possible. She stood at the top of the flight of stone steps that led down to the car park and took a few deep breaths of chilled air. The first light of dawn was beginning to creep across the frosted winter landscape, the early morning rays the same colour red as –

She stopped herself. The same colour as what, exactly? As the blood of a child she had seen in a dream? Because that was all it had been, she assured herself. A horrible anxiety dream, brought on by all those tests, all that worry, and most of all by Alex's wearing persistence, never failing to remind her that the next step in their life plan was for them to have children and that she would be the one to blame if they didn't.

Briefly, she wished she still smoked. A cigarette would feel wonderful here, amidst the calm of early morning. She was glad she didn't have any with her and to distract herself still further she skipped down the steps and, taking her heavy black overcoat from the car, set off for an early morning walk.

She wasn't surprised when her wanderings took her back to the church. The sunlight glittered off the frosted gravestones as she made her way between them, pointedly ignoring the route that led to the garden of dead children. This time the door to the church was locked, not that she had really wanted to go back inside anyway. She sat on one of the flat, broad stone markers, hugged her knees, and began to rock gently back and forth. The sound of footsteps on gravel caused her to look up and for the first time since she had come to the hotel she began to question her sanity.

There were people in the child cemetery.

Mourners

In Victorian dress.

The priest concluded the graveside ceremony and the tiny coffin was lowered into the earthen pit. As the entourage began to leave Laura could do nothing but sit, frozen, on the tombstone, while a procession from another age passed her by. As she exhaled as quietly as she could, her warm moist breath steaming in front of her, she realised she couldn't see the breath of any of the people passing in front of her.

When they were almost past, the final mourner, a woman, turned and looked at her. Laura recognised the nurse she had seen last night and hoped against hope that the woman was looking through rather than at her.

"We see you, you know."

The words, and the realisation that accompanied them, chilled her to the bone and turned her legs to water. Even though her brain was telling her this wasn't real, and her body was telling her to run from that terrible place, she found herself unable to move as she regarded this ghost woman from another age who was now talking to her.

"We see you," she said, "and we have a use for you. Both of you."

Laura wanted to speak, but the words caught in her throat. All she managed was a strangled croak as the nurse turned away to catch up with the procession as it made its way down the church path, out through the lychgate, and vanished into the mist of the forest beyond.

"For Christ's sake Alex we *have* to leave!"

"Because you had a funny dream? Because you went for a walk this morning at some ridiculous bloody hour and had a hallucination? Which isn't at all surprising considering how little sleep you've been having recently. For God's sake, Laura, listen to yourself! We've been planning this weekend for ages. We've been looking forward to it for ages."

Laura shook her head and bit down heavily on her right thumbnail.

"*You* have you mean."

Her response only made him worse.

"Well you should have been as well," he said, "and Christ knows why you haven't. This place costs a fortune to stay in, you know. And it's meant to be one of the most romantic spots in the country."

"Why, Alex?" she said.

"I'm sorry?"

"*Why* is it meant to be one of the most romantic spots in the country? Because the hotel's website said so? Because your friends said so? Or because you really and truly feel like that in spite of the fact that it must have been bloody obvious to you that I've been feeling fucking miserable ever since I got in the car, ever since I got out of that bloody clinic where they shoved God knows what instruments into me."

"So that we can have a child!" he said, his face creasing with either anger or frustration, she couldn't tell which. "My God, have you lost focus of that?"

"No, Alex. No I haven't. But this weekend isn't about us at all. It's about you and what *you* want. And since we've got here you've never once thought to ask me or consult me or wonder even for one second if perhaps, just perhaps, I might not want the same things as you."

"But we talked about this!" he said, definitely angry now. "We talked about it over a year ago!"

"Yes, and we haven't talked about it since then! Even though I've been unhappy. Even though it's been obvious to my friends, to my family, to everyone who knows me, everyone around me except the person who's the closest to me. Sometimes I don't know why I even bother trying to talk to you!" she screamed.

"I don't know why I even bother trying to listen!" was his response, looking as though he was close to the end of his tether. It was only when he reached to her for consolation and she pulled away that she realised she was seeing him properly lose his temper for the very first time. Later she was sure he would swear (to himself if no one else) that he never intended what happened next, that it was the combination of anger and pent up passion that resulted in his grabbing her arm and dragging her to the bed, not caring whether the door was locked or not as he pushed her face into the pillow to muffle her cries.

It didn't hurt as much as her visit to the doctors.

But it nearly did.

It was dark when she finally had the strength to pull herself from the bed. Finding herself alone she frowned. Had Alex been so violent with her that he had succeeded in knocking her out? She reached across to her alarm clock and hit the display button. The ice blue digits read back nonsense, and her wristwatch seemed to have stopped as well. She dragged herself into the bathroom, switched on the light and got into the shower, remembering to lock the door and prop a chair against it in case Alex returned.

She was under the spray for all of thirty seconds before what began as moans of physical discomfort quickly became screams of anger and frustrated misery, and by the time she was out she had resolved to get out of this place and as far away from Alex as possible. The car keys were gone but that didn't matter – she'd get the receptionist to phone a taxi that could take her to the railway station. She started throwing things into a case before she realised she didn't want to take anything with her, certainly nothing that reminded her that they had stayed here. In the end she pulled on some warm clothes, made sure she had her bag with her, and opened the door to the hotel room.

From which she found herself walking into another world.

It was a world she had seen before, but the last time she had only been half awake, had been able to put what she had seen down to a dream, a hallucination brought on by anxiety and lack of sleep. Now she had never felt more awake, and the cold bare prison corridor in which she was standing was as real as the pain she could still feel inside herself.

She made her way down the passageway and onto the landing as before. This time the floor below was empty, cleared of the surgical equipment she had seen being used last time. Her footsteps made little sound on the luxurious thick pile carper was she quickly descended the stairs, intending to make for the front door just ahead of her.

It was locked.

And now she could hear voices.

Laura made for the nearest room and almost sighed with relief when the heavy mahogany door swung open to reveal an empty study, dimly lit. She closed the door behind her and then listened to see which way the voices would go, all the while scanning the room for a possible hiding place.

The voices, presumably that of the couple she had seen last night, came closer. Laura's heart was beating so loudly that when they passed the study she could hardly believe they hadn't heard her. She waited until they had receded completely before relaxing.

She was about to try the door handle when something on the broad leather-topped desk caught her eye. It was not so much the subject matter of the flyer as the gleeful, self-righteous tone that disturbed her.

'The Abominations of God', ran the headline, followed by the equally salubrious 'Those little children who, through no fault of their own, will never enter Heaven on account of their Gross and Abnormal deformities may be offered a second chance by their Maker in the form of God's Blessed Servant and Surgeon Mr James Bridsoe. The good people of the town of (this was left blank) are hereby heartily encouraged to assist him in doing the Lord's work by placing into his care all infants who might be considered Unfit and Unseemly for Normal Life'.

The journal beneath it seemed to set out the twisted philosophy of the presumed owner of the house. Laura was too terrified to read much of it, but gathered that Mr Bridsoe believed that children born deformed were a 'sin against God' and therefore he had set out to encourage the delivery of such children into his hands that 'guided by my Lord' he might 'correct them'. This was horrible enough, but it was the final paragraph that made her shudder, the one that described what happened to the failures, the ones whom Bridsoe had presumably been unable to cure. It sounded as if there had been many, and their fate had all been the same – to be locked in the cellar to have their sin 'beaten out of them' until they achieved redemption so that they 'might be buried in the acreage of the property devoted to that purpose'.

And once a week, she realised, the ones who were still alive must have been dragged across to the church and chained to their seats while they were encouraged to recite the litany she and Alex had read on the wall – the specially rewritten Lord's Prayer penned by Bridsoe.

If she had left the room at that point then that was probably all she would have thought, but the sheer terror she still felt at the prospect of leaving the study made her turn to the leather-bound volume sitting on the desk.

It was the ledger she had seen the nurse writing in the other night.

As she turned the pages and viewed the painstaking line diagrams that had been reproduced within its thick vellum pages her stomach turned over. These didn't look like surgical procedures designed to cure anybody.

She didn't want to see any more, but she was unable to stop herself. The parade of grotesque images ended with the last operation to which she had been witness – a little girl whose thigh muscle had somehow been detached from her hip and reconnected much higher on her body so that she could now only walk with a twisted, crouching gait. Mr James Bridsoe hadn't been trying to cure any of those children at all, she realised as she stifled a gag of nausea at the back of her throat.

He had been trying to make them worse.

There was another noise outside the door, one so guttural and grating that Laura nearly vomited at the sound. The heavy slithering noise that followed suggested that whatever it was, it was now moving away from her.

And that it was huge.

Laura ran her fingers through her hair and tried to think. How many disabled children had Bridsoe managed to deform even further? Shortening bones, rotating flaps of skin, moving organs? And to what end? What kind of man had the temerity to rewrite the Lord's Prayer? To create an actual hell in the depths of this terrible place and people it with twisted, abhorrent versions of humanity? Was he some kind of religious lunatic who believed that redemption was only possible through extreme suffering?

She was about to reach for the door handle when she felt a barbed hook around her neck and she fell backwards into something soft. She struggled to get up, but with every movement she made she suddenly felt much weaker.

God, I'm bleeding, she thought. Something's cut me badly and I'm bleeding and this is the end.

But that was not the plan at all.

When she woke the brightness of the light being shone in her face made her shut her eyes tight. The chill of the table beneath the naked skin of her back made her realise she'd been stripped of her clothes. The two strong leather straps belted across her torso and legs made her attempts to rise impossible. She tried to look from side to side, but her head felt as if it was in the grip of a metal vice.

"Your husband was far more cooperative," said Bridsoe as his face came into view. "But then he always was the one who wanted children, wasn't he? At almost any price."

"What do you want?" Laura said. She was surprised to find she wasn't gagged.

"My dear girl, it is not so much what I want as what the children… need," he said, glancing around him.

Now, from all the corners of the room, as if in their short lives they had been anticipating this one event, they began to come forward. Those tiny helpless individuals who had been 'forsaken by the Lord', crawled on what remained of their amputated stumps, leaving trails of blood and other secretions from wounds that had never healed. Some emitted gurgling moans from what remained of their mouths; other could manage little more than a strangled cry from the gaping holes in their throats. Laura closed her eyes again but it was the noises they made, the horrible, crawling, squawking sounds, that made her realise she was surrounded by them.

"Those whom the Lord has rejected need a mother until they achieve their redemption," Bridsoe said, swabbing the soft skin of Laura's belly with surgical alcohol before taking a scalpel from amongst the collection of glittering instruments laid out beside him.

"You don't need to cut me for that," she said.

"My dear girl, that's not the purpose of this operation," he said.

There was a croak of anticipation from the shadows, from the grunting swollen thing that lurked in the darkness.

"The father I have created for them has been without a wife for far too long."

The Road Not Taken

The graves were quiet now, the church silent. If they were even the places where the story had come from. Now everything was back to the way it was before Robert had experienced the story.

Or was it?

He blinked. Wasn't the sun that little bit lower? Touching the horizon now, rather than hovering just above it? The sky was different, too. It was darker, a deeper shade of violet, the bronze hue leant it by the setting sun now almost entirely gone. As Robert got to his feet it faded completely as, suddenly, the sun wasn't there any more.

It was almost like being blinded. One moment Robert was standing in the graveyard, the gently descending grassy slope that led to what must be the hotel ahead of him, the next he was plunged into darkness.

Total darkness.

Robert blinked and raised his right hand.

Nothing.

He looked up, then down, then from side to side.

Still nothing.

He took a step forward. Whatever lay beneath his feet felt firm.

Another step. The same.

Was this it? The end? Was this void of nothingness his final destination? His building panic was tempered with a strange feeling of relief, as if a part of him had almost expected this. As he moved forward there was no suggestion he was about to plummet to some unfathomed eternal depths.

And so he kept going. If he was destined to spend the rest of his existence in this place at least he was going to keep fit. He had no idea why he should be treating his situation with such levity, but the feeling that he had received his fill of stories had caused a change within him. Whereas before his mind had felt almost hungry, as if no matter how much he ate he would never feel full, now his brain felt satiated, full but not overfilled. He could feel each of the stories inside his head, and knew that he only needed to think of one and it would be played out for him, in all its detail, in the blink of one of the eyes he presumed were still in his head. But it was even more than that. He could see all the stories, feel them all happening at once. There was no sense of confusion, no feeling of there being an assault on his senses. Instead, and despite having been deprived of almost any kind of sensory input, Robert had never felt more alive, more stimulated, and it was all due to the journey that he felt sure was now reaching its end. Perhaps this was even part of it, a final demonstration that he no longer needed the outside world to make him happy, or even to survive. Every emotion, every feeling, could be experienced inside his head.

As if to say this was the lesson he was supposed to learn, the lights came back on.

Only very small lights, and only far in the distance. As Robert squinted, he realised they were coming from the hotel. Gradually his surroundings reconstituted themselves, all a shade of the deep purple of a summer's night. Now he could feel grass beneath his feet once more. He looked up and saw stars. He didn't recognise their configurations, and the crescent moon that was slowly rising seemed to be slightly the wrong shape. He accepted it all unquestioningly, just as he knew that if he tried to turn around or stray from the path he would most likely be met with the same kind of resistance he had encountered out on the heathland. Not that he would have changed direction now, not for all the rewards that might be offered him. The building ahead held the answer, and nothing was going to prevent him from finding it.

The doors to the hotel swung inwards as he approached. His shoes made no sound as he ascended the stone steps, slowly, and with little effort, almost as if he was being lifted up them. Despite none of the light bulbs in the heavy overhanging chandelier being on, the entrance foyer was lit a dull crimson. Doors to his left and right were not only shut but heavy, almost cartoon-like bolts had been drawn across to emphasise that they were not the way he was meant to go.

That lay straight ahead.

The dining room was immense and beautiful and lit in gold. Again, the actual source of light remained a mystery, as the numerous lamps, bulbs and chandeliers remained unlit but glowed nevertheless in the reflected light that suffused everything. Three rows of refectory tables, laid parallel to each another and at right angles to the doorway, stretched to the huge bay windows far in the distance. In the huge fireplace to his left, logs burned yet yielded no smoke. To his right an immense mirror added size to a room that did not need it, reflecting Robert, the lights, fireplace, and the tables.

But not what lay upon the tables.

Here was what caused Robert to draw breath. Despite the opulent luxury of his surroundings, despite the gilt-veined marble that covered the walls, the curtains of rich indigo that mantled the windows, the exotic carpets that hugged the floors, it was what was on those long refectory tables that took all of Robert's attention.

Bodies.

They had been laid out head to toe, the heads pointing towards the entrance in which Robert was standing, the scalp of the each just inches away from the shoes of the one preceding it. Each was neatly attired and arranged with their hands clasped over their chest. Robert held onto the door post for support. Were they dead? Or just sleeping? As far as he could tell all their eyes were closed. If they were no longer alive shouldn't they have sheets over them? Or at least over their faces? He had no wish to get any closer but something made him take one step, then another, then another, until he was standing at the head end of the row of refectory tables on the left. His hand strayed to the black tablecloth on which the bodies lay. It was slippery, like silk or satin. Before he knew what he was doing his fingertips had brushed the forehead of the body of the man lying there.

The skin was like ice.

Robert snatched his hand away. How many bodies were there here? Fifteen? Sixteen?

"Actually it's twenty one. A number of ancient power that helps ensures the protection of their souls."

There was a person standing at the entrance to the dining room. No matter how Robert squinted or changed the angle at which he looked at them, he found it difficult to tell if it was a man or a woman. This was less to do with any specific features and more because those features kept changing. As the shimmering shape shifted through a variety of guises Robert realised he knew some of them.

No. All of them.

It was Mr Jeavons, the man who had told him the story about the golf course. It was Stokes the Newport art dealer. When Robert blinked he found himself looking at Dr Harrison, who had tried to point him in the right direction. Then he saw the landlord of The Winterman's

Arms, and a couple of the man's patrons, too. The figure was all of them and none of them. It held the important aspects of each and yet was more than just the sum of those parts. It regarded him with an earthy silence, waiting for him to speak. It was a moment before he could find the words.

"You're the one who brought me here."

"Many things have brought you here." Its voice was a mixture, too, the different sounds of all those different people fading in and out, intertwining with the mellifluous, otherworldly tone of whatever this being really was. "But none were as strong an influence as you yourself have been."

"Me?" Even as he said the word Robert knew it to be true. All Dr Harrison had said was that he should go where he felt he ought to.

"That's right." Could the being read his thoughts, too? "So much of it was up to you, and I'm so pleased. You did such a good job, you really should be proud of yourself."

Should he? After all, what had he actually achieved? Suddenly, a terrible thought struck him.

"No." The figure was shaking its head. "You haven't been in a psychiatric institution undergoing some form of deep hypnosis therapy and I'm not the doctor who's here to bring you out of it." Immediately Robert thought of something else. "And you're not dead, either."

"What, then? Where am I? Why am I here?"

The figure took a step forward. "You are at the crossroads, where life and death intersect. The point at which the recently deceased stop being trapped in this world and are given the strength to move on."

Oh very clever. "So I'm not dead but I'm dying, is that it?"

"Far from it. You are as alive as when you began this journey of yours." The figure pointed behind him. "They are the ones who are dead."

"Who are they?"

"Why don't you find out for yourself?"

Robert didn't want to, but now he found he couldn't help himself as he approached one of the tables, or rather approached one of the bodies lying on one of the tables. With a trembling hand he lifted the sheet.

The sightless eyes of William Martin, organist of Llanroath village, transported to another realm by things unknown, stared back at him.

"But he…"

"Has been waiting here for you. As have they all."

Next to Martin were two of the hikers who had met their end in the Welsh mountains. On the table parallel to theirs lay the body of Gemma Parkyn, who had succumbed to a terrible fate at the hands of Marion Morgan and her living dead son.

One by one he looked and one by one he recognised all of them. People that until now he had only seen in his imagination.

"And they look exactly like you expected, don't they?"

Robert replaced the last sheet and turned to the figure. "I still don't understand why I'm here."

"It's not to fill any vacant space on one of these tables if that's what you're thinking. Besides, there isn't one. As I said, the number twenty one is important for the preservation of their souls and any more would affect the ritual."

"Sacrifice?"

The figure chuckled at that. "Goodness me, no. Tell me, Robert, what do you think is important to ensure safe passage to the afterlife?"

He had no idea. "Living a good life to start off with?"

The figure nodded but that obviously wasn't the required answer. "True, but despite all our best efforts and our very best intentions, sometimes we make mistakes, perhaps through no fault of our own. Nevertheless, those mistake, those errors of judgement and the effects they have on others, can quickly build up. The chains can weigh heavy, so heavy that they prevent the right path being taken at the crossroads. Do you understand what I'm talking about?"

"You mean sin, don't you?"

"That's a very old-fashioned word for it but yes." The figure sounded pleased. "I'm so glad you figured it out for yourself. Before any of the individuals can move on in their journey, they need to be relieved of the burden that is weighing them down. That is where you come in."

"To hear their stories, you mean?"

"Partly. To use another old fashioned term those, if you like, have been their confessions. But they still require absolution."

"I'm not a priest."

"No. But you are able to offer them salvation."

The figure pointed over Robert's shoulder once more and he turned, to discover that the room had changed. The bodies were still there, but now the sheets had been removed, the subjects of the stories he had been told revealed.

And not just the subjects.

Placed neatly and meticulously on the chest of each body were a number of blurred objects. As Robert stared so they began to come into focus.

Food.

Each corpse in the room had the constituents of a small meal arranged upon it. Not much – some bread, a little meat, maybe an item or two of fruit.

"Just enough to represent their chains," the figure said.

"I still don't understand," said Robert. "Is this some sort of feast for the dead?"

"The feast is for you, Robert. To free the dead. To allow them to take the correct path on the crossroads where we now stand."

"You mean I have to…" Realisation had dawned. "But I don't know if I can…"

"You can, and you will. For that has been your purpose all along. What you were born for, if you like."

Robert found he could not take his eyes from the bizarre tableau laid out before him. "But what about me?"

The reply came from behind him. "You are the Sin Eater, destined to take the road less travelled, the one that, when you are finished here, will take you to where you are needed most. To hear more stories, more confessions and, in time, when you have heard enough, to return here to send more souls on their way."

He had known. Of course he had known, because he had done this before, so many times. The journey was not about him, it was about everyone else – the lives he learned about on the way. And as he was granted that single moment of clarity it was felt he deserved at this point in his allotted task, Robert, or whatever his name might have been before or would be after this, sat down at the first table.

He took one look behind him, just to check the figure had gone, before he started to eat.

Grim, Grim My Valley Now

Afterword & Story Notes

In 1939 Richard Dafydd Vivian Llewellyn Lloyd, better known as Richard Llewellyn, wrote *How Green Was My Valley*, a novel set during the reign of Queen Victoria about a mining family in South Wales. A Hollywood movie version appeared in 1941, directed by John Ford, and it was adapted for television by the BBC in 1960 and 1975.

The 1975 version is the one I remember.

Well, remember isn't quite right. I was only eight at the time & my staple television entertainments back then consisted of *Dr Who, The Six Million Dollar Man* and *Space: 1999*, but I remember my parents avidly watching How *Green Was My Valley* because it was set in Wales (true) starred Welsh actors (including hard drinking, hard-smoking Stanley Baker) and had been written by a Welshman (although later evidence has suggested this Mr Llewellyn wasn't Welsh at all).

My parents are Welsh.

Which means, of course, that so am I.

I was brought up in a household where things that were Welsh were, by definition, faultless. It will not surprise you to learn that we had a cupboard full of Tom Jones records as, I suspect, did many of the houses in our street and likely our town. Richard Burton was a hero, Ryan and Ronnie (look them up) were amongst the best comedians that ever lived, and if you didn't know all the words to the national anthem in Welsh you risked being burned at the stake whenever March 1st (St David's Day) came around, whenever Wales were playing rugby, or whenever Mrs Jones the school music teacher who walked with a limp and always had her tongue physically thrust firmly into her cheek when she dealt out punishment decided to put the second form at my junior school through its paces.

When I was young I always had a bit of trouble consolidating my 'Welshness', and that's a major reason why this book exists. I never had much of a Welsh accent and when I lost that (I suspect Christopher Lee and Peter Cushing were to blame) I was surprised to find how often I was considered English by my countrymen.

In Wales, this is not a good thing.

My lack of interest in rugby didn't help, of course. Perhaps some of you reading this will be familiar with trying so, so hard to like something you know you are supposed to like, only to know all along that it just isn't going to happen. In the same way that I was hard-wired for horror (and my goodness how my father hated that) I just wasn't hard wired for rugby (I don't think he was too impressed with that, either). My performances on the pitch were akin to Jacques Tati impersonations, and I had yet to discover *Monsieur Hulot's Holiday*.

I suppose the real revelation of youth came when I went to university in England and was surprised to discover that the obsession with certain public sporting events, and with where you came from and how you spoke, seemed to be far less important. Perhaps the odd comment and then moving onto other things rather than embarking on (what felt at the time like) lifelong vendettas against the country next door.

All the above may lead you to think that I hate Wales. Far from it. It's the place that made me who I am. The place where I was brought up had (and still has) some of the most beautiful countryside I have ever seen. Later on in life I discovered the works of Arthur Machen, who came from the same area I did, and if you want to know the real Wales, the mythic, pagan, beautiful, dreamlike Wales that I was lucky enough to enjoy as a boy, then read him. It really is a magical country. It rains a lot but that's the price you pay for living in a land of wizards and dragons, with landscape that look as if Cthulhu himself has scooped up the earth in a misshapen claw and dumped it unceremoniously to form a mountain range close by.

Over time my attitude has mellowed to the people, too. I still don't feel any tremendous kinship with the Welsh, but then I suspect my kinship lies with my own horror-loving kind rather than to any specific nation, so I can hardly give my own people a hard time when it's likely me who was, and still is, the weird one.

But still, those memories abide.

It had always been my plan one day to write something that would follow a similar structure to two books published by my friend Gary Fry's Gray Friar Press in the mid 2000s: *The Faculty of Terror* and *The Catacombs of Fear.* These were portmanteau books – short stories linked by an overall framework narrative that consisted of interludes and a wraparound. The arc plot of my book would be someone journeying through Wales, not knowing exactly who he was or where he was going, but being told stories along the way that illustrated for him different aspects of the darker side of the country in which he had found himself.

So here it is. I hope you've enjoyed reading it, and now it's time for the story notes. I hope it goes without saying that you need to read the book first before looking at this bit, but if you've somehow happened upon this section I suggest you go back to the beginning right now, both to avoid spoilers and to read the best bit of the book. What follows is the usual mix of reminiscence and rumination that I like to use as my way of not having to write an autobiography. One day I'll join all these notes up and the result may turn out to be one of the most curious memoirs ever written by someone from Abergavenny. Until then, for your entertainment and delectation, I present to you how *How Grim Was My Valley* (now you know where I got that title from) came to be.

On the Road

One of the principle routes into Wales (and the main one into South Wales) is via the M4 motorway, which runs from London to just before Carmarthen. I have driven its length many times. The most exciting/unnerving bit is a part that used to be referred to as 'the chicanes', an especially perilous concrete-sided windy bit as you pass through the Eraserhead-era David Lynch landscape of Port Talbot. They've improved the road quite a bit now but back in the 1980s, before the advent of speed cameras, that stretch of road frequently resembled a Scalextric track after an overly impatient five year old had been given the opportunity to play with it.

Wales is reached from England via a suspension bridge over the Severn estuary. There's a big safe one (now called the Prince of Wales bridge) which opened in 1996, and a smaller, bit more wobbly one that gets closed in windy weather. You are advised to take the safe one.

Mind you, that's the one Robert takes and look what happens to him. I wanted the book to begin with someone waking up in Wales and this felt the best way to do it. Of course, Robert could have asked to be dropped off at Magor services, which is before the hotel he finds himself at, but who knows what kind of story he might have been told at McDonalds?

A Cruel Summer

The first major landmark you come to once you're over the Severn Bridge and into Wales on the M4 is the Celtic Manor Hotel, famous for its golf course (the 2010 Ryder Cup was held there) and as a conference venue (the 2014 NATO summit). So it seemed the most appropriate place for Robert to begin his adventure. It probably won't surprise readers that the idea for a pit that holds prisoners from different times came to me in a dream, in this case while we were attending the marvellous Abertoir – the International Horror Festival of Wales, held in Aberystwyth every November. In previous portmanteaus I was keen that the first story should be a fast-paced pulp horror with a nasty ending. Here I wanted the mood to be a little stranger and a little more melancholy, to suggest that Robert's journey wasn't always going to be like leafing through a comic book (although there are plenty of comic book moments as the next story note will describe). Instead this one is deliberately a little strange. I've never played golf, but if I ever do, I have no intention of wandering off into the undergrowth.

Still Death

When I was around eight years old, a favourite ritual of mine was the weekly walk with my father into town to buy 'the papers', by which he meant the TV listings magazines for the forthcoming week (*Radio Times* for BBC1 & BBC2, *TV Times* for the solitary ITV channel) plus local newspapers that only came out once every seven days. Whatever the weather (including when the snow was so deep it came up to my little knees) every Thursday evening we would walk the mile and a half into town to visit the tiny newsagents that bore a startling resemblance, I realised in later years, to the one in Michael Powell's 1959 film *Peeping Tom* – the one where Miles Malleson goes to request 'views' of young ladies. And yes, the top shelves of this cramped little shop were filled with adult magazines and also items that I now realise must have been 8mm loops of the same kind of material for purchase. To my tiny self those top shelves looked as far away as the moon, or at least the top of our house. Fortunately the bookcase filled with Agatha Christie thrillers (the 1970s Fontana editions with that fabulous Tom Adams cover artwork) and Guy N Smith crabs on the rampage paperbacks was much more accessible. I wasn't quite old enough to read those yet, but I was already reading comics.

The horror comics were on the very bottom shelf.

American friends and colleagues talk fondly of discovering EC comics – *Tales from the Crypt* and *The Vault of Horror* – in their youth. Those never made it over here (or at least were never available in South Wales in the mid 1970s). The series that was on sale was Pocket Chiller, part of UK publisher Top Sellers' line that included Pocket Detective and Pocket Romance. Now I'm sure part of this is the rose-tinting of youth, but when I finally caught up with the EC comics it turned out the Pocket Chillers were better. Drawn by European artists (I later found out) and with the writers a mystery that will likely never be solved, Pocket Chiller stories brought the sensibilities of European horror cinema to the printed page. The women were beautiful Edwige Fenech-types, the men were handsome George Hiltons, and the level of cruelty and sadism on display was unforgettable. The secretary tortured by having her skin flayed off and her skull bashed in in "Everlasting Night", the hapless heroine attacked by the snake monsters at the end of "Evil Fangs", the unwise young grave robber who steals a ring and has to have his hand hacked off (in italics) to free his dead body from the grave he stole from. The man who only realises there's something wrong with his wife when she starts strangling the pets

I don't think my dad had any idea what I was reading.

And so we come to "Still Death", which was inspired a tiny bit by a Pocket Chiller entitled "Unholy Fiends" in which a woman in a large country house invites her son's ex-lover to stay because she's turned him into a zombie & he still wants her. I think the girl gets turned into one too and her sexy best friend comes looking for her. It all ends horribly. I used this as the starting point and at the time I happened to see *The Void*, the feature length Lovecraftian horror film from the team known as Astron 6. Mix both together and add a generous dollop of my predilection for works of weird art and "Still Death" popped out, which I intended to make as unnerving as possible. I hope the creatures with their heads tipping backwards evoked a pleasurable shudder.

The Men With Paper Faces

I had been asked by Justin Isis to contribute a story for a planned anthology tribute to the works of my friend and weird fiction author Mark Samuels. I've known Mark for many years and was happy to contribute. The first time Mark and I met we went on the guided tour of the famous bits of Highgate Cemetery. You can't go in on your own because of 'a bit of business' back in 1970 known as the Highgate Vampire case. Because of that, and because we were feeling in mischievous mood, we decided to pretend to be Romanian tourists. Whenever we saw a recognisable landmark we asked the guide if that was where Dracula was buried, insisting it was because we had seen it in a film. We fully expected to be thrown out but by some miracle we lasted until the end and the grave of Patrick Wymark, star of 1970's *Blood on Satan's Claw*.

Mark's stories tend to be grim, apocalyptic tales of crumbling sanity in a fragmenting world. I thought distorted and fragmenting faces that only one man could see would do nicely and Justin was kind enough to publish it in *Marked to Die*, published by Snuggly Books.

By Any Other Name

The themes of madness and a story about things only one person can see continues in this. My friend and fellow Welsh horror writer Mark Howard Jones has edited two volumes of *Cthulhu Cymraeg* – tales of Lovecraftian horror set in Wales. "By Any Other Name" was written for volume two. Part of the fun of writing a story like this is finding horror in the mundane and everyday – in this case water, extrapolated to the point that the lead character can see unnameable horrors even in raindrops trickling down a window. The Lovecraftian element in this one was provided by my friend Ramsey Campbell's enduring creation Gla'aki. His wife Jenny is the best one to ask to pronounce that name correctly, by the way, but obviously don't ask her to say it too many times in the presence of her husband or strange things may manifest…

Learning the Language

This one originally appeared in Paul Finch's *Terror Tales of Wales*, part of his excellent series of 'Round Britain' horror anthologies intended to emulate the (mostly) R Chetwynd-Hayes edited series of *Tales of Terror* published by Fontana in the 1970s. After growing up and Wales and then moving away to study, I moved back for a couple of years to work. It was only when I returned that the unusually strong dislike for the English by many of the Welsh people became truly evident. Perhaps it was because of where I was working, or perhaps it was because I don't have a Welsh accent (as I've mentioned above, I lost it when I was young, although my father did have reel-to-reel tape recordings of me when I was four and I sounded like something out of a Dylan Thomas radio play) but the very naked dislike of the English was at first something I treated with good humour, later presumed was a joke they were overdoing a bit, and eventually realised was a way of life that was actually profoundly irritating. So this story is a response to that. Whatever I may think of it, this story certainly has something – it disturbed Paul Finch sufficiently that he used the story to round off the Terror Tales volume, and it scared Johnny Mains so much he included it in his second volume of *Best British Horror*. My very Welsh parents, needless to say, absolutely hated it.

Somewhere, Beneath a Maze of Sky

The Brecon Beacons were a popular Saturday afternoon getaway for us when I was a boy. I well remember reading Ramsey Campbell's introduction to Clive Barker's *Books of Blood* in the Mountain Centre car park and Gary Brandner's *The Howling* one evening after a decent amount of walking, such that I now cannot get out of my mind the notion that his werewolf novel takes place in Brecon. This story started with the idea of a training ground for soldiers in World War II that had somehow become a ghost itself and could now travel around and appear whenever it needed fresh victims. The final result leaves things a bit more open as to what exactly is going on, but I like to think the assault course originated in Germany and could appear anywhere in the world. So just bear that in mind the next time you're out for a walk in the country.

The Church With Bleeding Windows

Steve Shaw asked me for a story for his Great British Horror anthology series published by Black Shuck books. I had no intention of writing a comedy, but sometimes stories come out a certain way and you as a writer don't have much say in the matter. The original concept combined two themes from the films of John Carpenter – a group of individuals trapped in a building (in this case a church), threatened by a chameleonic alien creature that was kind of like *The Thing*, but which could pretend to be anything to trap its victims, from a chair to another person. The way the story was going felt a bit too similar to the polymorph in the BBC comedy series Red Dwarf, so instead I made it into a demon familiar and mixed in a bit of Richard Stanley's film *Hardware* about a military robot that can rebuild itself using ordinary household objects. In this case the objects were people's diseased organs. From feedback I've had this one tends to be a love it or hate it story. Even after all these years it's still a thrill when something you've written has any kind of effect on people, so I'm equally happy with either reaction.

What Others Hear

I wrote this for volume one of Mark Howard Jones' Cthulhu Cymraeg series, inspired by the idea that, instead of vast unimaginable cosmic horrors, what if the creatures that threatened were so small they could walk along nerve cells and manipulate us? The seaside setting for this one is inspired by family holidays to West Wales, the furthest the Probert family ever travelled from where we lived, usually to spend a week in a rain-lashed caravan before making the trip home. I was always incredibly jealous of my school friends who got to go abroad to all kinds of exotic-sounding locales like Malta and the Costa del Sol while we never travelled further than Carmarthen. The ending is very much what the little me wished would have happened while we were there.

The Devil in the Details

Another story that was never intended to be a comedy. Instead I envisioned an old dark house murder mystery, where it turned out the killer was a young woman who was actually dead and possessed by the spirit of a demon that was bumping off those responsible for her murder. It turned out rather differently, didn't it? Devil in the Details was written for the Hersham Horror anthology *Demons and Devilry*, edited by Stuart Young.

Forgive Us Not Our Trespasses

This one was written for *The Eleventh Black Book of Horror Stories*. It turned out to be the final volume in that series, one which ran from 2007 to 2015 after which time its creator, publisher and series editor Charles Black, became beset with health problems that prevented him bringing out further volumes. A story of mine appeared in every Black Book apart from Volume Four (solely because I didn't have time to write one) and Charlie was kind enough to put two of my stories into Volume Five instead. The Black Book of Horror was a series intended to emulate the old British horror anthologies of the 1960s and 1970s including those published by Tandem and Fontana, but especially the *Pan Book of Horror Stories* edited by Herbert van Thal, which was both adored by and an inspiration to Charlie and many of its contributors. Charlie passed away in 2019. My wife Kate and I were with him at the hospice the night before he died, along with our good friend Kevin Demant of the Vault of Evil message board, a place where many of us like-minded pulp paperback fanatics first got to know each other. The Vault of Evil was also the springboard for Charlie's idea to create a series featuring the kind of stories we all loved. The three of us felt privileged to have been given the chance to have one last, lengthy conversation about the literature we loved before getting to say goodbye. You will have noticed on the way in that this book is dedicated to Charlie. The fact that he was kind enough to publish some of my stories is only one of the reasons why. He was a tireless defender and advocate of a pulp horror writing style that sadly receives neither the recognition nor the respect it deserves nowadays. He loved the gleefully nasty tales of authors like Sir Charles Birkin and Robert Bloch (as do I), but most important of all he was a very nice man, gentle in nature, always supportive, and someone who despite being in a business that requires putting oneself out there, had no real wish to be in the limelight. RIP Charlie my dear friend, you made the shadows a better place to visit.

The Road Not Taken

Robert's journey finally comes to an end, and it's apt that I've started talking about the *Pan Book of Horror Stories* because that was where I first became familiar with the concept of the sin eater in Christianna Brand's story "The Sins of the Fathers", published in Volume Five. Those of you familiar with the classic TV series *Night Gallery* may recall it was adapted for that show's second season in an episode starring Richard Thomas and Barbara Steele. While tenuously described in association with other cultures, the sin eater is most commonly seen in texts pertaining to Wales and so I thought it would do nicely to round off the book. I hope the ending doesn't come across as grim, by the way. After all, Robert has discovered his purpose in life, even if he's shortly to forget it and start the whole cycle again. With different stories this time, of course. Could there be another book in this? After all, Richard Llewellyn wrote four books in his Valley series. The final one was *Green, Green My Valley Now*, so now you know where the title of this section came from. If there was another names and locations would of course be changed. Perhaps Robert wouldn't even be a sin eater this time but have some other role that fulfilled the same purpose.

…and finally

It's the end of the book so time for the credits! Or at least the thank yous, because no book like this gets written without the help, advice and friendship of those who were instrumental in helping me get these stories to the point where you have them to hold in your hand in the form of this rather gorgeous book. So without further ado I thank:

Ian Whates of NewCon Press for being good enough to take this project on, and for his enthusiasm and expert help in bringing it to fruition. Ian, thank you so much - you were an absolute pleasure to work with and I hope we get the chance to do so again.

Elena Betti who didn't just provide a cover illustration that was beyond my wildest dreams (or rather, nightmares) but whose deliciously disturbing work also graces some of the stories themselves. Thank you, Elena, for giving the book such a touch of class.

Ramsey Campbell, that living legend in the horror world, for providing such a thoughtful, thorough and considerate introduction. When my wife Kate and I next visit Ramsey and his wife Jenny I will be sure to show my gratitude appropriately, likely by bringing along some obscure 1970s South American rarity on Blu-ray to entertain all of us, or at least myself and Mr Campbell.

The editors and publishers who were kind enough to commission and publish some of the stories in the first place.

Everyone I have ever met and ever known from Wales, but especially my parents and my brother Mark and his family. I don't find Wales that scary really, you know. Or do I?

And finally and most importantly my wife, best friend and partner in all things horror Kate Probert aka horror writer Thana Niveau, who has visited all the places with me that were used as inspiration in this book, and nothing horrible happened to her at all. That she has noticed. Yet.

And that's it. As always be good, take care of each other, and hopefully I'll see you all again soon. Leaving you with a twinkle in my eye and a song in my heart (both very Welsh things indeed).

– John Llewellyn Probert, who is Welsh
Somewhere in Gothic Somerset, (Not In Wales)
June 2022

Also from NewCon Press

Visions of Ruin – Mark West
Beautifully paced and full of deft touches that bring the 1980s setting to life, *Visions of Ruin* is a taut ghost story set during a rainy weekend at a caravan park on the edge of rundown seaside town. The author conjures a tale of subtle and unsettling horror.

May Day – Emma Coleman
Orphaned during wartime at just seventeen, May continues with the silly superstitions her mum taught her. Until the one time she doesn't; at which point something dark and deadly arises, and proceeds to invade her life, determined to claim her as its own...

Queen of Clouds – Neil Williamson
Wooden automata, sentient weather, talking cats, compellant inks and a host of vividly realised characters provide the backdrop to this rich dark fantasy, as stranger in the city Billy Braid becomes embroiled in Machiavellian politics and deadly intrigue.

Saving Shadows – Eugen Bacon
Award nominated collection of prose poetry and speculative micro-lit pieces by author Eugen Bacon. Complementing the written word are a series of full page illustrations by artist **Elena Betti**; thirty-five stunning images that enhance the reading experience.

The Queen of Summer's Twilight – Charles Vess
A mysterious man on a black motorbike rescues a rebellious teen from the streets of Inverness, setting in motion a series of events that will see contemporary Scotland clash with the realm of fairy, in this stunning tale inspired by the ballad of Tam Lyn.

www.newconpress.co.uk

Milton Keynes UK
Ingram Content Group UK Ltd.
UKHW010611060823
426385UK00004B/77